Noctilucents
Volume One

Martian
Blood

John Pahl

First published 2020
by Rowanvale Books Ltd
The Gate
Keppoch Street
Roath
Cardiff
CF24 3JW
www.rowanvalebooks.com

This Edition published 2024
by Rowanvale Books Ltd
The Gate
Keppoch Street
Roath
Cardiff
CF24 3JW
www.rowanvalebooks.com

A CIP catalogue record for this book is available from the British Library.
ISBN: 978-1-912655-62-5

To Tom, the star that burnt too bright

15 Years Earlier: Ben

The boy from an island lost beneath the seas reached out to touch the rocket to Mars.

Ben felt the cold, corrugated skin of titanium and carbon fibre containing liquid hydrogen. The tank's panel flexed and cracked, cries of tension between the super-cooled liquid and warm air outside. A valve hissed as it vented a stream of gas, easing the pressure trapped within.

He felt dwarfed: little more than an ant halfway up a palm tree, like those he had climbed back home. Only there wasn't a home, not since the water levels had risen and the hurricanes had blown his island away. Now there were just his memories and a point in the Pacific Ocean.

His mother, Cita, still raged at that loss, channelling her fury into new campaigns, first leaving him behind, then, when he was a teenager, not just letting him but encouraging him to join her. She'd been their island's leader, fighting for its survival. Having lost that battle, she now fought against the technologies that would kill all humanity – or so she said.

Ben had gone with her, but reluctantly. He had hoped that by being with her he could ease the endless anger and she would be the mother he remembered from his childhood: a calming presence, always there for him. But she was so angry, whatever happened, whatever he did.

Losing again had made things worse. This time it had been artificial intelligence, the AIs cooked up by technocrats.

"Ban them!" she'd cried. "Put humans first; protect the planet."

But that Dr Kasparov had prevailed – one of those slippery technocrats, or maybe more, for some called him leader of the London Revolution.

"Terrorist," Cita had said.

Now the battle was spaceflight, rockets like this *Prometheus,* on its way to Mars where the colonists waited for it. The first of many, built to cycle between planets, nuclear powered. It was the nuclear bit Ben's mother objected to the most, but with the global economy in free-fall, the project's cost played better with the millions of unemployed. There'd been riots just a few miles from the launch site on Cape Canaveral.

Ben turned to look out, away from the rocket. A seagull swooped by and his eyes followed it, envious of its freedom. If he couldn't be a dolphin, he'd be a bird of some form, flying like that, out over the oceans.

Arranged in four corners around the rocket were the lightning strike towers, one of which his mother was climbing with her banners. She'd do the messaging, she'd said; all he had to do was be there, on the rocket. They'd never launch it with protestors actually on it, particularly if one was a boy.

"Smile," she'd told him. "It looks better on the news."

He sighed. He'd rather be back in the Pacific, on one of the neighbouring islands to which his village had been relocated. There he'd go diving or surfing or maybe learn to navigate the traditional craft of his people, sailing for islands over the horizon, steering by the light of ascending and descending stars. Ben could just see the Atlantic swell crashing onto the beaches where they'd landed a few minutes earlier; it made him feel happy just looking at it.

Then the rocket exploded. The panel Ben was touching burst, flinging him up and out. Behind, he glimpsed the orange flames balloon out, starting at the base and heading up to the upper half which contained the nuclear engine. He heard nothing, instantly deafened by the violence of the sounds.

He felt no fear, which was strange; it was all unreal, like a dream where he'd suddenly be able to fly and join the birds circling in alarm. Tumbling through the air towards the hard ground, all he could see was the sky.

The sky was the fairest of blues, the colour of the waters of home, of Earth.

Then he hit the concrete and died.

Part 1

1: Tom

The thin sky hung over rolling hills scattered with rocks, red as blood. Tom, nose pressed against the glass, could feel the cold seeping in, but he continued to stare outwards until his warm breath misted the view. Unwilling to move or wipe clear the window, he stood for a few minutes until finally turning back to where old JT stood over the body.

"Not ashes to ashes, but sperm to worm," said old JT, with a farmer's son's uncompromising frankness regarding life and death. Maybe that frankness was how he was able to prepare the dead woman for the wormery tub while Tom only watched, seeing his friend Amina rather than a body full of nutrients. He could still hear her full-hearted laughs – the ones that had become rarer and rarer and were now lost for ever.

Unable to watch any more, Tom made his way from the greenhouse to the kitchen at the heart of Mars Base, where his parents were drinking tea.

"Want a cup?" his mother asked.

Tom shook his head. "It's not right, feeding Amina to the worms like that."

"We have to be practical," his father said. "We need to recycle everything; those are the procedures."

"Procedures? Is that all you think of? No wonder Amina hanged herself!" Tom exclaimed. "We're stuck on Mars and no one will ever rescue us."

"We're alive, aren't we?"

"You call this living?" Tom asked bitterly. It was the only world he knew, born on the planet nearly sixteen years earlier. "We haven't heard from Earth for eight years now."

"Don't say that," his mother said. "Tom, please, let's talk about this."

But Tom didn't want to talk about it, didn't want any of that mushy stuff that changed nothing.

In his bunk that evening he wondered, as he had night after night for years, how he could escape, how he could get to Earth. But despair engulfed his head, weighing it down, while nausea ate at his stomach; he was trapped in a prison that one day would be his morgue. *No,* he thought, *I mustn't give in; better angry than accepting.*

Suddenly frames from an old movie burst from his memory, with a wizard's gravelly voice demanding, "You will swear!" It had been a film of shining knights, valorous deeds, swords of power, love, lust and music that had stirred his blood.

"You will swear."

The words felt like a command. Crazy, yes, but when there was no hope left, doing something, however unlikely it was to change anything, was better than waiting for the end. But swear to what? On this dead planet there were no mythical powers that slept under the sands. It was the Earth and the Sun that mattered.

Suddenly he sat up and grabbed his tablet to start the astronomy app. Earth would be visible in the sky around dawn, the morning star. Tom lay back, his mind racing. It had to be strong, whatever he did, breaking all those rules his father lived for, and there had to be an offering – there always was. But what could he give when he had nothing?

Blood. He could offer his blood to the planet and leave the base at dawn like a thief. Suddenly he grinned and relaxed: he would go *outside.*

***

Early the next day Tom made his way from his bunk to the suit room, tiptoeing as quietly as he could. He wriggled into a surface suit, then stepped into the airlock, closing the inner door behind him.

For a moment he hesitated, gripped by doubts. Was this crazy? Was he? Then he realised he didn't care how stupid it was, how mad his parents would be or how many rules and procedures he'd break. He had to do something, anything, to fight against the trap.

Tom gripped the wheel that opened the airlock's outer door and turned it with all his weight, then, as it swung open, stood, looking out. The planet slept, dimly lit by stars, planets and two moons. Phobos and Deimos they were called, crossing the sky in opposing directions like the quarrelling brothers Cain and Abel, looking down on this dead world.

At first Tom could see nothing of the planet itself, the surface lost in darkness. The night's sky was dotted with stars, while towards the east glowed faint white clouds, reflecting the still-hidden sun. As the sun inched towards the horizon, these noctilucent clouds faded into nothing, but the sky slowly, gently lit up, changing from monochrome to colour – not the red of dawns on Earth, but blue. It revealed a landscape of countless scattered rocks and dunes all the way to distant rolling hills and low crags.

Tom stepped out of the airlock and walked across the red ground, his boots raising clouds of dust as he went, then stopped and looked back at the base, his home.

In the centre there was their greenhouse, sheets of glass containing the garden where they grew their food. On one side of it was a ruin, a hundred-metre-wide dome that was meant to have been their living space but had collapsed, its internal organs exposed to the hostile world. In the half-light it looked like it had been sacked in a war long, long ago. On the other side of the dome was the core of the base, a hexagonal grid of metallic modules with harsh, straight lines that reflected the pre-dawn sky. Its clean surfaces were broken by doors, windows, legs, cables, panels, ladders, masts and antennae. The base lay at the bottom of a cliff, into which stretched an access tunnel.

Dust had crept its way into every crack, over glass, under stones. Drifts clogged up the collapsed ruins and lay deep around the greenhouse, as if to bury it. The base was no longer the shiny silver of old photos but scarred and pitted with blown dust, its antennae and ladders tainted red as they had been changed by the planet, metamorphosing not into something new but something old. Even Tom's suit was ingrained with it, the glass helmet covered by fine scratches. Apart from Tom, nothing stirred but a handful of the dust blown by a gentle breeze. He was alone and he waited, watching for the dawn, hearing nothing but his breathing, isolated by an atmosphere too thin for all but the loudest sounds.

At last the first rays of light broke between the peaks of two faraway mountains on this, a new Martian day. Tom turned to the rising sun and searched for the morning star, the only one still visible in the sky. He stared long and hard at it, a despairing hunger in his eyes.

"Earth," he whispered.

He reached for the suit's tool belt and pulled out a knife. Its cutting edge was the one thing that was clean, sharp and bright.

Then he spoke. "I swear that I, Tom Tesla, will get off this planet. Whatever it takes, whatever the cost, I will find a way to get to Earth."

He reached down to his left glove and unscrewed it from the suit. The air – warm, life-giving air – rushed out, and the arm of the suit automatically sealed itself as it would if it had just been a simple leak. Automatic systems were triggered, and an emotionless voice said, "Warning, suit integrity breached."

Tom ignored it and looked down at his hand; it had already begun to whiten, the freezing air feeling like spikes driven into the skin. In the warmth of the glass helmet, Tom's eyes watered with pain.

"I swear," he said.

He brought the knife down so that the cutting edge lay against the skin of his hand, which began to tremble, partly from cold and partly from determination.

"I swear," he repeated.

With those words he forced the knife down and back, cutting deep into the palm of his hand. Bright beads of blood rushed out, spilling onto the rocks, droplets of bright red against the dull, lifeless surface. In the thin atmosphere they didn't freeze, but bubbled and boiled into the air, leaving a stain behind.

On Tom's hand the ever-present sand was blown into the wound, brown against the now blue skin, mixing into his blood the dust of Mars.

"I swear!"

Then a hand came from behind him and grabbed the knife.

2: Tom

Tom turned, instinctively pushing the knife towards the attacker.

"What the hell are you doing?"

Someone was shouting at him, battling to keep the knife clear from both of them. Suddenly it clicked: it was his dad, the one who never shouted, who was always calm, who was now loud enough to overcome the thin air.

"Have you gone crazy?"

For a moment Tom was lost for words, wrapped up as he had been in the oath, thinking himself alone.

"You're bleeding – show me," said his dad.

Tom wasn't in the mood to play nice. "It's nothing. Just leave me alone."

"What were you doing? Tom?" Tired grey eyes looked at him, seeking understanding.

"I just want to get off this stinking planet."

A stab of fear entered those grey eyes. "We all do, Tom. Let's go inside and talk about this, ok?"

Tom took a deep breath and nodded. But the anger remained.

At the airlock, before heading in, he looked round for a moment, taking in the view, the sunlight on the red soil. It was hard to turn away from that landscape, the openness so different from the constriction of their base: the feeling that he could walk and walk towards a horizon without end under an infinite sky. To return indoors was to be marched back to his prison cell.

In the shadows of the partly-lit suit room, he was met by his mother, Elena. Fear was in her eyes, too – fear for him.

"What was he doing?" she asked Tom's father, Michael. "Why was he out there?"

That's right; ask him and ignore me. Tom shrugged off her arms as they reached out to embrace him, putting his surface suit back on its rack.

Then she saw the knife and the blood in the palm of his hand, and her face went white.

"No, Tom, it's not that bad, surely?"

"I wasn't doing anything stupid like – *that*," he almost shouted at her, snapping. "I just wanted to go outside, to make an oath, to swear to Earth."

It was out there now, said. It sounded stupid put into words. His parents looked at him, perplexed. *Bet that isn't in any of the flight manuals.* But he'd had enough of their cloying love that suffocated him, keeping him a boy.

"Swear to Earth?" his dad echoed.

"Make an oath, for things to change, to be able to escape here." For some reason Tom felt that he couldn't repeat exactly what words he'd used, that they were to be kept secret.

His dad shook his head. "That makes no sense at all."

"Come and have some breakfast, Tom. Please," his mum pleaded.

He was hungry, starving, and there was a tempting smell of fresh bread that masked the base's usual aroma of dust and sweat. It was coming down the dimly lit hallway that led to the kitchen at the heart of the base, in its central hexagon.

Two others were waiting for them there, eating and drinking. Tom had hoped the numbers would ease the tension, but it seemed worse, as if they were a jury deciding his fate. Only old JT could be relied upon to be on his side, to give a friendly nod, sitting at the table with his mug of tea.

"Well?" asked Michael. Was he asking as Tom's father or as base commander?

"What happened?" That was Victor, pronouncing doubleyous as vees, not wasting his words, and standing even though there were empty chairs by the table. His face was lost in the shadows, only his nose showing, like the beak of a crow.

"Tom went outside on his own, then cut himself, deliberately." It was his mum, as if reading from a charge sheet.

"I was making a vow, to make something change." Tom spoke loudly, angrily.

"A vow? How unscientific," said Victor.

"But human," said JT.

"Did you know?" asked Elena, turning to him, accusing him.

"No one knew," said Tom. "It was my decision. *Mine*, not his."

"You're just—"

Tom guessed she was about to say 'a child', and the anger grew again. He was already a head taller than her.

"I'm nearly sixteen, and every single one of those years has been spent in this prison. We don't know if we'll ever be rescued; we have no comms with Earth – we have no idea what is going on up there."

"That is why we must be careful," said Michael. "Conserve resources, keep going, to be ready for when they come: you know that. When something's gone, it's gone forever."

"How many millions of times have you told us that? There must be more to life! What if we all end up like Amina or Mei-Li?"

"Oh my; I've forgotten Mei-Li," said Elena, hurrying out.

There was a silence after she left, and Tom helped himself to something to eat. Michael was lost in thought.

Mei-Li Wu was the second eldest after JT. Five years ago she had been buried under a sand-slide, trapped until her air had run out, leaving her with brain damage. Now the Nobel Prize winner who had been the first to identify Martian cyanobacteria needed Elena's help to get dressed. A moment later they returned. That was all of them but the Venezuelan, José, who kept his own hours.

"Tea," said Mei-Li, smiling.

Elena made her a cup.

"I made one for you," said Victor, handing Elena a mug.

She took it uncertainly, exchanging a worried glance with Michael. "Thanks."

"What did you think such a stunt would achieve?" asked Michael.

"I don't know," said Tom. "I just had to do something."

"He doesn't understand," said JT to Tom. "He only gets logic, only systems, not feelings."

"Then explain – tell me what I'm missing!" said Michael.

"We can't go on like this, can't you see that?" said JT. "We've been cut off from Earth for – what is it? Eight years?"

"Seven years, ten months," said Victor.

"Oh, thank you, *communications* officer," JT said, sarcastically. "They don't know if we're still alive – we could have died for all they know."

"So?"

"And for eight – ok, seven years, ten months – no lander has turned up on our doorstep ready to take us home. Maybe something's happened on Earth. Maybe it isn't going to come. Maybe it exploded like the *Prometheus*."

At that they froze, and the room seemed darker and colder than it was. In the silence they became more aware of the kitchen's failing lighting. Only four of the bulbs still worked, two of which flickered on and off. On the table was a simple lamp burning vegetable oil.

"It will come," said Michael. "We will go home."

"Home?" That was Mei-Li, looking worried; she could pick up the odd word and follow a conversation's mood.

"You say that," said JT. "But do you believe it?"

There was a silence.

"Belief needs nurturing; not just words, but deeds too. And that's what Tom was doing."

The mood shifted, and Tom realised some of his anger had gone with it. Maybe they could understand.

"We have to do something," he said. "We can't just wait."

"What? We can't just throw together a spacecraft from bamboo and thin air," said Michael.

"There is something," said Victor. "Bamboo and air."

Michael glared back.

"What? Dad? What can we do?"

"It's too dangerous."

"You can't not tell us – we have to know!"

"It's an idea Victor and I had."

"We need a working transponder," said Victor. "I know where we can get one. Michael does too."

"Is this true?" asked JT. "Is it?"

"Yes." Michael took a deep breath. "But not here. There is the possibility we could salvage one from a robot lander. However, the nearest – Sitefinder 3 – is about two hundred and fifty kilometres away. It would be a round trip of five hundred kilometres."

"In a surface suit? You'd never get there," said JT.

"No," said Victor. "But we could fly, couldn't we, Michael?"

Tom's dad looked trapped, but finally nodded.

"Yes," he said. "We could fly."

3: Tom

Tom's anger returned.

"You had an idea, then kept it quiet?"

"It's very dangerous. A hundred things could go wrong," said Michael.

"Tell them," said Victor.

Michael paused, then sighed.

"There's that old atmospheric research balloon – we could pump it full of hydrogen. Replace the sensor platform with a bamboo cage and attach two fans powered by fuel cells for propulsion. Add some fins and flaps to keep it going in a straight line, control lines, fuel cylinders, and maybe, just maybe, it would fly."

"That's a brilliant idea! I'll do it," said Tom. "Go on, Dad – let me."

"No!" Elena had gone white. "It's far too dangerous; I still say no."

Tom turned to her, furious. "You knew too? You kept this quiet too?"

"You should have told us," said JT. "We decide as a group, all of us, always: those were the rules."

"Then Tom came," said Elena.

"So?"

"Tom makes eight, and Tom's the reason we have to be especially careful."

"No, damn it! No! Not for me!"

"You should have told us."

"Ok, we should have, but we didn't!" Michael was obviously on edge again, close to losing it for the second time that day.

"What's going on?"

It was José Santos. He usually spent most mornings on his own, either in bed or working out in the gym.

"They had a plan to get a working transponder from an old lander, but kept it secret," said JT.

"Oh yes, the blimp idea: very dangerous." He turned to the kitchen counter and started slicing the bread.

JT banged a fist on the table. "You knew, she knew, he knew – you all knew but me and Tom!"

"Not just you two," said Elena. "Mei-Li too..." Her voice faded away. Suddenly embarrassed, she looked down. "Sorry."

"I should think so," muttered JT.

"Look, this isn't how we wanted you to find out, but after Amina we didn't want to risk any other lives."

"I don't care. I want to go. I want to fly the blimp," said Tom. His eyes gleamed at the freedom of being not just out of the base, but in an airship, flying the Martian skies. "Let's build it, now."

There was his vow. Whatever JT might say about the oath just being an act to build belief, Tom felt committed.

"We need to tell Earth we're alive, don't we?"

Michael looked cornered, but nodded.

"And we need to know that a ship is coming to get us?"

"They will come; I know they will."

"But we need to *know* that, to avoid another Amina."

Elena was looking scared – no, terrified. "You don't understand, Tom! It would require all day to get there and back, and the blimp could only take just enough fuel and air for one person. They'd be on their own out there if something went wrong."

"It could work," said Victor.

"Why would you say that? Why?" She seemed close to tears. "You know who'd have to fly it!"

Victor shrugged. "It could work."

"I'd fly it," said Tom again.

"No," said Michael. "I am the commander; I trained as a pilot. It would be for me to decide, and it would be for me to fly."

"We *have* to do this. We need to know what's going on – don't we, JT?" asked Tom.

JT scratched his chin. "I dunno, Tom, I really don't. I don't want to die up here; I just want to go home, someday."

"This is a safety issue: we have to do a risk assessment. We can't rush things – we must do it properly," said Michael.

"We should vote on it. I vote in favour."

"You're too young," said Elena.

Tom was suddenly furious again. "Don't keep saying that! I've had nearly sixteen years of living in this base, almost as long as any of you. I know how it works better than pretty much anyone." He almost certainly did. Lessons had been very practical, and they had taught Tom about everything from life support to thermal control. "You keep telling me about Earth: JT going on about life in Cornwall, sailing an old dinghy; José about the bars of Caracas and beaches of the Caribbean. Then you go on and on about Isfahan and Dad about Seattle, and Victor…"

Tom's voice trailed off. Victor Dubois rarely talked about his life back on Earth. Then, as Mei-Li barely talked, and with Amina gone, that was everyone. He hadn't talked with anyone else, ever.

"You have all those memories to fall back on, you live off those memories. I've got nothing. I want to experience the Earth you've told me about, not just exist in these boxes. And other people, friends and…"

Could he say girls? No, he couldn't; that would be too big an issue, even when worked up.

He'd had enough. It was time to leave. One parting shot to get in.

"What happens when those memories dry up – when you're left with the reality of life stuck here? How many more Aminas will there be?"

He stormed out, but there was nowhere to go, no escape from the rest of them and the inside walls of the base. Tom ran down the corridor that led to the nearest they had to open space: the greenhouse, their garden. He tried to imagine he was flying over the Martian rocks and craters, but the reality around him was too strong to escape the glass walls.

Without thinking, he found himself walking back to the suit room and the airlock with its window out to the Martian surface. He longed to get out there and walk – no, to run and run, until he was able to empty his legs of the energy that burned within his bones and be free of these cramped quarters.

Peering closely, hands blocking the reflections that could spoil his sight, he could just make out the morning star, Earth, still visible.

What's happening up there? he wondered. *Do they think of us? Is there someone looking back, wondering what's happening in their sky?*

4: Sophia

Even virtual reconstructions of exploding spaceships were a bit of a bore when they were homework. With a sigh, Sophia put on the data glasses and was in a simulation: a construct of Cape Canaveral fifteen years earlier. She'd been alive, just.

The boy; she wanted to see the boy again. Homework could wait.

"Replay from two seconds prior to the *Prometheus* explosion," she commanded.

She watched it explode, fire swallowing the spacecraft and its launch pad, the ball of yellow-white flame a sun on Earth, dwarfing the surrounding swamplands and the twelve protesting against the launch.

The burning sphere darkened, spitting out the radioactive core of the *Prometheus*, raining burning propellant and dark thorium dust. Where the fuel landed it exploded into more fireballs, spawning and splitting across the concrete where Sophia's virtual presence stood. Molten metal and razor-sharp fragments flew like daggers. Icons identified the radioactive hot spots, but she ignored the augmentation overlays, hunting for debris and bodies raining down, looking for one in particular.

The protestors who had reached the rocket itself had had no chance of survival. The closest had been incinerated, while others had only been identified by their DNA signature. Only a handful of bodies had been flung out even partially intact.

There he was!

The crumpled remains of the boy spun out of the core of the explosion, body blackened by heat and vaporised blood, and landed right at her feet: she had positioned herself correctly. Sophia made herself look at him. Most of his clothing had been blown away, together with the first layer of skin. What was left was red, raw, badly pixelated, and dying.

Most of those who had been tying banners on the neighbouring lightning towers were already dead. The towers had been bent over in the blast and then covered by burning fuel, flames licking upwards, the banners turned to ash. But one woman had survived, flung onto the hard concrete, breaking several ribs and one ankle. She staggered, not away from the disaster but towards its heart, hunting, looking, crying. It was a miracle the burning fuel missed her as it rained down.

"Ben?" she cried. She was going the wrong way, away from Sophia, for Ben was the name of the boy lying by Sophia's feet.

"Ben?" she cried again, this time a bit closer. Her voice was shrill, struggling to compete with the sounds of violence.

Sophia wanted to say something, but what was the point? This was all virtual, projections on her data glasses, constructed from recordings, not live. What would she say anyhow? He was dead or dying, his body already covered with a layer of thorium dust. There was nothing she could do; there was nothing anyone could do.

The woman was closer now, limping badly on her damaged foot, and partially obscured by flames and smoke. She peered around, hunting. When the clouds cleared for a moment, she was close enough to see the body, though not to recognise it.

"Ben?"

As the woman approached, the sensors she carried upped the resolution and the boy's square edges smoothed then sharpened, revealing the true extent of his injuries and making Sophia nauseous. She wanted to look away, but told herself not to.

"Ben?" It started as a scream and ended as a whimper of recognition. "No, no, no!"

The woman knelt by the body, picking it up and attempting to hold it in her arms. But she was too weak and too injured to manage it, and anyhow the body was too delicate and damaged, threatening to fall apart at a moment's notice.

She started to sob, rocking back and forth, the boy's blood soaking into her t-shirt.

"My baby," she cried, though he was no infant but a teenager, about the same age as Sophia.

Sophia's vision pixelated and then cleared up: the radiation was playing havoc with the electronics. For a minute time seemed to loop; the woman rocked back and forth amongst the clouds of smoke. Then something emerged from the smoke. A vehicle. Even though it was armoured and protected against such a hostile environment, it approached the woman gingerly. It came to rest behind her, and two figures emerged, humans turned into giants by their protective suits.

"Ma'am, stand away from the body with your arms in the air." The amplified voice came from one of the figures, male.

She seemed aware of them for the first time, turning around.

"My boy, my son, my Ben," she said.

"Stand away from the body with your arms in the air."

The woman stood up and screamed at them. "Murderers! Murderers!" Then her ankle gave way and she collapsed on her knees. "Help him – please. Just help him."

One of the figures came over to the boy and pointed a box at him: a Geiger counter. It began to crackle, increasing to a scream as he approached. The man stepped back, turning to the other.

"We can't stay: it's too hot. Let's take her and go."

"No!" the woman screamed. "I'm not leaving him."

"Take her other arm," the man ordered.

Together they dragged her to the back of the vehicle. They forced her inside, nearly throwing her in, before climbing in themselves and driving away, fast.

Sophia was left alone in the smouldering ruins of the launch site with the dead boy, who was beginning to pixelate again. She wondered about him, what he had been like and how his life would have been if the rocket hadn't exploded. And about his mother, whom Sophia's father hated. *Hated.*

Sophia had heard her name many times: Cita Stone.

Enough, thought Sophia, and took off the data glasses, returning to London.

5: Sophia

Sophia shook her head to clear it of lingering images of the Kennedy Space Centre. She was no closer to working out how to answer her history assignment, which was to describe the consequences of the explosion of the *Prometheus*.

She stretched, arching her back, loosening limbs stiff from lack of activity.

She took a sip of coffee from the mug on her desk and almost spat it out: it was cold. For a moment she thought of going to the kitchen for a refill, but that would just put off the inevitable, and now she'd started she'd better keep going.

She stared out of her window at the evening lights of the London City State and then around her room, looking for something else to do, any distraction. But unlike that of her messy sister Nina, her bedroom was already neat and tidy.

Idly, she double-tapped in the air in front of her to access her blipcoms, which flowed across her desk. Her friend Maria had already finished her essay; her angle was that the explosion had left the colonists of Mars stuck up there, unable to return to Earth. A software update was available for her electric speed-bike that promised a five percent improved sprint accel. Her sailing club's next race would be Saturday afternoon. The leaderboard flashed up; she was currently second. In tenth was her classmate, Zach, and his status showed he was studying too.

"How's it going?" she blipped.

"Stuck and bored," he replied. "Rather be sailing."

She laughed. "Me too. Join me in the construct twenty minutes before the explosion?"

"Ok."

She double-tapped the air in front of her. "Kennedy Space Centre, Launch Pad 39A, construct, simulation time twenty minutes before the *Prometheus* explosion," she instructed her c-agent, before putting the data glasses over her eyes.

Instantly she was hovering about the launch pad like a stationary seagull, watching the spacecraft fuel up, pressure valves gently streaming vented gasses.

"Shared construct request from friend Zach," her c-agent prompted.

"Accept."

Zach's virtual presence materialised beside her. He was in his most casual slacks, but at least he was respectable – almost.

"I've always wanted to visit Florida," he said.

"So original," she said, eyes rolling.

Layers of information covered the scene: the 2046 time-date, links to the Martian base and its colonists, descriptions of the nuclear-powered engine needed to speed them back to Earth, how the base has gone mysteriously silent seven years later, whole archives of speculations as to what had happened and why. Even more about who or what had led to the destruction of the *Prometheus*. Her parents blamed Stone, who in turn blamed Sophia's father.

"So, what's the plan?"

"Let's follow those protestors in from the sea," she said. "Get their perspective."

She waved her hand to dismiss the info-links. "Track Cita Stone and her son, Ben," she ordered.

Instantly the scene changed and they were a few miles off shore, keeping pace with a pair of racing hydrofoils powered by electric Yamahas. Both boats were packed with a rag-tag of protestors and their banners, bristling with sensors that recorded everything in beautiful detail. The hulls were lifted clear of the water, so they only left the faintest of wakes. The standard timeline noted the wind direction, light swell and how the hydrofoil's course had been selected so they had the sun behind them, hiding them from any observers on land.

"Neat," said Zach. "But why are we following this lot?"

"Why shouldn't we?"

"There are so many other stories from this day; why choose them?"

"They're important – I know it. You should hear my dad talk about Cita Stone."

"Your dad is so mysterious."

"My dad is a pain."

The boats raced on, approaching the line of white surf endlessly drawn towards the golden strip of beach and a green, flat horizon cut with the industrial lines of the launch complex.

"Get ready," called the driver of one, and Sophia saw it was Cita, with Ben standing behind her, holding on to a grab point on the hull, his wide face split by a broad smile. In the enhanced virtual reality they were glowing slightly, marked out for her attention.

As the craft approached the shore, Cita flicked the switch that retracted its foils so it could surf the breaking waves for the final few metres. Its momentum hurled it half out of the water and up the hard sands of Titusville beach. One of the protestors, labelled as Mark Vaughan, stayed with the boats while the rest ran up towards the Cape Road, crossing without stopping, heading for the launch site. They used wire cutters on the fences and began the half-kilometre run across the empty marshlands.

At this point the standard timeline would zoom out to get a tracking shot of them, tiny figures lost in the vastness of the site. But Sophia kept her focus on the Stones, mother and son.

"Can't we check out the control room?" asked Zach.

"You can," said Sophia. "I'm following these two."

He made a face, but said nothing.

Sophia noticed that they were becoming separated, as Ben ran faster than his mother. Maybe the angle for her essay could be how parents underestimate the abilities of their children?

As they approached the site, they split into two groups: one, including Ben, heading for the rocket itself, and the other led by Cita for one of the lightning towers nearby. Here they used lightweight ladders and climbing gear to ascend to the top, hauling a pair of banners as they went. *No nukes in space,* said one, while the other read *Don't pollute the universe.*

"The best bit's coming," said Zach.

"The *best* bit?" asked Sophia. She really had her doubts about Zach, despite them sailing together. "Dozens died."

The launch site was engulfed in the ball of fire, white and yellow. The lightning towers were bent back by the force of the explosion, and Cita was thrown from hers onto the concrete, smashing ribs and breaking her ankle.

"Yes!" said Zach.

This time Sophia followed the mother rather than waiting where the son fell, walking behind her, watching the debris and burning fuel rain from the sky.

"Morbid," said Zach with a sniff. "Surely it's over."

"Ben?" asked Cita.

Sophia couldn't stop herself watching.

"Ben?" The woman had spotted the body. "No, no, no!"

She knelt by the body, picking it up and attempting to hold it in her arms. But she was too weak and too injured to manage it, and anyhow the body was too delicate and damaged, threatening to fall apart at a moment's notice.

She started to sob, rocking back and forth, the boy's blood soaking into her t-shirt...

"Seriously, Sophia, what's up?" asked Zach. "Why this obsession with Cita Stone and her son?"

Sophia turned to him angrily, nearly fast enough to knock the glasses off her face. For a moment, virtual reality rocked.

"Don't you care what happened? Don't you wonder what happened to those colonists on Mars? Whether they're dead or not?"

He couldn't look at her – instead tried to kick a stone, unsuccessfully of course. His shoe went straight through it. "Stupid stone," he said.

The scene seemed locked in a loop, with Cita rocking backwards and forwards.

Sophia noticed that Zach's face had the beginnings of stubble on it, short black lines on a swarthy face: he, like her, was growing up. He looked back at her, eagerly, as if about to ask her something. Something dangerous and difficult that she didn't want to hear; something beyond friendship.

"Sophia," he said. "Can I ask you something? Are you doing anything—"

Nooooo! She didn't want this. Sophia began to babble. "Do you want to hear a secret about the colonists?" Without waiting for an answer, she continued. "My dad's AI says there's a seventy-five percent chance they are still alive and it's just that their communications broke down."

She shouldn't have said that, she knew it. It was dinner-table conversation they'd promised not to mention outside home, but Zach – though ok as a sailing partner – wouldn't be right for anything more, which she feared he wanted.

It was enough to distract him.

"Really? That's huge. If that's true, someone ought to send a mission."

"They are – that's the project my dad's been working on. He's constructing a spacecraft in Earth orbit that could bring them back home. It's almost ready to go; it just needs the lander to be launched."

Suddenly she stopped. What had she done? What had she said?

"Interesting."

It was a third voice, neither hers nor Zach's.

The woman holding the body in front of them stopped rocking and turned to Sophia. Her face aged.

Her hair became grey, then fell out, leaving just the odd patch behind, and her neck grew lumps – cancerous growths.

Cita stood up and approached Sophia, a smile of triumph on her face. Sophia was close enough that she could see every lump on her malformed face, see the half-healed scars left from the explosion long ago.

"So that's what Kasparov is up to, as admitted by his daughter: building illegal spaceships to go to Mars."

Sophia's mouth opened, but no words came out. What was happening? This wasn't in the timeline. How could Cita Stone be in her private construct?

"This will be useful," said Cita, and then she vanished.

For a moment Zach and Sophia looked at each other.

"What the hell happened there?" asked Zach.

"I don't know. I shouldn't have said that, about the mission."

"You weren't to know; this is a secured construct. She shouldn't have been able to get in."

Sophia looked around, trying to understand it.

"I was going to ask if you wanted to race a double-handed sailing skiff?" said Zach.

So that's all, she thought. *I could have let him ask that.*

There was a sudden scream of rage from outside the construct, out in the real.

"Sophia, you *total* idiot!"

"Who's that?" asked Zach.

"That's my dad," she told him, a cold lump congealing in her stomach. "I've got to go," she said, and took the data glasses off.

6: Sophia

"You are currently trending in the blipverse." That was her c-agent.

"Shit!"

"You are currently number one topic in the blipverse."

"Noooooooo! Undo! Undo! Undo!"

She could hear her father's footsteps approaching.

"Approximately ninety-one percent of the comments on the blipverse regarding you are either negative or highly negative."

This time she said nothing, frozen in panic.

Her bedroom door was flung open and there he was: Artur Kasparov, director of the embryonic space program, and her father.

"What have you done?" he yelled.

"I was just doing my homework…" she began.

"What the hell were you thinking?" he demanded.

"What've I done now?"

"Don't play innocent with me, Soph. How many times have we told you *Don't trust the blipverse, don't tell anyone about the Mars mission*? But I've just seen a vid of you all over the blipverse talking about how I'm building a rocket to go to Mars!"

"But that was only just now, and in a private construct, honest!"

"What was just now?" His face was inches from hers, red, angry. Close up she could see the augmentations inside his eye, polysilicon irises tracking her.

"I need some coffee." It was a distraction, to get them to her mother, who was the calmer of the two parents.

"No – you tell me right now."

"Shouldn't Mum hear about this? She's the legal one."

She could see the augmentations in his eye glow with data as he considered her words. "Come on," he ordered, and she followed him, replaying the scene in her head, hunting for clues.

In the kitchen, her mother, Anna, was looking at the display. The data glasses – she had refused embeds – were glowing with images for her eyes only. Sophia spotted herself on the display, and her stomach muscles contracted painfully.

"You are *so* in trouble," said Sophia's younger sister, Nina, sharing a cake and a hot chocolate with their Granny Milla and enjoying the moment.

"So what?" she said, deciding on attack. "They'd have found out soon anyhow."

On the display she saw two spinning spheres orbiting each other: the ident of Humai, her father's Artificial Intelligence.

"But we've lost the ability to manage the agenda. Our #castaways image-crafting campaign is archived now, and we're in damage-limitation mode," it said.

Her father was in augmented conferences, eyes out of focus, concentrating on images created by nanomachines built into his irises and beamed directly onto his retina. "We can't deny it unless I force my daughter to perjure herself, tempting though that is. I'll blip you back; first I need her version of events."

Both parents turned to Sophia, and her mother took off her data glasses.

"I was just doing my homework – you know, on the *Prometheus* explosion. And I couldn't work out what to say so I thought it might be helpful to talk it through with Zach."

"I don't know why you bother with him," said Nina. "He's a B at best, maybe B-minus."

It was usually best to ignore these interruptions.

"We'd entered the construct and we got talking at that point when Cita Stone finds out her son is dead – you know?"

They nodded impatiently.

"We were just talking about the colonists and stuff, and then Cita changed, *aged,* and turned to me, and it went live rather than construct. She said what I said was 'interesting' and then she vanished. That's all."

"You skipped how you told Zach about the mission to Mars – breaking your promise."

Sophia's father pointed at the display, which was now looping back to her comments about how he was "constructing a spacecraft in Earth orbit".

"They've missed a bit," she said. It was a straw, but worth grasping for.

"You said *more*?"

Maybe that wasn't such a good idea.

"Just before that, I said something about how they're probably alive up there."

He sighed. "That's the bit we wanted to get out there first, at the right time, to build support for a mission to rescue them. Of course they wouldn't release that bit; now it will look like we're just saying it as an excuse to return. No one but us thinks they're alive up there."

Blip alerts were queuing up on the display, flashing urgently. He sighed again and rubbed his eyes as if trying to remove the images they projected into his head.

"Could the leak be Zach?" he asked. "Could he have been a construct, or rigged to relay to the Earth Firsters?"

"Records suggest he's clean," said Humai, its ident glowing on the display as it spoke. "I've checked the construct that Sophia and Zach were using, and there are unverified components that suggest root-level intercept and intrusion tools."

"Which is *just* why we told you not to trust the blipverse and not to mention to others about my work. You messed up, Sophia."

He tapped twice in mid-air to initiate a private blipverse conference, or blip-con. "Dr Khujandi, what's the damage?"

Sophia couldn't hear the reply, but she noticed her mother dash for her data glasses to follow the conversation. She sighed. It wasn't really her fault. Why was she getting blamed? And why couldn't she have had ordinary parents who weren't always away or in blip-cons?

"That wasn't very clever," said Granny Milla, handing her a coffee.

"Duh," said Nina. "If I had augmentations, I'd be able to spot tag-along spoofing. Why don't you tell Mum you think that's a good idea?"

"You're too young for embedded tech," said Granny Milla.

Anna took off her glasses long enough to say, "No sockets, no embeds and no nanobiotics."

Sophia shook her head. Even Nina should have known that wasn't going to fly.

"Of course – I should be there," said Artur. "We could move to Justinian to lobby for the mission."

"What about us?" asked Sophia.

"I'm not sure I could look after them again," said Granny Milla.

"I didn't mean to set your shawl on fire," muttered Nina.

"Nina, she was in it at the time," Sophia pointed out.

"We'll all move to Justinian," said Anna.

Sophia almost choked on her coffee and exchanged a wide-eyed look with Nina.

"You're kidding!"

7: Sophia

"You can't mean it," said Sophia.

"We've been thinking about it for a while," said Anna. "It was always a possibility for your father around the time of the launch."

"What about your job?"

"The Global DNA Databank is based in Justinian, so in a way it would be easier."

"But my friends are here. This is home – Granny Milla is here. This is London… Justinian is nowhere."

"It's the home of the Global Council," Anna said.

"Where would we stay? What about school? What about my friends?" The questions seemed to pour from Sophia.

"That's nonsense," said Artur. "Of course they didn't get Mars plague."

It wasn't for them: he was in a blip-con, no longer their father but head of Transworld Aerospace's special projects.

"Why are you punishing *me?*" asked Nina. "It was Sophia that blabbed in the construct."

"Let us work this out," said Anna.

She put on her data glasses and tapped twice in mid-air to begin blipping again. "Search: schools Justinian," she commanded.

Nina shrugged and cut herself some more cake.

"I'm going to the garden," said Sophia.

Their apartment was two floors above the 50-storey Alderman's Tower's mid-level garden block. It was spring, the time when plants awoke from their long slumber, filling the glass-caged air with the scents of life.

Sophia put on her data glasses and got her c-agent to blip Maria and Zach. They augmented into the garden, their images mixed into the scene around her, walking among the knee-deep grass, where the long, fine blades caressed their legs.

"I didn't do anything," said Zach. "I swear."

"It's ok. Dad is blaming me," said Sophia. "What do the others say?"

"Most of them are jealous you're blipverse global; some are even saying you did it deliberately for the attention," said Maria.

"They're crazy. Who'd want this? My blip-stream's gone wild. There are all these horrid, horrid blips, and my parents are talking about us moving to Justinian."

"No way," said Zach.

He was still in his slacks, that almost-stubble on his face. Was he really a B/B-minus?

"Who'd move from London to Justinian?" asked Maria.

"It was all a secret, but as you've heard, my dad's been working on a mission to Mars."

"Which is crazy; all the colonists are dead – Mars plague or something," said Maria.

"Says who?"

"Everyone. It's all over the blipverse."

"No one knows," said Zach. "Do they?"

Something in the eastern sky caught Sophia's eye. In her augmented view, her semi-aware c-agent had decided to overlay a marker pointing out Mars.

Distracted, she took off her data glasses. Her friends vanished with indignant calls of her name, but she ignored them. She could see Mars with her own eyes, a red dot low in the darkened sky, a solitary echo of the multitude of lights across the city. Up there was the base, silent for eight years.

What has happened on Mars? she wondered. *Is anyone still alive, looking back at us down on Earth?*

Part 2

8: Sophia

The plane rose swiftly above London and into the air; Sophia was on her way to Justinian, press-ganged into her father's battles.

The plane was a recent-year jet from her father's company, Transworld Aerospace Corporation. Its carbon exoskeleton was melded into a shell of smart glass, all avionics and intelligence hidden within the wings. The plane could be made transparent, a bubble in space, though today they had the top and bottom plates opaque.

Sophia sat at the front, where in the old days the pilot had flown the plane – before smart systems took over such drudgery – and watched the familiar curve of the Thames below her and the glittering muddy brown of its estuary. The plane banked sharply to the right as it turned towards the south-west, allowing her to look down at the fishing boats, a fleet of yachts racing with their spinnakers set and kite-powered merchant ships that dotted the water.

She loved flying; not just the feeling of freedom and speed, but the ability to see a whole city, province or even country in a single glance. As they climbed, the plane broke through a layer of clouds which sped past on either side, a blurring rush of white and grey, broken in two by the bubble of glass in which she travelled. Unafraid, she stood as far forward as she could, revelling in the feel of their motion, putting her hand up to feel the cool glass in front of her. Then they were above the clouds, which merged into one white sheet, and as the plane climbed higher, the feeling of motion lessened. Sophia lost interest and turned away to join her father.

This last week, he hadn't stopped reminding her of her mistake. It hadn't been much fun. She didn't like being the centre of attention for all the wrong reasons, and moving to Justinian hadn't been in her plan for her future. They'd banned her from most of the things she enjoyed, like sailing, and confiscated her electric speed-bike, which she had thought they didn't know about.

Halfway back, one side of the plane had been made opaque to avoid the distracting glare of the cloud-tops outside and was projecting the ideograms of the Transworld Aerospace Corporation's AI, Humai, together with someone Sophia recognised – a Dr Khujandi, whom she vaguely remembered as being chief designer of the spacecraft.

"Listen, Artur," he said, "this isn't good; the interplanetary transfer window is closing. The lander will be ready to launch tomorrow—"

"I'll be there," interrupted Artur.

"—but the politicians are getting cold feet, saying the mission needs further study. Can Justinian really block us?"

The news that TAC was putting together a mission to rescue the lost colony on Mars was dominating the news feeds. The Earth Firsters had denied leaking the story to the blipverse, which no one really believed, but it had caused such a stink that questions had been raised in the newly-built Global Council at Justinian.

"The Collapse made them feel they have to be involved in anything risky, such as space travel. The techno-luddite Earth Firsters are whipping up rabble-rousing nonsense about Mars plagues."

"Fearmongers! Could they really stop us? Oh, hi, Sophia."

"Hi," she said. "Sorry and all that. Can I do something?"

"Get that Mr Bevan to change his position and support us," said Dr Khujandi. "His EuroCore block is logjamming us."

"All sorted," said Artur. "Our intel is that he's suspicious of Cita's hardliners. They're going to switch to neutral, accepting a mission to Mars if it's automated and we agree to only bring back any survivors; no rocks, no samples."

"Are you sure?"

"Yes, no doubts about it," said Humai, its twin rotating spheres orbiting each other.

"But it will be an off-blipverse agreement," said Artur. "I've been invited to a private meeting with Mr Bevan. Officially there's been no mention as to agendas, but as you know, we have ways and means…" He looked over his shoulder to find Sophia watching him, and said no more.

"Hah," said Dr Khujandi. "Those ways and means of yours, very helpful. Do they know if Cita has heard of this?"

"That is less clear," said Humai. "We suspect so."

"That woman. I wish we could cast her away on Mars," said Artur, rubbing the bridge of his nose as if it itched.

"On another matter," continued Dr Khujandi, "I've been approached by representatives of Bella Cloud Corp again, asking for exclusive blipverse access rights to all space missions. They seem very insistent, threatening even, saying Felix Fernandez himself won't be happy."

"We should be cautious," said Humai. "BCC has significant influence, but what they want would give them a monopoly on the space blipverse."

"Never," said Artur. "I'm not going to let the project be derailed by Cita Stone or even Felix Fernandez. Offer him the full version of Sophia's blab in the *Prometheus* construct."

"What? You can't do that! Anyhow, surely it was deleted."

"I extracted it from your c-agent's cache," said Humai.

Huh?

"You said you wanted to help," said Artur. "It's got the bit about the Mars colonists probably being alive, which is the bit we want out there. I'll see him in Justinian this evening at the BCC event at Cloud Heights – tell them that. Tell them I'll raise it with Felix myself."

He was insistent, commanding, and Dr Khujandi nodded his head in agreement. Sophia was rather impressed by her father's energy and authority, even while furious with him for using her private logs for his own schemes.

"What event's that?" she asked.

"Business for those like me who meet with Felix, a party for everyone else. Maybe you can go – if you've finished your assignment." He stared at her, as if commanding her too.

With a sigh, she made her way to another work station and opened a window on her virtual desk. She read again the opening lines of her essay:

The Prometheus *explosion did not cause the Collapse; rather, it was the firing gun of a decade of destruction. The casual system of international governance was unprepared for repeated blows that would destroy the easy affluence of the first decades of the twenty-first century. Droughts were followed by floods as global warming kicked in, shortage of oil aggravated economic meltdowns, conflicts over water became battles over food, and the piles of dead were already mounting before the pandemics hit in earnest…*

It was no good; she couldn't concentrate. Sophia sent a blip off to Maria and Zach, asking for an update on what people were saying. The replies kept her distracted from both her assignment and her father's business until they were on the final approach.

When she made her way to the front of the aircraft, she could see the three linked artificial islands of Justinian in front of them. Built in the middle of the Sea of Marmara just south of Istanbul, close to Europe, Africa and Asia, it represented a fresh start after rioters and looters had gutted the old UN building in New York.

The islands were circular, six kilometres across, and their aircraft was banking to line itself up with the runway on the third, officially called Cephisso. It was named, together with its sisters Borysthenis and Apollonis, after the three muses, but everyone called them A, B and C Islands. They were equally spaced apart, like the points of an equilateral triangle, connected by maglev trains continually looping around and between each island.

Sun glinted off the buildings, and in the distance, in the park at the centre of A Island, Sophia could just make out the top of the One Earth statue's observation platform. It was surrounded by the Global Council buildings, the World Courts, museums, embassies, concert halls and conference centres. To her left was B Island, where the ambassadors, delegates, resolution crafters, lobbyists, blip-con artists, server farm execs, cleaners and all their families lived, played and slept. All three islands seemed to glow with newness under a spring Mediterranean sun, surrounded by sparkling sea.

On landing, Artur's qID got them waved through all the layers of the airport's security straight to the maglev station. The train crossed the six kilometres of bridges in just a few minutes, flying over the water like a bird skimming the waves on one of the planet's wide oceans. It was strangely peaceful after the flight.

They shared the maglev's long carriage with a family from Africa with dark skin and long, colourful robes. One of the younger children recognised Sophia and gave her a long, hard, serious look. She smiled back. The child was astonished at first and started to point at her, before grinning in return.

The train began to decelerate, arriving at A Island. "Warning," it said. "All of A Island should be assumed to be blipverse global public."

Then they began to hear the noise. It was a deep rumble at first, like thunder far away, but when the carriage doors opened, it hit them like a wave, as loud as the sunshine was bright. Shouting and screaming, whistles and chants from waves upon waves of protestors, held back by the blue-uniformed JustSec police force. They made two lines, clearing a path to the Global Council complex, a hundred metres away across Democracy Plaza.

Sophia could just hear a voice speaking on a megaphone. It was hard to keep track amongst all the sounds of all the different chants, chorusing the slogans on their banners: *No nukes in space*, *Mars rocks/Mars plagues* and *Humans not machines.* The crowd pushed again and again against the thin line of JustSec officers.

Then the protestors saw Sophia and her father and recognised both of them, breaking out as one in boos, followed by jeers of contempt. Artur seemed unconcerned, as if confident in his victory and their defeat, though Sophia certainly wasn't. In fact, she hated it. The voice with the megaphone spoke out, louder than before, the speaker hidden from view, so it was as if the crowd itself was crying out.

"See him! See that polluter of the universe! See that Artur Kasporov – the one scheming with AIs to infect the peoples of Earth with the plagues of Mars: plagues from the planet of the dead!"

Suddenly Sophia recognised the voice. It was Cita Stone. Despite herself, she was shaken.

"Ignore her," said her father.

But it was hard to ignore a crowd feet away, screaming at her, raging at her, held back by only a thin line. This was much, much worse than the blips, crazy though they had been. This was in-her-face hate: raw, visible, dangerous and violent.

Then the line broke, and the mob was all around her. JustSec pushed through to make a circle around them, but they were struggling with the mass, and Sophia found herself squeezed by their bodies on all sides. Fists beat against her, bruising her arms, shouting faces inches from hers. Sophia could hardly breathe, terrified she could trip and fall under the rush of feet, lost under a stampede. She tried to push away those next to her, to create some space. Someone behind her pushed back, and she spun around and was about to lose her footing when she was caught and thrust into the arms of a boy, who held her tight.

She looked up, and saw that his eyes were blue, skin golden, hair curly and expression confident – as confident as her father, but with the hint of a mischievous smile. The same age as her; no, maybe a little older.

"Leave her," he said, and they stopped.

There was an intensity to the experience, of her reading his face and character in a split second, of him responding, of their bodies feeling, creating memories, locking into the moment.

She smiled, cautiously, and watched the answering expression flicker across his face.

Then from behind the JustSec lines, a squad of heavily-armed soldiers pushed through and grabbed her, dragging her away from him, through the crowd and towards the GC building, leaving him behind.

Was that fear she had read? Fear of her or fear for her?

And who was he?

9: Tom

Tom ran and ran.

Under him, the treadmill made an ugly screech as ageing electric motors struggled to keep the track flowing.

On and on he ran, yet the metal wall, covered with scraps of bamboo parchment, remained one metre away, never getting closer, looming in his face to remind him where he was. The tiredness in his muscles felt good, overpowering the terrible itch in his bones, the anxious urging ache to do something, to escape. Left foot, right foot, left foot, right foot... each came down with a satisfyingly solid thud on the rolling rubber strip.

They were meant to exercise every day for an hour or two to avoid muscles wasting away in Mars's light gravity, but in the long years some had stopped, taking the easy route to adapt and become a person of this planet – a Martian.

Tom was one, his body never having known what it felt like to be pulled down by the standard one-g on Earth. But he loved the running machine, an escape valve to release the energy that boiled within. The only one in their little gym more often than him was José, who had turned away from the rest of the castaways to focus on his body and its fitness. At the other extreme was Mei-Li Wu, who hadn't exercised at all since her accident. Tom's dad had, of course, done exactly the amount regulations said he should, as regular as clockwork, by the book.

He stretched out the strides longer and longer, legs reaching forward and bare feet landing to grip and pull the track towards him. The machine adjusted its speed higher, matching his pace. Faster and faster Tom ran, and his breaths became deeper while sweat drops burst from his forehead. They trickled down his face, which he shook from side to side to keep his eyes clear.

Tom gasped and slowed slightly, wishing he'd brought some water. He had put on many more weights than normal, and they dragged him down as if he were running under Earth's gravity, nearly three times his normal weight. But it was his choice; it made Earth itself that bit closer, and the pain made him feel he was doing something, as if it could make the vow come true if he pushed hard enough, if he suffered enough. Tom pictured that moment when he had stood outside, looking up at the Earth, that bright star in the morning light, the day he had made that oath.

"Whatever it takes," he muttered to himself, increasing the pace, pushing himself just that little bit harder.

On and on. He checked the screens and wondered what he'd see if he travelled those kilometres for real. He had never been allowed to go more than a few hundred metres from the base.

What is Earth like? he wondered. In his mind's eye he pictured it, running open under the sky. For a moment he felt dizzy and paused, nearly tripping over as the treadmill whisked his foot from under him before he managed to lunge back into balance. Here on Mars, to be out in the open without a surface suit meant death.

His footfalls echoed around the chamber while the equipment creaked in protest.

"Tom," said a voice from behind him.

Snatched out of his reverie, he turned to see his father, then mis-stepped. Without mercy, the machine dragged his foot in one direction as his body fell in the other, pulled out of balance by the weights. Tom crashed onto the treadmill, which spat him out.

"Sorry – I should have warned you I was here," said Michael, picking Tom up.

"It's nothing. I wasn't paying attention."

There was a moment's silence as they sat on the floor, looking at the running machine. Tom took the time to catch his breath and wondered if he was expected to apologise for his earlier outburst, then decided with a burst of anger that he wasn't going to, that he didn't want to.

"It's the momentum," said his father.

"Huh?"

"With all that extra mass you get the weight of Earth, but your momentum's three times as much, so your balance is all wrong."

"What?"

His father snorted. "Stupid me; you don't know what is normal, you've never felt Earth gravity. It's why you've grown so tall."

"I know—"

"Yes, you know, but your body doesn't."

Suddenly Tom's father turned to him and gave him an unexpected hug.

"I'm sorry, Tom, you never asked for all this. We all volunteered – ok, not expecting to be up here seventeen years waiting for the return trip, but we knew the risks. Of course you want to escape; we all do."

Tom nodded, not knowing what to say or how to respond to his father when in this mood, transparently showing affection rather than giving curt instructions.

Michael shook his head before turning to Tom, holding his neck gently so that he could peer at his son, and he in turn could see his father's sad eyes under the grey hair.

"You don't know how tough it's been to keep going. Keeping the machines working is to be day in, day out fighting a battle that you know you can't win, and the price one day will be your life. That makes it harder to motivate everyone here to make an effort that could be meaningless. And not least to cheer up your mum." Michael looked away. "And to keep going myself… that's a burden that has a price." He paused. "Sometimes I wonder if we didn't make it – if at some point we all went mad and none of this is real; if we're locked inside our minds, not these cells."

"Don't be crazy, Dad. What could be more real than all this?"

"Yes, this is real – our reality. So maybe you were right on the blimp too. Maybe we should take that risky flight and learn whether we're doomed to be stuck here forever or not."

"Dad, let me go. I'd love to fly a blimp across the Martian surface."

"No; this is mine. I'm the commander. I decide. I'll go."

For a moment Tom wondered if this was right; if his dad's initial take that it was too risky had been the right one. But he told himself that it wasn't his decision, it was his father's. It was *his* responsibility. And it was a choice that would help him towards Earth.

"Whatever the cost," he whispered.

"What? What did you say?"

"Nothing. It's nothing."

10: Sophia

Sophia walked into the Global Council building in a daze. Either side of her were members of the elite JustForce, Justinian's army, growling with eagerness to clear the plaza.

"Soph? Are you ok, Soph?"

It was her father; she nodded absently. She discovered she was trembling.

"What the hell? That was crazy – I thought they'd kill me or something."

"But you're fine, right?"

"Now it's you that owes me, big time."

"Don't be silly. No one's hurt, and I was the one that got the JustForce squad to snatch you back. Bit of rough and tumble, but we're both ok."

He seemed to have relished the action, unfazed by the violence, his suit as sharp and crisp as it had been this morning. Her shirt was rumpled, the matching trousers ripped, and she could still feel the hands on her. She looked back, wondering if the boy had followed her in, but the protestors were outside, kept back by the JustSec's re-formed lines.

"Anyway, welcome to the GC."

Sophia looked around and found herself in the entrance hall of Justinian, the meeting place for the peoples of the planet and gateway to the Great Chamber. Like a rabbit warren, there were lifts, escalators and corridors heading off in all directions, to smaller halls, committee rooms and offices, but they all were connected to this one spot, the heart of the Global Council – or, as Artur put it, the GC.

Standing at its centre was a statue of Athena, the work of gene-splicing artist Tocado Muzanki. Cell printers had been used to sculpt yew to the form of a 15-metre-high woman, holding in one hand a steel sword and in the other a bio display on which slowly scrolled the constitution and conventions of the Global Council. She seemed to be looking directly down at Sophia, who stopped to stare up at those giant, expressionless eyes. Outside, the sun broke through a cloud, and bands of light came down through the glass matrix roof to give the goddess's skin a reddish-golden sheen, as if for a moment she were alive.

Totally auth.

Sophia was brought back from her reverie by the hubbub coming from the delegates crossing the hall's wide space, chatting and arguing. Her father had already started work, standing at the bottom of one of the busiest escalators. He seemed alive to a degree she'd never seen. Every other person who went past, whether heading up or down the moving stairs, seemed to know him. Moving between the delegates were the staff robots, taking coats and hats, bringing refreshments and then cleaning up after the messy humans spilt them.

My father is a... Sophia stopped, wondering what words to use. Manipulative schemer, or a great man betrayed by his own daughter? The trembling was gradually easing. She went to join Artur as he talked to a rather stout Indian woman in bright orange sari, whom he introduced as Bina Thakur. Sophia got the impression of a no-nonsense organiser, something like a schoolteacher.

"Delighted to meet you, Sophia," Bina said "You must meet my family – maybe at the BCC event this evening? Artur, surely you'll be coming? I will be there representing Bangalore Systems, not the committee, for once."

"Bina is chair of the Space Access committee, Sophia," said her father. "So she's pretty busy today."

Bina gave a crisp laugh, almost a bark, then wagged her finger at him, leaning slightly forward.

"And it's all your fault, Artur, isn't it? Off in London and Iran, secretly building rocket ships to go to Mars."

"It was you who suggested sending us to the Iranian desert – to 'keep an eye on us', you said."

"But you weren't unhappy, given their cheap power – and it didn't stop you getting into mischief, did it?"

Artur smiled. "Come off it, Bina, we all know you love refereeing these battles."

"But where is Anna?" asked Bina, straightening her back. "We haven't had the pleasure of seeing her in Justinian for – what is it? Three years?"

"She's coming later – no doubt to tell you we should never have given you all that power over deep space missions."

"Not me – I'm just the chair! But I know, I know, you're not happy, but the Earth Firsters were equally dissatisfied by that post-*Prometheus* compromise. And speaking of which, I spot Mr Bevan."

She waved at a man who had just entered the building. He was wearing a fine, long, black cloak with a hood to protect his face from the sun. Apart from a beaky nose, the rest of his face was obscured in shadow, hard to make out with eyes accustomed to the bright sunshine.

"Mr Bevan, come and join us."

The face under the hood nodded. "Madam Chair, my apologies, but I must talk to Dr Kasparov before the meeting."

"Please, call me Bina, and let the robots take your cloak."

One of the robots stopped and put an arm out towards Mr Bevan. The smooth, matt metal skin reflected dully the light pouring down from above as its fingers opened and wrist rotated in invitation.

The newcomer stepped backwards, away from the machine.

"No, no, Madam Chair, I want no help, need no help," he said.

He pulled back the hood, unbuttoned the cloak, then seemed unsure what to do with it. With a smile of exasperation, Bina took it from him and passed it on to the robot.

Mr Bevan gave a slight bow. Underneath the cloak he wore a dark, formal double-breasted suit with tails and a tie: he seemed vastly overdressed for the Mediterranean warmth.

"I hope your journey from Wales wasn't too troublesome?" Bina asked.

Aha, thought Sophia, *I knew he must be from somewhere cold.*

He paused, as if considering how to answer. "All travel is an inconvenience, but this was a necessary inconvenience."

"We haven't moved our position," said Artur. "The Mars mission must fly."

"And the quarantine of Earth must be maintained – but we have a proposal. It is… er… delicate. I have booked an off-blipverse meeting room, if you will join me."

Artur acted surprised. Sophia nearly grinned at it, amazed that the others would be taken in; but then again, she did know her father a lot better than they did.

"A proposal? Well, we're certainly not in the mood for compromise, but we will listen to any suggestion from EuroCore."

"Good, good," said Bina. "You two go and make progress, and then the committee will meet afterwards."

"You better wait in the visitors' gallery, Sophia, just up there," said Artur, pointing towards a corridor that led upwards.

All of a sudden Sophia was alone as delegates came and went, their displays and data glasses aglow with information.

Huh.

Feeling a bit left out, she made her way in the direction her father had indicated till she was in what felt like the audience of a concert hall, a ring of seats around the open chamber below her. She was soon lost in thought, wondering who the boy had been and whether their meeting had meant as much to him as it had to her. Should she talk it over with her friends in London? It seemed too soon, as if talking about it would damage the delicate, just-created memories.

Sophia was deep in a reverie when she was distracted by activity on the floor. She could spot her father making his way to the London City State desk, with its familiar flag. Looking around, she was able to find the long, dark-suited figure of Mr Bevan already at the EuroCore desk. She put on her data glasses, which became awash with information: one stream following where her pupils were looking so they could flash up the affiliations of the delegates she gazed at, while another trickled more slowly the committee's business.

32nd meeting of the Space Access Committee, Agenda, Minutes, Chairman's Report... The text scrolled remorselessly upwards.

The meeting dragged on, and very soon she was bored again. She tapped twice on the desk to read some blips from her friends, but then their faces split into a pair of spinning globes.

"Well, well, what do we have here?" said a familiar, amused voice. "Doing a bit of gossiping?"

"Shut up, Humai!" she hissed. "Stop listening in, and stop interrupting."

"Who, me? I just thought, seeing all the trouble you made, you might actually like to hear the big decision. But," and the AI sighed, ideogramming tears, "alas... ah, the youth of today."

"Ok, shut up, I'll listen in."

The images of the spinning globes dissolved into a spray of teardrops and then vanished, to be replaced by scrolling text:

Resolution GC/SAC/32/2061/4: *The Committee authorises the Transworld Aerospace Corporation to send a single automated mission to Mars, and if any of the human colonists are found alive, return them to Earth. Condition of authorisation: no return of Martian materials.*

She heard Bina's voice announce the resolution and then her father officially support it.

"And any comments from EuroCore?" asked Bina.

"EuroCore supports the motion," said Mr Bevan.

"Well, that's nice to see, the Technocrats and Earth Firsters working together," beamed Bina. "That should make things easier; we can go straight to a vote."

There was a burst of graphics on the board above Bina's head as the icons of each country's flag lined up on either side of the podium. Almost all were in favour.

"The motion is passed," said Bina, and there was a scattering of applause.

"And so, history is made," said a smug voice, as two spinning planets emerged on the desk in front of Sophia, surrounded by firework icons.

"So what, am I meant to be impressed?"

"Ah, I see you don't get it," said Humai. "Probably just as well. That's the irony; you, who can leap up and shout, don't want to, while I, who do want to, am unable to move, let alone leap."

"Oh, I'm so sorry for you," said Sophia sarcastically, getting up. "Tell Dad I'll meet him in the entrance hall."

"Will do," Humai said, vanishing in one final burst of exploding fireworks.

Sophia tried to retrace her steps, but she soon got lost wandering the maze of corridors. Eventually she found herself in a dead end and on her own, lost in a dull stillness away from the echoes of voices that had resonated in the main halls. A sign pointed the way to the off-blipverse meeting rooms, and out of curiosity she followed it. Along a corridor were a series of huge doors, looking as impressive as airlocks. Next to each was a display; the first said 'MR-1, Reserved, Bevan' with an image of his stern face. Sophia smiled in recognition.

Idly, she walked down, examining the other doors, till she stopped in shock. The display by the meeting room at the end had a photo of a face she recognised:

the boy from the protest outside. And there was a name – he had a name; Alejandro.

She knew his name, and she knew where he would be. Here – now.

She pulled open the large door. It opened slowly, heavily, and she saw not a room but a short mesh walkway across a void to a large, mirrored box that was hanging, separated on all sides from the rest of the building. The box was suspended by wires and was not fixed but moved slightly from side to side: a room floating in air.

The box also had a door. Sophia nervously walked across the void and struggled to open it. An automated voice spoke.

"MR-3 is an off-blipverse meeting room. To enter, please put all your blip and comms devices in the secure container at the back of the outer door. It will be keyed to your quantum ID."

Sophia closed the large outer door. It felt like locking herself in the deepest vault of the most secure bank. The door gave off a very faint light – enough to find the container the machine had mentioned. She took off her glasses and put them in the drawer indicated. It closed with a snap.

"No smart, data-aware or blipcom devices detected; you are free to continue."

She hesitated, slightly overwhelmed by the intensity of the process, feeling naked without any of her tech. *None of that. Time to get a grip.* She walked the final steps to the floating room and opened the inner door.

Inside, her eyes had trouble comprehending what she saw. Were there many people there or just one? It was hard to see, as the room was lit by candles, naked candles, wax and flame.

Then it clicked into place. There was just the one person there, not the boy she'd hoped for but an old woman, and all the walls, the floor and the ceiling were mirrors, reflecting the scene to eternity. And there were just two candles and an infinity of their clones. Behind her the door closed, sealing shut, and from outside there were the sounds of pumps and air rushing out.

"An unexpected guest; how nice."

It was the woman who spoke, walking towards Sophia on the mirrored floor, her shoes snapping on its surface, echoes continuing as if an army were on the march. It was an uneven step, for the woman was limping slightly. Her face was a mess of cancerous scars and growths, and on her skull-like head were tufts of mud-grey hair.

Suddenly Sophia realised she recognised her.

"Well, well, it's the Kasparov girl," said Cita Stone.

She was getting close to Sophia, who backed away.

"Hello," she said.

"And hello to you too, Kasparov girl. Let's have a little chat," said Cita. She waved at the room; in the flickering candlelight there seemed to be an infinite line of Citas, stacked like a force of nature. "Isn't this room lovely?" she said. "Nothing electronic is allowed in here, and when the door closes the air outside is sucked out so this room is hanging in a vacuum. No one outside can hear us or detect us: a space for just you and me."

She advanced on Sophia, who found her back to a wall.

"Now tell me, how is your father funding this spacecraft to Mars?"

"How what?"

"Come, come, don't play games. You've just flown in with Kasparov from London – you must know."

"I have no idea what you're on about."

"You should tell me, for all our sakes. How many more sons must die for humanity's hubris?"

"Daughters too," said Sophia, then regretted it, remembering Cita's son, Ben. "Oh, sorry, forgot about your..."

She watched Cita's face, inches from hers. Lips curled, revealing yellowed teeth, then uncurled, hiding them. Cheek muscles twitched. Eyelids closed, then opened to reveal crazed eyes staring at her, unblinking. Sophia felt that the other woman had slipped sideways, mentally crossing an invisible line into a world of grief and rage, a loss that was an open wound, a force which couldn't be controlled.

Suddenly her hand shot out to grab Sophia's neck and thrust her against the glass wall, hard. The back of her skull banged against its surface, and in the impact Sophia bit her lip, filling her mouth with blood.

"Now, you *will* tell me," snarled Cita, her eyes inches from Sophia's. "Why did your father destroy the *Prometheus*?"

11: Tom

The corridors were dim, the shadows deeper than normal. And the base was freezing, far colder than it should be. Tom was wrapped in every spare layer of clothing he could find; his breath was frosting in the air in front of him. He passed doorways into the other cubicles, caves that ominously swallowed the light.

But Tom was for once happy, for the dimness was good news, one of many very small steps towards Earth. He had woken early, anticipating the excitements of the day, and decided to make sure his father was awake for the dawn departure. He banged on the door to where his parents slept – not so much a knock as a victory drum roll.

It was the day his father would fly over the Martian dunes, returning with the transponder that would resurrect the dead comms, opening a window back to Earth.

It had been a great week: all of them working together to prepare the blimp for flight with the hope of rescue to come. He remembered the first meeting, working out who would do what and how. His dad had never seemed so alive, less the play-safe, do-it-by-the-rules commander than a risk-taking leader.

They needed hydrogen to fill the envelope and oxygen for the pilot, and both to power the engine's fuel cell. That meant water, and more of that precious liquid than the closed system could spare, so more would have to be mined, split and stored. Records would have to be checked to find the exact location of the

Sitefinder lander, controls to steer the craft designed and created.

"Ok," Tom's father had said, standing by the bamboo parchment chart on which he'd drawn a timeline of what must be done and when, "this is what we're going to do."

There was something for everyone, apart from poor old Mei-Li Wu.

"José, we need water; sounds like a job for you."

José had simply nodded, knowing what that meant. The base had been built in the Maja Valles at the bottom of an escarpment that was riddled with rills, signs that at one time water had flowed down their sides. It was permafrost soil, rock and ice in a mixture as solid as concrete.

At the back of the base an airlock led into the hillside, where a tunnel had been cut into its heart. Freezer-cold, it was usually not a place to stay long. But in all directions from the main tunnel were drilled narrow holes into the rock. And once in a while, when they needed more water, the tunnel would be transformed. Heaters would raise the temperature of the tunnel's atmosphere, first to barely freezing, then to the tropical warmth that José relished. Fingers of sultry air would explore each of the cracks and crevices of the drill holes, waking the ice into liquid water that would flow down to a collecting drain in the centre of the tunnel.

Tom had helped José, sharing in his simple pleasures of warmth and work. He'd smiled as he'd raised the drill bit to the solid rock, relishing the noise, the sweat, and the chance to use the strength that had come from those long days in the gym.

Then, as they had sat, listening for the joyous sound of trickling water, José had abandoned his usual reticence to tell stories of his early life in Venezuela, of canoeing down the Orinoco River and surfing the beaches of the Caribbean.

From the tunnel the water would be piped to the garden and JT. Pumps, coolers and pressure cylinders were his tools, storing the gases that hissed from the splitter, energy and water converted into hydrogen and oxygen.

JT was serious about the task, and Tom had to struggle to raise a smile from him.

"Won't it be great to have comms back?" he had asked, as they changed the filters on the algae tank.

All JT had said was "Aye", so Tom had tried again.

"Don't you wish you could fly in that blimp too?"

At that JT had stopped and thought. "Maybe, if I had to. If I really had to."

Tom hadn't asked any more questions, and they'd worked in silence under the garish pink of the hydroponic bed's LED lights.

But others were more supportive of the blimp mission, and Tom found he had a surprising ally in Victor. He worked ceaselessly to manage the base's power to feed José's and JT's work, switching off everything deemed optional, which he decided included heat and light.

"What can possibly go wrong, Elena?" he had asked, smiling at Tom's mum, who hadn't replied.

She was in charge of life support, and thinking up things that could go wrong was how she had spent her time. Oxygen, pressure, heating and water: without them her husband would die. Should something medical go wrong out there, he'd die. The calculations always said the same thing: the blimp could only take the one, and return with one and the Sitefinder transponder. There'd be no one to help, and there'd be no chance of rescue.

She hadn't been much fun, so Tom had preferred to spend his time helping José, JT and his father. Michael had been busy removing the weather sensors and modifying the controls so the blimp could be flown by someone in a surface suit strapped to a bamboo seat, wide enough for a pilot and the recovered transponder.

"Isn't it great?" he'd ask, relishing his new alter-ego, acting out the walking, talking space hero of the books and movies that had fired Tom's imagination, the old rule-book commander forgotten.

And Tom had agreed, trying the controls himself, going out in surface suits with his dad to the swelling balloon and sitting in the pilot's seat, moving the control stick from side to side as his father checked that the engines pivoted correctly. He imagined flying it himself, and itched to try the blimp, to fly off from the base into the air, to see the plains of Mars below him.

As well as the stick, there were three valves. The left one vented hydrogen from the envelope so it would descend, while the centre one opened the gas tanks to inflate it and ascend. The valve on the right dumped some of the water ballast for rapid ascent.

"See, it will be no problem. Vent hydrogen to land by the Sitefinder probe, dismantle the comms we're after, attach it to the blimp by this cable, then dump water to get airborne again and head back to base."

And at that thought Tom and Michael had grinned at each other.

But on the day of the launch, as they breakfasted in the cold and half-dark kitchen, Michael's smile was more a grimace. The alter-ego was lost in the shadows, and the old worrying base commander was back.

"We should give the blimp a name," said JT.

"No," said Michael. "No point."

JT shook his head gloomily but said nothing.

Elena fussed around, making sure Michael had eaten enough for what would be a very long day.

"I'll be fine; leave me be."

They hugged in the airlock. "Take care," she said.

"You know I will."

Tom, JT and Victor went out with him in surface suits to the readied blimp. The envelope was fully inflated, creases filled out by the pressure of the gas inside. Cables were wrapped around rocks and the legs that held the base up above the soil. It trembled gently, swaying from side to side in the soft breeze that came in the morning.

Victor and Michael conferred, helmets pressed together so that sound could be transferred where the glass met.

Victor nodded, and Michael turned to Tom, bringing his helmet closer so that its glass just touched his.

"Good luck, Dad!"

"I'll be fine – look after your mum."

"Will do."

There was a pause as Michael stood back, looking at Tom; then he came back for a moment.

"It will all work out, trust me."

Then Michael clapped Tom on his shoulder, which he barely felt through the suit's thick material, and turned to the blimp. For a moment he looked up at it, watching as it strained against the cables, then he moved towards the cage underneath and strapped himself in.

He looked over at the other three and then reached for his torch. With no working radios, they had chosen to communicate by flashing Morse, a dead language from Earth brought back to life on Mars.

KEEP CLEAR.

They walked backwards towards the base as Michael tried the engines. The port and then the starboard engines slowly began to spin their propellers. Clouds of red dust were raised in their wake, gently spreading over the rocky plain.

READY 2 GO.

Tom, JT and Victor moved to the cables, loosening them but keeping a wrap around the rock or base leg so they could use friction to control the weight more easily.

Michael raised his hand, and Tom's heart began to beat faster. This was really it; in a moment of terror the risks became magnified, and he wondered if he should call out to his father that it wasn't worth it, that he should stay here safely on the ground with them. But there was no way his words would be heard: he was alone in a glass bubble.

Then Michael dropped his hand and, on the signal, all three let go. The blimp jerked into the thin air, nodding gently back and forth as it explored its freedom.

It continued to rise above Tom, glowing gently in the morning sun, trailing the three cables. He watched his father working the valves, adjusting them to control the ascent until the blimp settled at a height of about one hundred metres.

Tom could see Michael turning to look down at the three figures and the base – its seven hexagons, the greenhouse with its garden, the tunnel heading into the hill behind, the cables heading off to the black cube of the thermonuclear power plant. He seemed to inspect what had been his kingdom, and then blinked a message at the watchers below.

ALL SYS GO.

They waved back.

Michael turned to the control stick and pressed it forward. The propellers began to spin faster and faster, till their blades were a blur. Through the thin atmosphere, Tom could hear a gentle *thrump, thrump, thrump* as the blades cut the air. Gradually the blimp built up speed, and it turned away from the sun, heading west.

As it disappeared behind the hill, there was one last message.

BYE.

Then he was gone, and Tom was alone with JT and Victor.

12: Sophia

Sophia blinked hard as she tried to get her eyes to focus and remove the watery film between her and the world. She could feel a hand holding her around her throat, and the pain throbbing from the back of her head. It must be a mistake.

"Thwat?" she asked, her mouth full of a warm liquid.

"It is for the best – go on, just tell me what you know." The speaker was shorter than her, but her grip was like steel. Sophia could make out tufts of grey hair and two dots of eyes. Stone, Cita Stone: that was the other's name.

She struggled, pushing the older woman back, but her head was slammed against the mirrored wall again. She heard glass crack.

"Go on," the other whispered. "Tell me, tell me now."

Panic filled Sophia. What could she tell this woman that would satisfy her enough to make this stop? Then anger: she wasn't going to stand for this. Sophia ignored the questions and focussed on the woman, using her strength against the solidity of the wall behind to push the other away, hard. Cita was flung back, falling onto the ground.

"Leave me alone!" said Sophia.

From outside came a whistling of air, and then the door opened. It was her father, eyes questioning, who saw her standing over Cita, threatening.

"Well, well, like father like daughter – violent thugs both," said Cita, getting to her feet.

"I saw you go off-blipverse into this room. What happened?"

"She attacked me. She asked why you destroyed the *Prometheus* and then she attacked me."

For a moment anger could be seen on his face. "She was asking what? That we'd destroy our own spacecraft?" He turned to look down at Cita, candlelight flickering across her face.

"We know an AI was involved; that means you. Devious AIs, manipulating us, careless of the lives of humans. No more AIs – no more spaceflight."

"Didn't you hear? We got the resolution approved."

"That fool Bevan was weak; we knew he was. Well, you'll have that one mission, then we'll see. And you've made more enemies today."

Artur looked at her, as if judging how to react. Then he remembered Sophia. "Were you hurt?"

"She banged my head against the glass." Sophia pointed at the cracked mirrored wall.

"Let me see," he said, examining her, checking for a cut. "No blood, just a bruise." He turned to Cita. "But that's my *daughter* you attacked. You should be more careful when you're alone in an off-blipverse room."

He began to roll up the sleeves of his fine-cut suit. "Sophia, I think you should leave us."

"No – not like that!"

Sophia's mother sometimes talked about what Artur had done in the dark days of the Collapse, when London had fought and won its independence: a rough lad from the wrong side of the river, the lighterman's son.

"She is right, the girl of yours. I've company coming; you'd have realised that if you were thinking straight. A witness."

Yes, he *is coming. That boy, Alejandro.*

"We should go, Sophia, and leave this woman well alone."

"Before you go, you wouldn't like to clear some things up – such as what you were really doing on the Forward Project?" asked Cita. "With a team of twenty and a dedicated AI, all you came up with was a mission to the planet of the dead – seriously? And now the Technocrat movement's AI expert is the director of a *spaceflight* mission?"

Cita was watching Artur closely. She saw his expression change, the confirmation that these were good questions to ask.

"So," she said, nodding her head.

"We know the *Prometheus* was secure from our side," said Artur. "It can only have been sabotage. You and your team are the only suspects."

"My son was killed in that explosion! It was your rocket that failed – or your AI double-crossed you."

"You're crazy; we checked both. It could only have been your lot. Come, Sophia."

Cita Stone waited until they reached the door. "There will be other days – know that. One resolution is not enough: I will come back, and things *will* be different."

Sophia looked back one last time to see the old woman alone in the room of mirrors. Lost in her thoughts, surrounded by her many reflections, lit by two candles and their thousand copies.

Back in the sanity of the Justinian corridors, her father strode ahead, but Sophia caught a glimpse of the boy, Alejandro: he had been watching them leave the off-blipverse room. He was thin, she realised, as if stretched. She didn't know what to say, trapped between the desire to return to where the world was normal and not crazy and wanting to say hello. In the end, her father's exasperated "Come on, Sophia" snapped the spell and she walked on, leaving him behind again.

"What was that about?" she asked, as they made their way out, back to the reception hall.

"Not here, Sophia." Her father was walking fast, not stopping even when other delegates came up to congratulate him and grabbed his hand to shake.

"But could it have been an AI that…?"

"I said not here!" he snarled, stopping to glare at her. "How many times must we tell you not to blab in public spaces?"

Sophia fumed, but said nothing. She was in the wrong, again, but her father was crazy, she thought. What would her mother say? Condemn her or him? She had time to reflect on the monorail back to their apartment on B Island. Had she put her foot in it again? At least there was a party to look forward to.

Their apartment was on the 18th floor of Troy Tower, one of three residential blocks shaped like cooling towers, their hyperboloid walls creating natural cooling in the inner courtyard. The Kasparovs' windows faced north and west, so they could see both the setting sun, its limb just resting on the horizon, and the blood-red-tinted buildings of A Island.

The apartment was sparsely furnished, giving the impression of being rarely used. One of the few ornaments was the tapestry her parents had commissioned, showing the Collapse and London's battles for independence, back when they had been student activists. It took almost the length of one wall.

Sophia sank gratefully into a comfy chair by the window, looking around with interest.

"That's where the tapestry went, then," she said.

"Humai?" asked her father. "Are we secure?"

On the wall appeared the twin spinning globes, rotating around each other.

"Yup, Artur, all clear; I've checked these rooms, so go ahead."

"Open an encrypted blip channel to Anna."

Sophia's mother, augmenting into the room, was concerned. "I thought you'd be out celebrating the resolution."

"Cita Stone assaulted Sophia – she hit her," said Artur.

"Why? Sophia, what happened?"

Sophia looked at her parents, wondering what they knew that she didn't.

"She was asking about the *Prometheus*. She said she knew an AI caused the explosion."

"Not that again," said her mother. "Her lot blames AI for everything."

"What's this all about?"

There was a silence.

"Well?" Sophia asked.

Her father's eyes gleamed. Sophia could tell that he wanted to tell her, wanted her more involved, but her mother sighed.

"Artur, how can we explain? She's too young to be mixed up in your plans."

"I'm not," Sophia said, automatically.

Two lights spun on the wall, turning into two rotating, orbiting globes. "If you're to make the BCC event at Cloud Heights, you better get ready soon."

"Yes, you'd better go and change, Soph," said her father. "Anna, don't go, I'll give you an update." As he went into their study, her image followed him, leaving Sophia alone.

"Huh. Gee, thanks, Humai."

"You're welcome."

"Do you know why the *Prometheus* exploded?"

"No. Not yet."

She remembered her father's behaviour in the off-blipverse room and wondered for the first time if there were things he wanted that were more important to him than his family. Sophia shivered. If that was the sort of thought that all this led to, then maybe she didn't want to get 'involved', as her father called it.

He returned, along with the image of her mother.

"So, Sophia," said Artur. "We've got a choice for you. Would you rather head back tomorrow to London to your mother, or join me for the launch?"

Was she to have a choice after all? Or was it one of those fake choices, when her real preference would be neither, but for them not to move to Justinian?

"The launch? Of the spaceship heading out to Mars?"

"Yes."

What did she want?

She remembered seeing Mars bright in the sky above London. The launch! That wouldn't be all confusing like today; that would be an adventure, to discover what had happened up there in the sky.

"Of course, the launch, yes."

Her father smiled – the smile he showed after winning a poker hand – while her mother's shoulders dropped a fraction.

For a moment on the wall were projected the faint images of two rotating planets, orbiting each other. One was blue and the other red.

And then they were gone.

13: Sophia

Humai's taste in clothes was excellent, thought Sophia. It had secured create rights from the Vinci fashion house and printed off a close-fitting knee-length dress, fine material with a silky shine, dark with a green tint and retro Alexander McQueen styling. To match it, her father gave her a smart pendant which glowed like the setting sun. She got the feeling it was a concerted effort to be nice to her. *What else could I wrangle out of them?* she wondered.

In the robocab on the way there, she could feel her father's tension. He was still in his sharp suit, indicating that to him this was 'work'.

"So why are we going?"

"Because, Soph, Felix Fernandez is rich and his Bella Cloud Corp powerful, and we've just turned down its request to exclusively mount BCC sensors on all our space missions. A few honeyed words might be diplomatic."

"Uh-huh."

"Don't worry; these events are parties, really. All the important stuff is done on the lower levels where you needn't go."

Ahead, Sophia could see searchlights playing up and down a tower.

"So that's it?"

"Yup. Cloud Heights."

It was about a kilometre high: a thin pencil of nano-carbon with glass elevators continually ascending and descending. At the top of the pencil was centred a squashed cylinder that looked like a checkers piece or thick coin – more the latter, as it was coated in gold with milling around the edge. On top of it were two more disks, the first identical to the one it rested upon but half offset, hanging outwards. The second was smaller and also offset to leave a space between them, where Sophia could just make out what looked like trees.

The small disk acted as a landing pad for the continual stream of helicopters, helistats, STOLs, blimps and hybrids arriving and departing. Lights shone from the upper disk, its windows and the space between it and the landing pad: the pulsing, multi-coloured signature of a party. The lower disk was featureless, with no windows and no lights.

"The main cylinder contains the Cores: a bit like a private off-blipverse store for BCC; custom plate arrays. Data goes in but never out. You've heard your mother and me talk about being careful what traces you leave on the blipverse – well, this is why. BCC can run its trawlers over anyone at any time. There is also the lattice farm that creates forty percent of all blip-soaps followed worldwide, which pays for all of this."

At the base was a queue of guests, a qID check and security scan (rather overkill, Sophia thought, given that there was clearly nowhere on the dress she could hide anything) and then a brief pause for the elevator. She saw her father crack his knuckles, then shrug the shoulders of his suit into place.

The elevator – or rather car, as it was cableless, a vertical mono-rail – had not just glass windows but a glass floor and ceiling too, and accelerated knee-bendingly fast. The view was wonderful: the sun had just set, leaving broad brushstrokes of gold and rusty red over the western sky. She could see planes descending and taking off on C Island, while over on A Island the top of the One Earth sculpture could just be seen, reflection glinting off its globe.

Then, all of a sudden, the car started to decelerate, so aggressively she felt nearly weightless. The view disappeared, and all was dark for a few seconds as it plunged through the lower cylinder to arrive on its upper surface – the garden Sophia had spotted.

"Welcome to Cloud Heights," said an attractive woman waiting for them.

"Would you like a drink?" asked the male companion at her side, handing out glasses of something fizzy. They both took a glass.

"Be careful now, Sophia," said her father. "Just the one."

"Mr Fernandez is expecting you, Dr Kasparov," said the man. "If you would follow me, please, into the Cores." He led Artur down a staircase that vanished into shadows.

"I'll find you," said Artur to Sophia over his shoulder. "I think the main party is on the upper level."

She was tempted to explore the garden. In the evening air the scents of roses and clematis wafted attractively, and there were burning torches lighting pathways between trees and gurgling water features.

But the other guests were heading upwards, so she followed them on the curving escalator that took her up to the upper level, a single open space as large as a ballroom, glittering with gold paint and glass chandeliers.

There were hundreds, if not thousands, of people in there – what felt like half of Justinian.

At the centre was a circular bar, freely dispensing more bubbly and cocktails which changed colour as they were drunk. In between the guests coasted robots with plates of delicacies from around the world. The first to approach Sophia had a tray of sushi: "Rare or extinct?" it asked. She shook her head, remembering stories her mother had told her about a BCC team buying the last known stocks of selected fish species before they became extinct and then charging Anna's project for DNA samples.

On other plates was real meat, not vat-grown stuff, in the form of finely sliced carpaccio and recreated dodo mini-burgers, oyster taster selections, white asparagus with truffle, chocolate-covered locusts, live termite dip and, rather prosaically, Spanish churros.

Around the edge of the great circular room was the entertainment – you just kept walking until you found something you liked. To one side were blip-soaps, live streams with the top actors from the most popular shows, with specially commissioned storylines linked to the event. Anyone walking round the left side became an extra, whether they liked it or not.

Sophia chose to go right, where there were performances of music and dance. First she found a group of dancers, clones from China, created by the body programming artist Xu Ming. They had nanobots inside all their muscles, allowing them to be programmed to enact any choreography at will, remotely synchronised. Xu Ming himself, flown in especially for the event, was inviting guests to select which performance they'd like to see.

There was a gap between acts, a window with a luxurious seat plumped high with dozens of cushions where guests could admire the views out over the sea. The next act was a Mali jazz quartet, which was playing Jakatan composer Sumarno's Famine Fifty-Four mash. It was struggling to compete against the background mutterings of the crowd and next-door musician – a DJ with the latest mixes for some enthusiastic dancers. A sign requested that timing and rhythm augmentation be used by anyone entering that floor.

In alcoves around the wall was artwork: sculpture from the transparent school and paintings commissioned by the New Revolution countries (Sophia recognised, with a smile, several works from London).

On the far side of the room from the entrance, the roof was retracted to create a more relaxed space where couples and groups could talk, lying back in the easy chairs and sofas so wide they looked like beds. Here a charcoal burner glowed, and lights were dimmed so that the stars, just coming out, could be seen. Sophia could see why, in the darker edges, many couples were locked in close embraces.

At the far side of the upper plate, the marble floor gave way to wooden decking, as if this were just some large balcony, a bit bigger and higher up than most apartments. Sophia made her way to the edge and, steeling herself, looked down.

"Don't do that."

She turned, and her pulse seemed to skip a beat. It was the boy, Alejandro. He'd changed his outfit since the morning and was now wearing the latest gen blip-wear: pin-striped trousers and adaptive cloth jacket with striped blue sneakers. The blue matched his eyes.

"Hello, Alejandro," she said. She'd said his name. He was real.

"Hello, Sophia," he said.

There was a moment as that soaked in, their eyes locked. Then the pause had gone on a fraction too long.

"You know my name?" she asked.

"You know mine."

"It was on the door – the off-blipverse room."

"Ah-ha. Clever," he said.

"Mine wasn't."

"Didn't have to be – you've been all over the feeds."

"Don't. My dad's been giving me such grief for that."

"Now that's something I'm familiar with."

He smiled, and she smiled back.

"Can we get away from the edge for a bit? Please?" Alejandro asked.

"Isn't it safe?"

"Oh, it's safe; I just don't like heights."

"What are you doing up here then?"

"I live here."

"Here?" Sophia looked around at the ballroom.

"Well, not here – downstairs," he said.

"In Cloud Heights? Your family?"

"Well, there's just me and my father."

"Alejandro *Fernandez*?"

"Sophia *Kasparov*?"

She laughed. "Touché – parents do impose themselves through their surnames."

"Mine is rather good at keeping my name off the blipverse – amongst other things," he said. For a moment, a shadow crossed his face. "Please, let's sit here," he said.

They sat away from the edge, on benches carved from tree trunks lying around a charcoal burner, designed to give the feel of a forest glade.

"Hi, Alejandro," said a boy, coming to join them. He was with a girl, and Sophia saw that both were about the same age as her and Alejandro, dressed smartly but not expensively.

"Pepe, Yeliz – this is Sophia," said Alejandro. He seemed to guess her thoughts. "Relax; these are my keep-me-grounded friends, not high-flyer-involveds like you and me."

For a moment Sophia glowed, but then stiffened. There was something about his tone…

"Pepe's dad was my father's head of security in Barcelona before things took off."

"Here he's just a heavy, but the pay is even better," said Pepe. He had a strong Spanish accent – or was it Catalan?

"And Yeliz's mother is in charge of host entertainment."

"Congrats," said Sophia, "this is amazing."

"Oh no," Yeliz said. "This is guest entertainment." She said no more, pointedly, and there was an awkward silence.

"Come on, Yeliz," said Pepe. "I want to try that human kite."

With a smile and wave, they had gone.

"They seem nice," said Sophia, cautiously.

"They are."

There was another exchange of glances, then silent staring into the fire. Where to begin?

"So, where's home for you?" asked Alejandro.

"London for now – but there are plans to move us to Justinian," said Sophia. "You know, parents, they come up with these ideas."

"Tell me about it."

There was another shared smile.

"Tomorrow I'm off to see the launch of the spacecraft – you know, the one off to Mars?" Shit, she'd done it again, blurting stuff out.

"That sounds amazing – I'd love to see it," said Alejandro.

Sophia froze. She could ask him, but she didn't know him, really, not more than just the surface. Wouldn't it be better to give it time, to think it through?

"Would you like to come too?" she asked. She was really on a roll.

"That sounds great. How could my father say no?"

His eyes flicked around the deck, then caught Sophia's again. They both grinned, and in triumph Sophia drank deeper from her glass than she normally would. *Really, Sophia!* she could hear her mother's voice saying in her head, but she decided that she had earned it.

"I like your outfit," he said.

"It's new: retro from house of Vinci."

"My mother had a dress like that."

There was a deadness in his voice that made her think of suppressed emotion. His mother?

Then they weren't alone anymore; her father arrived, followed by Pepe and Yeliz.

"Come, Sophia, time we should be going," said Artur.

"It's still early," protested Sophia.

"We're done here," her father insisted.

"I've invited Alejandro to the launch," she said. Best to just say it.

Her father's eyebrows rose, then he gave her a frown and glare, before looking at Alejandro as if calculating. He wasn't in a party mood, she could tell; he was at work, calculating the strategic benefits. Then he offered his hand to shake.

"Alejandro, a pleasure to meet you. I've just been talking to your father, and if we can help him out in other ways, that would be great."

Maybe she had got away with it; maybe she'd even helped.

"I'll see you tomorrow," said Sophia.

"Tomorrow, then," he agreed.

With a half wave and smile she turned away.

When she turned back again, Alejandro was ignoring Pepe, who was talking of moving on to a club on C Island. He was watching her leave, and she detected both an urgency and sadness in his blue eyes.

14: Tom

Never had a day seemed so long, or Tom so full of doubt.

They had calculated it would be a five-hour flight there, then an hour to dismantle the lander's comms and attach it with the cables to the blimp before another five hours home.

Everyone was quiet that day. Mei-Li Wu asked again and again, "Ok? Ok?", to which Elena had to reassure her as best she could.

One of them had to keep watch, just in case Michael returned earlier than planned. Tom had expected to enjoy the task, but in fact he was miserable, questioning his judgement and wondering what was happening out on the plain. For more than two hours he stared out of the airlock window at a landscape where nothing moved apart from the odd flurry of dust blown by the wind.

In his mind's eye he followed his father's flight: the blimp gliding over the Martian surface, navigating using a prepared sequence of craters and canyons as landmarks, hunting for the glint of sunlight on metal that would show that he had arrived.

Lunchtime, that's when Michael should have reached the Sitefinder. It was a silent meal in the kitchen of the base, after which Tom's mum gave him a long hug. He wasn't sure if it was for his benefit or hers.

With the airship away, the constraints on power were relaxed; gradually the temperatures inside the base rose and lights were switched back on. José returned to the gym to work again on the muscles he was so proud of, while a grim-faced JT decided it was a good day to clean the shrimp pool.

The sun, which had climbed to its peak in the sky, began to sink towards the west, measuring out the hours left. With it went Tom's spirits.

He tried to reassure himself: maybe no news was good news, meaning the expedition had gone as planned. But then a cold fear ran down his spine – maybe his father would just vanish, and not only would they never see him again, but they'd never even know what had happened. He'd never really thought of his father as mortal, as having an ending, but now he was overwhelmed by thoughts of loss. *Is this how my parents worried about me,* he wondered, *when I went out for that oath?*

At the hour when he was due to return, a grim-faced Victor appeared in the airlock.

"We should wait outside; the light is fading."

Outside they waited, wrapped in the protective surface suits which separated them into three cocoons.

They stood in a line, all three facing the west – the direction in which Michael had left, the direction he should return from. The weather seemed unsettled, gusts of wind blowing from one direction and then the next, raising clouds of dust that obscured the view for a moment before settling back on the ground. As the shadows lengthened, the wind seemed to be picking up, raising bigger clouds for longer. A red fog descended on the scene, blocking out everything except the nearby airlock.

"Come on! Come on!" Tom muttered, but there was no way for the others to hear.

He looked around in all directions, to check that they weren't somehow mistaken or that the blimp hadn't circled around to come from the other direction. As he scanned round to the north and the hills behind the base, his eyes were caught by a face in the airlock window, white with fear: his mother. He couldn't bear to look but locked his eyes on the western horizon, the line at the bottom of the sky to which the descending sun was getting ever closer.

Another sandstorm whipped up, clouds of dust whirring around them; a faint whistle and rustle of particles could be heard hissing along the ground and battling against the glass of his helmet. Tom felt he was suffocating in a red blanket. The wind blew the sand round and round, gaps opening and closing where the sun would be visible for a moment and then disappear. In one of the moments of clarity, he saw a shape against the bright disk, and his hopes rose.

But what was it? Was it maybe one of the two moons eclipsing the Sun?

Then he saw JT point excitedly. He, too, had seen something.

As the cloud of sand moved south, the view cleared and Tom saw the blimp, silhouetted against the setting sun. Below it on a line swung a dark object, which he realised must be the much-sought-after lander.

He pointed as well, nearly jumping with excitement, and now he could look back at the base towards the waiting, worried face in the window. *It's all right,* he wanted to say. *He is returning, he is successful, he is safe.*

Larger and larger the blimp appeared as it got closer and closer. It was hard to see with the light behind, but in the shadows a light appeared, flashing.

SLOW FLIGHT WIND WEIGHT.

Now it was closer, they could see that Michael had brought most of the lander with him. It must have been impossible to disconnect just its comms; maybe it had cold-welded together in the long years on the planet. One end of the cable was knotted around the bamboo frame below the blimp, while the other was attached to what looked like a structural support bar of the lander. It was clearly heavier than they had planned for, and it swung slowly back and forth, like the pendulum in a giant's grandfather clock. The blimp rocked in time, accelerating as the probe swung back and then decelerating as the weight below it rushed forward.

The engines were worn after the long day as much as the human occupant. Tom could just hear the thrump-thrump of the propellers again, but their rotation was now slightly asymmetric, and there was a grating of sand trapped within their drive shafts.

Tom, JT and Victor moved towards their allotted places, spreading out to catch the lines as Michael eased the blimp down. Tom could make out his father's face through his suit's glass visor: a strained face, worn out by the day.

Just as the knot in Tom's stomach was easing, Victor suddenly pointed urgently at something behind him, and turning, Tom gasped. A dust devil – an enormous swirling column of sand, dark red with shadows of an ominous purple – was rushing towards them over the rocky plain, larger than any he'd seen before. It moved towards them as if alive, as if there were a malevolent intelligence in its heart, its foot a hungry mouth that sucked up sand into the air, waking the dead land with a roaring hiss.

But Michael had seen it and begun his descent early, trying to move a craft that could not be hurried, that had a timing all of its own, a timing dictated by the swings of the beast carried below it. As the dust devil approached, it began to suck the blimp into it, dragging it sideways through the air. Tom could see Michael trying to fight the controls, battling harder and harder to keep the ship under control.

Then the dust devil was upon him. The blimp was thrown sideways like a rag doll thrown by an angry child. Caught within the vortex, the blimp began to spin, round and round, faster and faster, the heavy payload below it circling, the line between them taut under a tension that rose and rose as the speed increased.

Then the carcass of the lander bounced onto the ground, raising a cloud of dust – a cloud that was sucked, spiralling, into the storm above, crackling with short bursts of electrostatic lightning. It bounced again and was then caught fast by a rock, locking like an anchor, stopping the blimp directly in its tracks with a jerk. It was too much for the bamboo cage underneath, which fell apart, splitting on one side and spitting out the human within.

Michael flew through the air, head first, straight into the base. He hit the corner of metal above the airlock; his face mask shattered on its sharp edge, glass and blood flying in all directions.

He hit the corner of metal above the airlock; his face visor shattered on its sharp edge, glass and blood flying in all directions.

For a moment, as the body fell to the ground, falling past the window where the watching, horrified Elena screamed a silent cry, Michael's hands struggled wildly, grasping at shards of glass, trying to do something, anything.

But by the time the suit hit the soil it was over, and the figure lay still. His blood continued to pour out through the open wounds onto the rocks around where he had fallen, blood that bubbled and boiled like some witch's poisonous brew.

Tom and the others ran over to where he lay, but they were too late.

There was no time for last words, no time to say farewell, no time for a last look into eyes still full of life. As it often chooses to do, death had come before they were ready for it. Michael, the man who had once been the mission commander, Elena's husband, and Tom's father, was dead, killed by the base he had struggled for so long to keep alive.

The sun set, the light faded, and darkness descended like a curtain.

Part 3

15: Tom

They dragged the body over the rim of the airlock. Michael was lying head down, arm locked under his body, cracked face plate splintering on the dusty metal floor. A fragment broke off and slithered off into the shadows.

JT closed the door, and automated systems kicked in, hissing air into the room – the air that would have saved Michael's life.

Tom gulped, trying to stop the waves of nausea, the knot in his stomach so tight it threatened to propel its contents upwards. *This cannot be, it cannot be, there must be some mistake. When we turn the body over,* he thought, *we'll see the mask isn't that badly broken*; he'd have an emergency mouthpiece, something, there had to be something – his father just could not be dead. Not dead, killed by the mission that Tom had asked for, to get a lump of dead metal, to risk his life just because his son had asked him to.

It could not be.

But the blood was gently expanding from the downward-facing suit: no longer bubbling but spreading, fingers flowing outwards then filling, mixing with the Martian dust to make a syrupy mud.

When the light above the door went green and pressure was restored, JT and Victor opened their suits' masks, but Tom was frozen, unable to move, just staring at his father's body.

It could not be.

The inner door of the airlock opened and his mother, white, shaking, and with tears running down her face, knelt by the fallen figure. "Michael," she whispered. "Michael."

"There was nothing we could do," said Victor roughly.

JT reached down and pulled at an arm, trying to turn him over. "Help me," he grunted. With Victor's help he turned the suit over, adjusting the arms and legs so they were lying naturally, as if to ease pains that Michael would no longer feel.

"Oh," said Elena, reaching out a hand to touch his bloody, battered face, then drawing it back. "Oh, oh, oh…"

"Come on, lad," JT said, turning to Tom. "You can't stay in there for ever."

"It can't be true."

"It can and is. Now let me help you."

Together they climbed out of their suits and packed them before hoisting them onto the racks around the room.

There was a moment's silence, as if all were wondering what to do next. Tom felt crushed by guilt, unable to move or speak, filled with nausea.

From outside in the corridor came a wailing and regular thumps. Turning, they saw José and Mei-Li, who was hitting herself hard, hands battering her face and chest.

"Ai ai ai!"

"Stop her, José," said Victor.

The Venezuelan gently grabbed her hands and held them tight. "Easy… easy."

There were two more wails, then a sniff.

"Come," said José, pulling her away, but she wouldn't move – just stood there looking, watching the others.

"We'll leave the body in the garden, ready for the wormery," said Victor.

"No!" said Elena.

"We can't afford to let his nutrients go to waste; we have to recycle everything, even Michael, just as we did for Amina."

"Not the wormery. Not Michael."

She stood up, facing him. She was about a foot shorter, tear-covered face looking upwards.

"That's not what he wanted. He wanted above all to return to where he left, back to the Kennedy Space Centre in Florida – that's where he'd want to go."

"Don't be a fool, Elena: to survive we must be sensible, and I am base commander now. I decide."

"No, Victor, please." She reached out and touched his arm. "For Michael."

"For Michael? No. For you, maybe."

Elena made no reply, turning away to look down at the body.

At that the spell on Tom broke. "Kennedy. He should go back to Kennedy – that's what we must do," he said. It wouldn't ease the pain, the hurt, but the wormery would have been worse, inconceivably worse.

"We should at least wait until we try to contact Earth," said JT. "We can put him in a body bag and bury it in the dust outside – it'd be as good as the coldest deep freeze. The collapsed dome would do, in the shadows, covered by sand."

Victor gave a nod. "Ok, but it's dark now. We'll do that in the morning when we go for the transponder."

"Damn the transponder! You shouldn't be worrying about the comms when Michael has just died."

"Call me sir, Trevelyn: you will call me sir."

"Tomorrow."

"No, today, *now*. I am the commander." Victor's head twitched to one side as if flicking off an invisible fly, eyes locked on JT's.

"Don't fight, please don't fight, I can't bear it," said Elena. Tom moved to her and they hugged, holding together, one pair of eyes closed, the other averted from the figure at their feet.

"Ok, tomorrow." Victor shrugged, then grabbed one of Michael's limp arms. "You," he said to JT, "take the other arm: we'll move him in his suit to the garden."

Together they dragged the body through the corridors to the garden. Behind them walked Tom and his mother, followed by José and Mei-Li, a silent procession of four. The only sounds were their footsteps and the thumps as the body was dragged over the rims of doors and down steps to the garden floor. In the wider space under the glass, Victor and JT walked further apart, eventually coming to a stop with Michael's arms outstretched as if crucified.

They spread out in a circle around the figure.

"I will stay with him," said Elena. "Can someone get a mattress here?"

"I'll stay too," said Tom.

"Thank you, Tom," she said, holding him tight.

"I'll get them," said JT, disappearing back into the main base.

"Are you hungry?" Tom's mum asked him.

"No." In truth, he felt he couldn't have drunk a drop or eaten a crumb. His stomach lurched at the thought of food. As its knot got tighter, its pain began to spread: muscles tightened, ready for either flight or fight, a pain that was spreading to his head.

"I will get some food," said Victor. "I am hungry."

With that he left, and after a bit of coaxing, José managed to get Mei-Li to follow. "Sorry," she said. "Very sorry."

Then she turned away, to leave them alone.

They stood for a moment in silence, then Elena knelt down and gently removed Michael's helmet, putting it carefully to one side. She ran her fingers through his hair, then took out a hankie to soak up the blood and clean up his face.

"It's all my fault." The words burst from Tom's mouth before he could stop them.

His mother turned to him. "No, Tom, don't say that; it was his decision. You mustn't blame yourself."

He wanted to tell her about the oath, about swearing to get to Earth whatever the cost. But he didn't trust himself to say another word as he struggled to halt the tears that rolled silently down his cheeks.

"Oh, Tom," his mother said. "He loved you very much; he'd want you to know."

Tom exploded, throwing himself against the seed beds, pushing them over, plants and dirt spilling over the floor.

"Don't say that! I don't want that burden!"

"Tom…" His mother was unsure. "Don't, Tom, it will be ok."

But it was a lie. It wouldn't be ok, for his father was dead. Never again would Tom hear his voice, have him ruffle his hair, know he was there protecting him against an indifferent universe. There was nothing between Tom and death now; they were face to face.

When JT returned a few minutes later they were more collected, and he said nothing about the mess, just laid two mattresses nearby. He then left again and returned with two cups of tea, which Tom found he was ready for.

"I nearly wasn't on the flight – did I tell you that?" said Elena.

"No."

"I was the backup; didn't really want to go. I'd had enough of being stuck in metal tubes for months on end. But then Neda, who was meant to go, got shot in the Second Iranian Revolution – it was a big thing at the time. And Michael, my parents and government officials were so keen for me to take her place that I said yes."

They sipped their tea and watched the body and thought about what might have been.

Later that night JT wrapped the body in its bag and Elena and Tom kept watch on its dark mass, illuminated faintly by light from the corridor outside and the stars above the dust-scarred glass roof. Neither wanted to talk or sleep, though Tom did lie down at his mother's insistence so that he could rest if his body relented.

As he lay there, Tom became aware of the smell: the smell of decay, the smell of death. He knew it must be the garden's compost heap, where organic waste was broken down, turned into nutrients for the next generation, but he couldn't escape the feeling that it was his father. He was dead because he had loved Tom and wanted to give him hope. And if it hadn't been for that love, love that Tom didn't deserve, Michael would be alive. Love had killed him as surely as that dust devil.

During the night Tom kept one hand wrapped around the pendant his father had given him for his tenth birthday. It was made of rock, its multicoloured layers worn with age. It had been part of the Origin Stone, one of the oldest they had found on the planet, a relic from just after Mars had formed.

Tom tried to imagine how time could continue second after second, day after day, year after year, for so long. A century, even a hundred years, seemed beyond measure: but a couple of thousand million years – how could one grasp that?

His father had been alive for just fifty-six years, a blink of an eye for the universe, and now he would be still for the many billions of years that time had yet to run. What difference had that life made? All lives must end, someday. What difference could anyone make with such a short time? What difference could he make?

His sleepless eyes stared into the night, watching the slow turn of the stars.

16: Alejandro

"You failed me."

"Yes, father." Alejandro knew this was all he would be allowed to say. 'Sorry' was deemed weak, explanations were useless: his father saw everything, knew everything.

They were alone in the Cores. The guests had gone, taking their life with them, leaving Cloud Heights to silence and shadows. They were in the memory room, which was apparently empty, curved blank walls ready to be painted with information from the BCC's endless reservoirs.

"This was how simulations said it should go," said Felix Fernandez.

He made no gesture or command: he didn't need to, his body stuffed with every neural interface and augmentation his money could buy. Alejandro had data glasses; everyone had to have data glasses or embedded nanotech when in this room.

The images of two people materialised in the room. Alejandro and Bina Thakur.

"My father welcomes you to Cloud Heights," said the simulated Alejandro.

"Thank you; it's a pleasure to be here," said the simulated Bina.

"He followed your business today closely, as he has an interest at stake: including space in the blipverse."

"I'm here representing Bangalore Systems, not the Committee."

"Ha!" said Felix. The simulation paused as he spoke. "That was my prediction: she'd try to duck out of responsibility for the Mars decision by switching hats. Did she think she could get out of it that easily?"

The simulation of Alejandro continued. "Of course, but my father said he'd like to discuss the space update to the BCC plates. Maybe Bangalore Systems would be interested in bidding?"

"Not the core systems, of course," said Felix, forcing another pause. "We'll still develop them in-house. Don't want anyone else getting their hands on our crown jewels."

"We'd definitely be interested; please send me any information you can."

"My father says it would be best if you came for dinner at Cloud Heights."

The simulated Bina looked wary. "I'd be delighted, of course, but must check my diary. It is easier to schedule events that are blipverse global public like this."

"Not stupid, that one – thinks we'll put the squeeze on her," Felix interrupted again. "Staying away won't help."

"My father says he likes his contractors to be close, available to him. Shall we say next week?"

The simulation froze.

"That was how it was meant to proceed, with a sixty-three percent likelihood of her saying yes. But this is what you did instead."

Alejandro's heart sank. *No, please, don't show this.*

The simulated copies of Alejandro and Bina Thakur were replaced by recordings from the earlier event, in the main ballroom.

"My father welcomes you to Cloud Heights," said the recorded Alejandro.

"Thank you; it's a pleasure to be here," said the recorded Bina. She was shorter than him, and he politely leant down toward her.

"He followed your business today closely, as he has an interest at stake: the space blipverse."

"I'm here representing Bangalore Systems, not the Committee."

"I was right," said Felix, gloating. "And you should have stood taller, not bent over like that. Act, boy, act. In the world outside this room, you must behave as if you're on stage."

The recording paused as he spoke, then restarted.

"Of course, but my father said he'd like to discuss the space update to the BCC plates. Maybe Bangalore Systems would be interested in bidding?"

"We'd definitely be interested; please send me any information you can," said Bina.

"But what happens here?" Felix asked.

The attention of the Alejandro in the recording shifted, having spotted someone behind Bina.

"Excuse me," he said, then walked towards the disk edge, where a girl – Sophia – stood peering over the edge.

"Don't do that."

The recording continued, covering the whole dialogue. Alejandro's stomach felt as if it were empty of all that was good and instead filled with stones. He couldn't leave, he couldn't say anything, he could only watch.

"So, Alejandro, you ignored my specific instructions and instead made small with a girl. Not just any girl, but the daughter of the man who turned down BCC's space blipverse request. Explain yourself."

There was nothing to say. He'd been here a million times before. The only solution – no, it wasn't a solution – the only *option* was to say nothing.

"You do remember I'm trapped in here? That while I remain in this disk, these archives, linked to my augmentations, count as my memories and hence are outside those ridiculous privacy laws? I have to rely on you doing my bidding, and yet again you've disappointed me."

Don't say it, please don't say it, Alejandro prayed, but in that room there seemed to be no God, only Felix Fernandez.

"What would your mother have thought?"

Don't do it, please don't.

A new figure appeared in the room with them, a beautiful woman with dark eyes and dark hair in a light green dress. She looked disappointedly at Alejandro, her sad eyes filled with tears.

"Look what you've done to her, boy."

She was just a simulation, Alejandro tried to remind himself, just a construct. But she was so real, and he missed her so, that these images, however painful, were precious to him.

"Always do what I say, boy, or there'll be trouble."

His father replayed the end of the conversation, beginning when Artur Kasparov had joined them.

"Kasparov thinks he's so in control, able to turn down even me," he said softly. "Kasparov has a lot to learn. You can go to the launch, but you must wear a full suite of BCC sensors. Everything you see, everything you hear, I want a copy of. Imagine me with you every second of the time you're with the Kasparovs."

He could imagine it. How low could his heart sink? he wondered. At what point would it become lost?

Then his father rewound the conversation and focussed on Sophia. *Please – oh, God, please no. Don't, not her.*

"Good-looking girl: growing up nicely. Maybe you're a chip off the old block after all." Felix smirked, and something inside Alejandro became frozen. "Next: the meeting with Stone. A strange character, not someone we'd want to be seen talking to. What did she want?"

"She says we have a common enemy and she can help, but she wants resources." Alejandro was finding talking difficult.

Felix frowned. "She is stirring, and not always in directions that help BCC. But she could be an ally, and there would be dangers in not working with her."

In the air materialised Sophia again, with her father in this recording, racing through the Global Council.

"But could it have been an AI that...?" asked Sophia.

"I said not here!" her father snarled, stopping to glare at her. "Wait until we're in the apartment."

Felix pondered.

Alejandro's legs felt tired from the long day, but there were no chairs. His father had upgraded to the best-toned muscles on the market, and looked like a fat old man squatting in a young, athletic body.

"Ok, let's see where this goes. I'll call in favours from some of my... ah... more capable connections. The... exotic nanobiotics need field testing, anyhow."

Felix Fernandez stretched, and moved those artist-crafted legs of his.

"That's enough for one day. Call host entertainment: tell them to send up girls five and eight. Oh, and I want some churros – make sure they are fresh. There's nothing worse than cold churros."

"Yes, father."

At least he could go to the launch, to see her again; but with his father watching, recording, judging, capturing her for the archive, his memory.

Oh God, please help me.

17: Tom

Tom had wondered if the night would ever end, but it did, as they always would, time remorselessly moving forward. He might even have slept, though he was hardly sure: parts of the night seemed to have disappeared from his memory.

He also found he was starving, and his stomach had settled, so he was able to eat and eat and eat. Tom wondered if that was right – how should he behave and act the day after his father had died? That hadn't been in any of his lessons.

But Victor had no doubt how he would behave, taking charge over breakfast.

"This is what we will do. I will say some words, then Mr Trevelyn, then we take the body outside."

"Call me JT. Everyone does – everyone has since I was younger than Tom."

Victor looked at him coldly. "Your proper name is Jim Trevelyn, and you are no longer a child. I will call you Mr Trevelyn, and you will call me sir."

There was a silence.

"Is that understood?"

"Yes."

"Yes what?"

"Yes, sir." It was said quietly.

"Right then."

Later they all stood around Michael's body, the bag unzipped enough to show his face. Tom's mum was comforting Mei-Li, so Tom stood by himself, feeling small and alone.

Victor said a few perfunctory words, all about Michael as commander and how he had done his job professionally – nothing about Michael as the man – before nodding at JT.

JT nodded in reply but for a moment stood there, still, gathering their attention.

"Michael was many things to many people. Most of them cannot be here today: his family back in Seattle, his friends and colleagues from when he trained for the job he loved.

"I remember the first day I met him, when we worked on L-DOM – that's Lunar Deep Operations Mission, for the likes of Tom that weren't there. We always knew he'd be the one to lead us to Mars."

At that Victor Dubois stirred; his head twitched before he controlled it, forcing himself to be still.

"He was the all-American type, and for him it was true. He was open and friendly, welcoming us into his family with open arms. And Elena too; as they started dating, he introduced her to his parents, to his brother and sister, and they opened their hearts to her, aye, and her to them too."

At that JT paused: there was a sniff from Tom's mother, but while she stirred, she didn't speak. Tom pondered on these recollections of the time before he'd been born and of people he'd never met, wondering how much he really knew of his parents.

"So, we flew through the void to this world where we stayed, for year after year, hard times when death was ever-present, stalking across the wilderness of rocks and windblown sand. And it was Michael that glued us together, a pillar of support we all relied upon during the dark times when we realised we had been marooned here."

JT shook his head slowly, then straightened up and looked at Tom. "But there was also joy there, with the coming of Tom, and if Michael was proud of what he had achieved, it was nothing compared to how he felt about Tom. He was proud of Tom; he loved Tom, truly, as a father should be proud of and love his son."

Tom's eyes smarted and he wished he could hide, escape these words that stung as they shone.

"Michael was our commander; he was my friend; he was Elena's husband and Tom's father."

JT slowly zipped up the body bag, and the face disappeared forever.

"We will all miss you, old friend."

Then, in a procession that reversed the one from the day before, he and Victor dragged the body bag to the airlock, where all but Mei-Li and José suited up. Mei-Li wasn't trusted in a suit, and someone had to stay with her.

Tom took a spade to move the sand, while his mother held a rough cross, two bamboo stalks bound together by vines, crafted by JT somehow during the night.

Outside, Victor and JT pulled Michael in his bag through the dust towards the ruined dome. It had been intended to double their living space, created by blowing up a hemisphere-shaped balloon, then covering it with a mixture of sand and water that would set like a dark reddish-brown igloo. But the balloon had burst in the process, leaving fragments like a broken egg, increasingly covered by the relentless Martian dust.

They dragged him through the gap that would have been the doorway to its interior and then found a hollow between two curved sections of the dome, cupping the central space like a pair of hands.

Here JT took the spade from Tom and dug a ditch into which Victor pulled and pushed the body bag. With each moment, to Tom it appeared less and less like his father and more like a thing, an object to be buried out of sight.

They all took it in turns to shovel sand and rocks onto the bag, until it was covered and disappeared into the soil.

Victor gave a nod and walked back to the airlock.

JT stayed for a moment with Tom and Elena, placing the cross above where Michael's head would have been, before following Victor, leaving them in peace.

So, thought Tom, this was it. Part of him wanted to end this awful waiting and return, but then he didn't want to leave his mum. Again, he wondered: what should he do? How should he react?

In the end, he decided to focus on remembering his dad, how they had played hide and seek in the garden when Tom had been little, how he had always been there, forgiving Tom's many blunders, giving lessons on everything so he knew how it all worked. Some things he had yet to understand, like people and leadership, or how to control your emotions in a crisis, but his father had known all that and more.

His best memory was the most recent: of Michael the hero preparing for his last mission. It was a memory tinted with shades of guilt, and the full weight of his loss seemed to crush Tom.

He remembered instead when he'd been very young and first tried to get out through the airlock. Michael had shouted at him, catching him just in time, angry because he cared, because he loved him. And Tom had betrayed that love, used it to get what he wanted, to get the comms working again, without thinking of the consequences.

Then Elena turned to him and bumped together their face plates so they could talk.

"Ok? Shall we go in?"

He nodded, and they headed back without looking behind them.

Inside they were called by Victor into the central hexagon, where they sat around the table expectantly.

"Right, enough of that: it's time to get organised, to run this place properly," he said. "None of the slack routine we had before."

His head twitched again, as if the invisible fly had returned. But there were no insects in the base.

"Trevelyn, Santos, we need to audit our supplies; get to it. Tesla, clear up this mess and keep Wu out of my way; I'll be getting that transponder from the lander outside to rebuild the comms systems. Trevelyn, you will help me deflate the blimp, recycle the remaining hydrogen."

He paused, then looked at Tom. "Oh, yes, and then there's Tom: you'll work like the others, harder maybe. No time for lessons now; we're one short." Victor smiled, as if he had remembered a happy thought. "The wormery – yes, that's a good place to start. Clean out the wormery today, and then tomorrow the human waste system."

"What?" Tom asked.

"Victor, is that necessary?" asked Elena.

Victor's head twitched again.

"Is there a problem?" he said softly. "Have you something you want to ask of me?"

He stared at her, challenging her. She couldn't match him and looked away, downwards.

"Ok, then," said Victor.

Tom was gripped by a new fear, a fear that didn't come from the dirty work ahead, a fear that added to the sorrow and the grief: a fear not for himself, but for his mother.

What was he meant to do?

18: Sophia

Sophia followed Alejandro down the aircraft steps, bouncing two at a time, feeling the blast of heat on her skin as she looked around. So this was where the road to Mars began: the space port of the East Iranian desert.

She was excited but also frustrated. The journey had been tiring and her father had been preoccupied. He hadn't worked, not for a moment – all displays off – even though she knew he wanted to, but had continually drummed his fingers, cracked his knuckles and snatched half-looks at Alejandro.

Alejandro had been worse, extremely tense and edgy, not keeping up the easy-flowing conversation of yesterday's meeting on Cloud Heights. There was a look in his eyes; a lost look of misery, if not despair. Strangely, it made Sophia just want to find out more.

"Sophia?" It was her father, calling her back to the plane. "Just a moment – sorry, Alejandro."

Back in the plane she saw that the displays had awoken, with Humai's logos spinning as usual.

"What's up?"

"It's Alejandro," said Artur. "He's completely wired, recording absolutely everything – multi-viewpoint, multi-band, audio, visual, IR, EM, you name it."

"Look at this," said Humai. It animated a figure of Alejandro, rotating with animated overlays highlighting features. "He's got active clothing, smart fabric in his jacket, recording glasses, and his BCC badge is packed with sensors."

"Why would he do such a thing?" asked Sophia, feeling sick. This was pretty disgusting at any time, let alone for what surely must count as a date.

"We don't think it's his idea. It's Felix's way of reminding us of BCC's power – that we can't ignore it or expect just to get away cost-free from turning him down. Felix gets Alejandro to do everything for him."

"He could have said something." She could have waited before inviting him, used the careful consideration she was meant to be known for.

"No doubt Felix wouldn't have been at all happy about that. But Alejandro must know we'd spot at least some of it, and hence alert you. We're going to give you two a tour of the public domain stuff. Just be careful."

Her father must have been right, because afterwards Alejandro seemed to relax just a fraction, as if glad she'd been warned, with eyes that begged, pleaded for forgiveness, understanding.

Huh. Explanations first.

They were met by a man with a grey beard and long white shirt, or shalwar, who shook their hands warmly.

"Sophia, this is Dr Khujandi, chief designer of the spaceplane."

She had already recognised him.

"Very pleased to meet you, Sophia and Alejandro; you've arrived on a very special day."

He pointed them in the direction of the nearby hangar. Sophia had spotted it from the sky, admiring its tent-like structure, silver canopy mirrored to reflect the sun's heat. It was only when she was on the ground near it that she got a sense of the scale of the building.

"The Mars lander is being prepared in the hangar. We're very pleased with it – room for ten spaceplanes inside, though at present we have just the one, with two more in orbit."

Ten? wondered Sophia.

Alejandro followed behind, bashful, clearly ashamed about what he'd brought with him.

Dr Khujandi led them in through the first door of the airlock to the main building. "Bit dusty today – wind blowing in over the sand dunes; we need to keep that away, particularly during final payload integration."

When the door was closed, fans started blowing a gale over them, whipping Sophia's hair into streamers as it sucked any particles of dirt towards waiting filters. For a moment she saw the despair leave Alejandro's face, and one of his hands was raised a fraction towards her uncontrolled hair; then there was a click and the storm subsided.

"After you," said Dr Khujandi, opening the second, inner door.

Sophia stepped through into the refreshingly cool hanger. It seemed nearly empty. "Wow, how large is it?"

"Five hundred metres long by two hundred wide, two hundred and fifty high."

Dr Khujandi and Sophia's father led the way, and they followed but more slowly, turning around and around, their gaze upwards. The canopy fifty metres above was supported by ten carbon fibre poles, dividing the space into two rows of identical bays, each with a giant doorway in front of it.

The first bay was occupied by a vehicle with black fuselage and surrounded by equipment, gantries and walkways. Just above the craft, a white rectangular box was suspended by crane on a white track that stretched from one end of the hangar to the other. Above the door in front of it was writing – just the one word: *Phoenix*.

The next two bays had their gantries and walkways but no craft present, and above them were written *Zumrud* and *Firebird*. Around the *Phoenix* swarmed maintenance robots doing their final checks. The rest of the building was empty, bare concrete floor dimly lit from down lights near the top of each of the support poles.

Sophia felt like a mouse in a museum. She smiled at Alejandro, realising that despite the circumstances she was glad he was there.

"Are you all right?" asked Dr Khujandi. "It's a bit disorientating the first time you come in here, but it's wonderful to have a structure like this; you can do everything in the cool under one roof. Spaceplane repair and maintenance in the same place used to integrate it with the payload."

He was rather serious, but Sophia didn't feel intimidated. He seemed gentle and only partially with them, as if the rest of him was forever wondering about the numbers and designs as he unconsciously ran his fingers over his beard.

"Can I see the spacecraft – the bit that's actually going to Mars?"

"Of course; come this way. You're lucky, as we've just finished the decontamination procedure and are about to seal it away for the launch."

"Decontamination?"

"Yes, the Earth Firsters that your father is battling with were very insistent that there'd be no contamination of Mars with Earth lifeforms, so we irradiated the landing craft: we just finished this morning, but it should be down to safe levels by now."

Should?

Artur intervened. "But I think you'll find there is only room for one guest. Maybe Alejandro would like to come for me for a bit?"

Alejandro seemed only too happy to agree.

"See you – tell me about it, sometime – later, that is." He wasn't very coherent.

Dr Khujandi led the way up a metal staircase to a higher-level gantry where teams of engineers were working, checking instruments and tapping away at slates or talking to their c-agents. They climbed upwards until they reached the white box, where they entered another airlock.

"This is the payload room, so I'm afraid you must put on these overalls and hat if you go any further."

Feeling a bit like she was going to a fancy-dress party with a 'doctors and nurses' theme, Sophia put on the clothing as requested.

"And here we are. This is the lander."

Sophia followed him along the walkway, then gasped as she looked down. She was above the spaceplane, looking into the gaping hole of its cargo bay. In front of her was the Mars spacecraft itself, ready to be lowered into the hold, its bronze heat shield towards her, silver landing legs behind it, retracted like those of a dead spider.

"So that's going to Mars."

"Yes – the final component of the spacecraft is being built in Earth orbit, with room for any survivors. It will head out under autopilot, pick them up and then bring them back to the main craft for the journey home."

"What's it called?"

"The main spacecraft is called the *Odyssey*, while this lander we've named *Boreas*, after the north wind."

Then Dr Khujandi's blipcoms went off and he excused himself, leaving Sophia alone for a moment. She wondered about the long voyage the craft would take and what it would find when it got there. She reached out to touch it, then wondered if she should. After a moment's hesitation, she lightly stroked its cold metallic surface. And then, moved by some inner urging, she whispered "Good luck, *Boreas,*" before leaning forward to give the nearest panel a gentle kiss.

She could see faintly the greasy stains her lip gloss had made, and was about to reach out to scrub it away when Dr Khujandi returned.

"Don't touch, Ms Kasparov, don't touch!"

"Of course not," she said hastily, and with a guilty glance backwards, followed him out.

When they left the payload box to climb down to the hangar level, she found her father and Alejandro deep in conversation with a young woman who reminded her a little of Dr Khujandi.

"Ah, Forough, here you are. Ms Kasparov, this is my daughter."

She had a strictness of her tone and bearing. "Has father showed you the Phoenix? And were you impressed?" she asked.

After Sophia had admitted she had been, Forough added, "But has he shown you the caravanserai?"

"You show that to these two, as I must borrow Dr Khujandi for a blip-con," said Artur.

Forough led the way back out of the hangar into the open air, baking hot in the afternoon sun. As they walked, their footsteps kicked up clouds of sand. A short trek along the dusty path led out to the desert and a series of mounds, the remains of mud buildings, which Sophia could make out must have followed a rectangular layout.

"These were built many hundreds of years ago – inns for travellers crossing between India and the Middle East."

Sophia looked out across the dry landscape, trying to imagine what it would have been like.

"It must have been a long and desolate trail," said Alejandro. It was the first thing he'd said unprompted all day.

"Indeed. It's a great reminder of the depth and passage of time. Have you read the *Rubaiyat*, by Omar Khayyam?"

"Some of them."

"In one he wrote: *'Think, in this batter'd caravanserai/Whose portals are alternate night and day,/How sultan after sultan with his pomp/Abode his destined hour, and went his way.'* But now no one remembers the name of anyone who stayed here."

It had been recited as a performance: Sophia and Alejandro exchanged amused smiles.

Sophia thought of all those hundreds of years and thousands of travellers on this bleak spot in the middle of the desert. She looked around, her eyes watering as the wind gusted a cloud of hot dust in their direction.

"Watch out for the djinn," said Forough.

"The what?"

"Dust devils – columns of twirling wind and sand. It used to be thought they were djinn, demons of the desert. Now, of course, we talk of conservation of angular momentum."

A beeping went off on Forough's blipcoms.

"The spaceplane is ready: I must go back. Maybe you and Alejandro can watch the launch from the viewing gallery?"

The control centre was on a rocky hillock above the runway, with a viewing gallery on its roof. Sophia and Alejandro could see the spaceplane inching its way out of the hangar, taxiing to one end of the runway. All around the space centre, as far as the eye could see, were the solar farms that generated the power needed for everything, from fuelling the spacecraft to her home back in London.

The parched landscape appeared still and lifeless, yet Sophia reminded herself that compared to Mars it was a fertile oasis. Why was her father so keen to fly to a dead world?

The spaceplane's cylindrical fuselage was nearly a hundred metres in length, and with its two stubby wings had overall a diamond shape. The entire airframe was a rich, dark black that seemed to suck light into it, a hole in the radiant sunshine flooding the desert. It seemed inactive apart from the nav lights patiently flashing, one at each wing-tip and a third on its tail.

Sophia wasn't sure how to handle Alejandro, and he seemed frozen in doubt too.

"I'll watch the augmented overlay," he said at last, putting on his data glasses.

"Good idea," she said, following suit.

After instructions to her c-agent, Sophia saw displayed the launch status and digits counting down, one by one, smaller and smaller numbers until they reached zero.

Suddenly a cloud dust was flung up behind the vehicle, and a second later the sound reached her of the machine coming to life: a building, rumbling roar. With a jerk, it began to move, slowly at first, twin cones of flame emerging from the engines on each of its wings. In her glasses, darkened against the bright late-afternoon sunshine, she could see overlaid gleaming lines of the launch corridor and constantly updating figures giving position and velocity. Faster and faster the spaceplane accelerated along the runway, all numbers green, dead in the centre of the invisible pathway its designers had laid out for it.

Then, with a sudden tilt of its forward canards, it was airborne – climbing, streaking upwards, its engines a scream loud enough to rip the air in two.

Without thinking, caught in the moment, Sophia leapt into the air, hands punching upwards.

"Go, *Phoenix*, go!" she shouted, grinning at Alejandro, who echoed her words, but their sounds were lost within the crescendo of noise from the rocket ship in the sky. There was a bang that rattled the bones within Sophia's body as it went supersonic, accelerating ever faster, climbing ever higher, forever beyond reach of her words.

She ripped the glasses from her face to peer into the sky, and with a hand above her eyes, she searched for the disappearing dot, following the contrails, looking for the twin glows of the engines.

"Good luck," she whispered, thrilled, wishing despite her doubts that one day she could follow it on its long journey.

Then she turned to Alejandro to see elation in his face too, the launch having blown away his demons and self-consciousness, as if he, like her, felt that anything was possible, that sometimes even gravity was defeatable. For a split second their faces drifted closer, until as one they remembered and jerked back.

Then something seemed to snap inside Alejandro. He grabbed the BCC badge, pulled it off and threw it away, followed by his jacket.

"I won't do this anymore – hear me? I can't!"

He looked nervously at Sophia, who smiled – no, grinned – back. Things were going to be ok.

"There're probably lots of sensors left," he said.

"I know. We'll have to find another time, when you're without them."

Sophia looked up again, her eyes hunting for the *Phoenix*. But it had escaped; its black diamond had vanished into the infinite, unending, silent dark of space.

19: Alejandro

"You disobeyed."

Alejandro was back in Cloud Heights, in the Cores. He was physically in the room with his father and yet appeared to be standing on the runway in the desert, immersed in a virtualised launch.

"You disappointed me."

He was speaking softly, and the quieter Felix was, the more careful Alejandro had to be.

"It was very simple: say nothing of the sensors, just let them listen and watch – let me listen and watch. But you couldn't even do that."

It was a trap; he was trapped; there were no ways out.

"I could crush you. You have no secrets from me: every moment of your life is mine. I could ruin anyone that tries to befriend you. I could make a soap character with your name and face and make Alejandro shorthand for a global joke."

He could do it, Alejandro knew. But that wasn't what he feared.

"Look at me."

Alejandro made an effort and looked at his father, clothed in figure-hugging, soft, black material, cut to show the expensive physique at its best.

"Ah, so you have the guts to do that. But can you look at Bella?"

No! Not her!

They were joined by the image of a beautiful woman with dark eyes and hair in a green dress.

"Oh, Alè, my sweet, how could you do your father so wrong? He has given you everything. Maybe you don't love me anymore."

Alejandro couldn't stop himself from looking at the simulation of his dead mother, transfixed.

"If you don't do what your father says, then we won't be able to see each other anymore. Why would you want that?"

"Mama?"

"You heard her, boy. If you don't behave, it will break your mother's heart – again."

"No, Papa, it wasn't me…"

"Don't you *dare* talk to me like that!"

There was a silence, only broken by the woman's gentle sobs.

"I could wash my hands of you, banish you from here. No more Bella, ever."

Alejandro's heart felt compressed into a stone. To never see his mother again, to be cast adrift, even by his tormentor: then there would be nothing left of his life.

No! There was Sophia. He picked up his head to confront his father.

"So, boy, you haven't realised yet what I could do."

There was no clicking of fingers, no barking of commands. His mother just vanished, to be replaced by a simulation of Sophia. Felix lifted a finger vertical and Sophia stood straight. Then he twiddled the finger around and Sophia spun around and around on cue, dark hair flying out.

No – not her! But Alejandro's screams were silent, locked deep inside him where even his father's sensors couldn't reach.

"The living are almost as malleable as the dead. I could predict word for word what Bina Thakur would say – until you screwed up. I can do the same for little Miss Kasparov. You would lose her too."

The finger stopped spinning, and Sophia stood still.

"What shall I do next? Or have you learnt the lesson?"

What could he say? What options did he have?

Then his father twitched, nose raised as if to smell the wind. The images of the desert vanished, to be replaced by graphics of the Solar System and plain, old-fashioned, two-dimensional video.

"So, they *are* alive…"

"What?"

"Listen up, boy, this is important. Communication incoming from Mars – yes, there really are survivors."

It was a newsfeed, real-time public global, starring Felix's second-favourite construct – the feed host Honeyed Semtex, skin literally glowing with health in the way that was impossible for those really alive.

"This just breaking, TAC Earth stations are picking up transmissions from Mars. Yes, you heard right: Mars. They are alive. Decoded, the data stream contained basic video and audio. We will replay from start corrected live minus six-point-three minutes. Note, this is *not* available as full blip-immersion."

"Is it on?"

There was a face, close to the camera: a woman.

"Yes, get back here so they can see us all." A man's voice. The woman stepped back to show a grainy picture from inside the Mars base, the communications hexagon.

In the centre was a grim-faced man.

"This is a test message from the Mars Base on the Maja Valles. My name is Victor Dubois. I am the base commander."

There was a muttering from one of the others there, too weak for the words to be picked up by the microphones.

"We have been unable to communicate for the last eight years after the final transponder failed. We only recently were able to salvage a replacement from one of the Sitefinder probes, but at the cost of the life of Michael Tesla."

At this the woman began to cry, then stopped herself, drying her eyes.

"We also lost Amina Sissoko, and Mei-Li here has been seriously injured." At the sound of her name,

Mei-Li started forward expectantly, confused, looking around. She was led away by the woman.

"However, as well as me, survivors include Elena Tesla, José Santos and Jim Trevelyn."

"JT," said the oldest one there, a man with white hair. "Just call me JT."

"There is also one other, Tom Tesla, who as you will be aware was born here on Mars, but" – at this the man, Victor, pursed his lips – "decided not to be present for this message – is that right?"

The woman, Elena, returned, shaking her head. "But he has grown. He is no longer a child, but is nearly sixteen."

"A typical teenager," said Victor.

"Oh no – yes, I mean." That was Elena.

"We will listen for another ten minutes for a return communication, then repeat this sequence once an hour.

"Is there anyone down there on Earth listening to us?" asked Victor.

The communication stopped there.

"More updates on this *thrilling* story coming soon: stay with us!" said Honeyed Semtex. Then she was cut off and the sequence rewound from the start, playing again, this time without sound.

"And to think those image rights could have been mine; ownership of those words could have been mine. All those rights, exclusive, forever, just as they were for the *Prometheus,*" said Felix. "And with *Odyssey* on its way, all the blipverse rights of the landing, the rescue. It's enough to make one anti-space." He shook his head sorrowfully. "This changes things. I need to get someone inside those Technocrats, to find out about their plans and what that AI of theirs is up to, something I can use to negotiate for my lost rights – or stop their space missions if they say no."

"They won't trust me if I turn up with sensors again."

His father paused at that. "True." Then he began to laugh. "I'm good, I really am."

Alejandro was terrified. *Laughter!*

"Listen, Alejandro, I can fix even your mistakes. So, you let them know about the sensors – they will know I'm angry. They will even understand if you were to – say – move out for a bit. You could stay with Pepe and his family in the workers' compound."

Alejandro couldn't follow him: it sounded too good to be true; there had to be a catch.

"They might even help you, get you non-smart clothing without any of my lovely sensors. They might then trust you."

Oh, shit.

"But of course, you couldn't be seen coming up here to me."

Then how–? Oh, of course…

Bella was back.

"Oh, isn't that so kind of your generous father! You and I will have our little chats, and you can tell me everything. It will be so nice to spend some time with you, dearest Alè."

"Do you understand?"

Alejandro nodded. At least this way he'd have a chance, and maybe Sophia wouldn't say anything; maybe she'd never talk about Mars or what her father was up to.

"But remember, boy: you must tell your mother all you know. I will find out if you hold anything back. You will not see me, but I will always be watching, anywhere and everywhere. No secrets, or you lose everything – forever."

"Ok."

There was one parting shot.

"She's too young for me, anyhow – for now."

His skin crawled, but it was done. He was free to go.

Alejandro packed a bag of things, but before descending he visited the upper disk to look around the ballroom one last time. Empty and deserted, dark and silent as a morgue, it was hard to believe that yesterday it had been thronged with life, music, and the happy sounds of people. He and Sophia had talked for the first time over there, where the roof could be rolled back.

Enough of this, he thought, turning to leave, not looking back. He took the monorail from Cloud Heights down to ground level: it was late evening and the lights twinkled all over Justinian. He found he was shaking, slightly but uncontrollably, and not just because of the vertigo.

Pepe already knew about the arrangements before he arrived, showing him to a basic room in the apartment block at the base of the pencil: home for the guards, cleaners, entertainers, cooks, medics, attendants and all the many others needed to keep Felix Fernandez alive. It was bare, painted concrete, a narrow, steel-springed bed and little else, like a prison cell. To Alejandro it was beautiful.

"So, Al, you've been caught misbehaving with the lovely Sophia and sent down here for punishment – how'd you wrangle that? Nice one!"

Alejandro nodded, desperate to release the tension, to fill the emptiness, the hollowness, to enjoy every second of his freedom.

"I feel like a drink – many drinks; maybe more."

"And I, my friend, know just the place. It's over on C Island, where the posh people don't go, and where you can get everything you want, if you know who to ask."

"Sounds just right." He would contact Sophia afterwards, when the shakes had gone, when he was calmer.

They headed out into the night to take the monorail across the water, heading towards C Island.

20: Sophia

For some reason Sophia wasn't as unhappy as she had feared about the move to Justinian. For a few weeks their apartment in Troy Towers was chaos, rooms filled with boxes of things that they couldn't leave behind.

"This is so stupid," said Nina. "Why did all of you bring so many *things*? You could just get the MakeIt! machine to print a copy."

"It's not the same; these things have memories," said Anna, unpacking family knives and forks from her childhood.

"But you could just scan them, then print them out this end! Why transport atoms when there are atoms here too?"

"One day you'll understand," said her mother, which Sophia knew would really wind up her sister.

Artur was bursting with energy at the news from Mars.

"They're alive! They're alive!" he said, bouncing around the rooms in a fighter's crouch, boxing invisible enemies.

Anna had to control him too. "Calm down, Artur; you're just like your father after a few drinks celebrating London's independence."

Sophia didn't get that bit. All she remembered of her grandfather was an old man coughing hard between gasps for air, hankie to mouth to catch the phlegm, dying of cancer, his life wasting away along with his once-strong muscles. It was scary to think her father could be like that one day.

But the news from Mars helped her finish the assignment, giving a nice upbeat twist to the end: namely that the *Prometheus* explosion hadn't been final; that its replacement, the *Odyssey*, had been successfully launched. She could even provide blip-vid taken first-hand from the launch, getting extra credits, plus kudos with her old London friends.

She missed Zach, Maria, and the others, but there was always the blipverse and blipcoms to keep in touch. For reasons she wasn't entirely sure about, she hadn't yet told them about Alejandro. Indeed, she wasn't sure what to say, how she felt about him, not knowing how to restart things with him.

In the end she needn't have worried, as she saw him almost at once at the International School in Justinian. She was rather nervous, but it went off ok; she said hi to Pepe and Yeliz, who were there with him, and avoided Nina, who no doubt would have messed things up somehow.

"How'd it go with your father?"

Alejandro froze, eyes slipping away from her, lost for a moment.

"Not good," he said, sheepishly. "I've moved out of Cloud Heights – it's ok, honest; I've got a room in the worker block, along with Pepe."

Snap, thought Sophia. The Kasparovs weren't the only ones moving, then. She volunteered to help make the room presentable, but the visit there was a disaster. It felt so empty and soulless compared to Troy Towers, let alone the luxuries of Cloud Heights. And just being in his bedroom – that raised too many issues. She had offered to use their apartment's MakeIt! machine to create a few decorations, and left quickly. Pepe and Yeliz hadn't helped.

Yeliz seemed to attract boys like flies, but she battered them away with her harsh scorn, and towards Sophia she behaved only a little better.

Pepe seemed very different to Sophia, enjoying cheap jokes and walking with a swagger. He'd just got nano tattoos that could be programmed to be any pic or vid anywhere on the body. Some had designs based upon famous artworks, but instead Pepe showed a set of circles that flowed along his arms, legs and face from some central point.

"They radiate from somewhere – guess where?"

Uh oh, thought Sophia. "Your tummy button?"

"No," Pepe said, grinning. "Lower."

Gross, she thought, but when Nina heard about the nano tats, she again demanded that she be allowed to get some implants. She was only quietened by a promise from Humai that it would help her with her AI project when it came round.

Alejandro didn't mess things up, though, not pushing her, but asking about her interests, trying to find out something they could do together.

"We have to do an assignment."

Huh! I've just finished one.

"Why don't we do one together?"

Hmm… that doesn't sound too bad.

Together they came up with the idea of an analysis of the art and symbolism of Tocado Muzanki's sculptures, the prime example being the statue of Athena on A Island. They were allowed to escape school early and headed off on the monorail for an afternoon that started with a quick inspection of the woman made of yew before breaking for a coffee and chat at the GC café.

"Any sensors you'd like to tell me about?" Sophia asked.

"None, honest – all clothes newly printed, sensor free."

"Just the two of us?"

"Well, the whole of A Island, café included, is officially global public. But one advantage of being Felix Fernandez's son is that you know where the gaps in coverage are. Like this particular table, and other little-known corners of the One Earth Park."

"Clever!" Sophia wondered what to talk about. "So, those on Mars – they say two have died up there."

Alejandro didn't seem interested.

"What did you do in London, Soph, apart from studying and looking totally auth?"

Sophia grinned, before telling Alejandro about her electric speed-bike, the sailing and the skiing.

The school wasn't the only one giving Sophia things to do. At home her father was worrying about the non-appearance of the boy, Tom, the youngest of those castaways on Mars.

"You wouldn't believe the blip threads on the subject. Total crazies, saying they're afraid to show him as he's been infected with Mars plague and turned into some sort of monster."

"Poor boy," said Anna. "To be forced blipverse global at his age, on all the world's feeds with every moment analysed to death – that would be hard, even if he hadn't just lost his father."

"This meme needs to be controlled, quickly," interposed Humai. "Sophia, can you help us out?"

"I've already got a new assignment."

"Just the one blip," said her father. "He could be your blip-buddy – just think how impressive that would be to your friends."

"But make sure he says something we can release global public. It can be something as simple as 'Hello world'," said Humai.

"Ah yes," said Artur, grinning, "an AI's birth cries."

"Ok, ok," said Sophia. "I'll do a quick blip."

It had to be quick; she had too much on. Over that coffee with Alejandro, Sophia felt they had laid the foundation stones of a new relationship, slower but surer, getting to know each other by doing things together. And that was going to require time. There were so many new things to handle, from new home, new school, new friends to new emotions, even new types of relationships.

She loved the outdoor activities on offer, and one day managed to get Alejandro to join her in sailing a foiling catamaran around B Island. She thrilled at its speed, hitting well over twenty knots as they skimmed underneath the monorail bridges.

Alejandro wasn't the best of sailors, though he was game on her behalf, which she felt was something. But just doing something together helped turn the surprise at finding herself with him into something like comfort, though her heart still skipped a beat when she saw him.

He was more into the clubs and nightlife, which required a bit of negotiation on Sophia's part to get out at what she felt was a reasonable hour. "I'll be sixteen in a couple of weeks" was parroted so often that Nina would try to wind her up by finishing any of her sentences that began with "I'll be...".

She invited him home to meet the rest of the family, which had been awful in anticipation but actually went off ok. Her mum and Alejandro had strangely connected somehow, and Artur had seemed to think his presence meant he'd won a battle over Felix Fernandez.

Needless to say, Nina had been a total pain.

"An A-star-minus-minus," she'd said. "I feel sorry for him, really."

She wouldn't say why.

One day Alejandro managed to wangle an invite to the Sky Beach's late club, the hip2hip. They offended Pepe by ditching him, and then her parents by staying out way beyond the agreed curfew.

But it was worth it, for as they lay on the Sky Beach's warm sands Alejandro kissed her: a long and intense kiss, a kiss that was followed by many more, a kiss to which she responded with kisses of her own, holding him tight.

21: Daniel

Daniel stared at the closed door, wondering what he should do next, where he could go.

He could hear those on the other side: the hum of children, voices calling for quiet, then the rhythmic sound of learning, the drone of the teacher-bots.

"I'm sorry, Daniel," Reverend Pasteur had said before he shut the orphanage door. "You are sixteen now; you can't stay with us anymore."

He'd been lucky to be taken in at all, to have a home amongst the wreckage of Miami, cut off when the *Prometheus* exploded, then forgotten after the Collapse. He had lost everything when Hurricane Gladys, stronger, hotter and angrier than anything seen before, had blasted its way through Florida, turning Cape Canaveral into an island and taking his surname, along with his parents. All he remembered of the time before was running round their house, crying out "T" over and over again.

The alphabet. The children inside were reciting it aloud, just as he had.

"…R-S-T…"

He smiled at the memory, but turned away. There was nothing more to be done here, and he was hungry.

The hot and humid air blew from the Gulf of Mexico across Miami and into his face as he ambled through the familiar streets. Blip-booths, corner shops selling Geiger counters or second-hand sockets, and the bright and noisy open market: the fish stands with their stink and flies, packed with hawkers, vendors crying out their deals of the day, entertainers, pickpockets, beggars and hassled shoppers.

On the roof of one bungalow, Daniel spotted a shrivelled coconut shell, washed up there by Gladys's storm surge, after drifting from heaven knew which faraway island.

There is a world outside, he reminded himself. *I will find a way out of here.*

He passed the mall slums, where the homeless had turned the abandoned, empty shops into a dense mass of alleyways that the uninitiated and uninvited could get lost in. Daniel had spent a month there living in the remains of a Hallmark store.

A drone flew overhead: a local gang's, out on a delivery, funded by black-market qIDs, stolen from those who could be murdered without being missed. You had to keep your wits about you to avoid the gangs. Charity kids were not popular, but Daniel had learnt when to hide and when to run. After Gladys, Daniel had survived as best he could with packs of the hungry, boys and girls scavenging just inland amongst the rubble – hoping to be protected by the strong rather than picked on.

There had been one persecutor in particular, a boy from the trailer parks who called himself Nails, who wrestled wild dogs till they accepted him as their pack leader. Nails still had the scars that came from those battles, with great chunks missing from his chin and his right earlobe lost – presumed eaten, as he'd remind Daniel as he stole his food. Everyone thought about food a lot, in this lost corner of a failed state where there were many mouths to feed.

His eye was caught by the poster on the window of what once had been a Walmart:

The Earth Needs You!
Join the Defenders of the Planet
Meet at the old robot factory

"Don't go," said a voice.

Daniel turned. It was a woman, casually standing at the door and watching him read it. She was one of the Wally mother-clan that had taken over the building. They were ok: a matriarchal commune, tough as gator skin, handling twice the number of kids as the orphanage. From inside he could hear a blip-soap blaring in the background.

"Why?"

"They're a crazy lot. I had a sister go to a meeting and she was never the same again. Last I heard, she'd gone off to Atlanta or something. Started babbling away about Mother Stone; nothing could stop her."

A baby started crying, and she left.

Crazy was bad, but what did she know? It sounded interesting, and could be his way out of here. He wouldn't be sucked in; he'd just listen and learn. There might be food.

There were many who thought as he did. All ages, creeds and colours turned up, men and women equally hungry and thin. There were so many that those too old or young had been turned away at the entrance by organisers in military-looking uniforms, black with green stripes.

Inside the factory only the skeletons of the robots remained, rusting like bones discarded by scavenging animals. It was roasting hot and soon everyone quietened down, saving themselves, hoping for water, any drink.

"Lemmings!"

Daniel could see it was one of the rejected, an old man, shouting at them through fencing from the outside.

"You're all lemmings!"

He was chased off by the organisers: things were beginning to happen. There was a raised area like a stage on which two figures appeared, a man who also wore a uniform and a woman.

"Welcome," said the man. "I am Captain Mark Vaughan of the Defenders of the Planet, and today is the day that will change your life." He spoke with the slick confidence of someone who could sell anything to anyone.

People started to stand up, to get a better look.

"But you are thirsty," he continued. "First you must have something to drink."

The uniformed ones, who Daniel guessed were the Defenders, came round to everyone there, handing out little bottles. A shrivelled little woman with a closely-shaven head handed one to Daniel: he raised his to the light and could see inside a grey liquid with tiny specks of silver that rose and fell, glinting in the sun.

"What is this?" he asked.

"Holy water and dust," he was told. "Drink up."

A handful of those there refused the bottles and were kicked out.

It was hot and he was thirsty, so Daniel drank.

When all of those that remained had finished, the woman stood up.

"I am Cita Stone. I am here to call you to arms to defend your planet. Enemies are coming: demons from the sky from the planet of war, Mars, threatening to contaminate this Earth with their plagues."

From the ranks came a growl.

"But you will not just contend with the demons from Mars, but also traitors. Traitors that have polluted the Earth and now want to bring these diseases down from the sky; traitors in league with the artificial intelligences, plotting to steal this, our home, our planet, from us. Will you stand it? Will you watch your world taken by thieving traitors, machines and demons?"

"No!" the ranks called out, and Daniel found himself saying "No" too. Her words appeared in his vision, letters of flame that burnt into his head.

Traitors. Machines. Demons.

"No, you will not! For you will fight for what is right – fight to protect your planet, your lives, your future."

"Fight," said Daniel, and the letters fired inside his skull. *Fight.*

"Protect the purity of humanity against the impure machines, for you are Defenders now. You will fight for us, with us!" she said.

"Mother Stone," cried out the uniformed Defenders.

"Mother Stone!" echoed Daniel with all the others, speaking as one.

He felt alive, sure of who he was and what his mission was. It was all so clear, so obvious, and he felt one with the crowd around him.

Afterwards Mother Stone and Captain Vaughan walked amongst them, and they cleared a way.

He stared at the woman, transfixed. Now she was close he could see the growths on her neck. They bulged like malformed vegetable roots, the ones that would taste bitter and be useful only for animal feed. Her mud-coloured hair was scraggly and thin, with most of her head bare and an angry red.

She stopped in front of Daniel, a look of wonder on her face.

"I had a son who looked a bit like you, and was about your age when..." Her voice trailed off, and her hand reached out to his cheek. "He would be thirty now – no, thirty-two."

The hand slid down, stopping on his neck.

Daniel looked at her with wonder. Did someone care about him in a way he hadn't heard since he lost his mother?

"But of course he's dead."

Dead.

"Vaughan, send this one for special training. He could be useful, later. You'd like to help us, wouldn't you?"

He agreed. He was so pleased that he could help the woman with all those growths on her neck.

The woman whose words burnt within his head.

The one they called Mother Stone.

22: Tom

The work was dirty, the work was smelly, the work was hard, but to Tom it was a relief rather than a punishment.

In the days that followed the funeral, Victor chose Tom to clear out the wormery and then the human waste system. If anything could have matched how Tom felt about himself, then those two tasks were perfect.

Nothing seemed right to him. His vision seemed slightly skewed, with vertical lines becoming angled and time moving at a rate that defied measurement, as if out of joint with the universe. There was a pain behind his eyes and a heaviness in his movements, as if the gravity on Mars had doubled or someone had attached an anvil to his forehead, dragging him down.

It was hard to believe that Michael had gone; he could clearly hear his voice in his head. Tom kept expecting him to appear in the kitchen, thirsty for tea, or pop his head round the door as he studied, checking on his progress. It was as if they were playing hide and seek and Tom was always searching, never finding. One night he woke covered in sweat: he had been dreaming he was the storm, whirling his father round and round, throwing him against the base like a child throws a toy.

He deserved the worms, he told himself, deserved the chores that Victor seemed so keen to give him. The sweat that ran down his body felt good, as he laboured with a minimum of clothing to save it from becoming stained by the base's muckiest waste.

Don't think about it, he told himself, but there was no escape. Again and again the images would flash into his head, unbidden. His father flying through the air to collide with the base, grasping for air as he fell to the soil. His father lying in the body bag as JT spoke at the funeral. The black bag being hidden under shovel-loads of red sand.

Then they would start again, pictures of a figure flying through the air and crashing against metal.

JT had offered to help, but Victor had had none of it – it was Tom's job, and strangely Tom had agreed with that, even as he increasingly loathed the officious new commander. If he hadn't sworn that oath, he might not have driven Michael to go on the doomed mission for the transponder, and they might have played it safe until the rescue ship came. He deserved all he had got, he thought.

He didn't want company, didn't want to "talk about it", just wanted to get on and do what had to be done until he was so exhausted he could sleep. Tom knew that JT and his mum both meant well when they asked how he was keeping, but he didn't want that. He felt like shouting at them but knew it wasn't their fault – it was, after all, his. It was his father's love that had done this, and if pushing them away kept their love away, then maybe it would keep them safe too.

He wasn't the only one working hard; there was much to do. He was dimly aware of what the others were up to from the morning briefings that Victor so relished.

JT and Victor had gone out and deflated the blimp. Together they had brought inside the remains of the lander, and in the repair shop they were able to disassemble it, extracting the transponder that had cost Michael's life.

After a day of soldering, Victor had got the comms back on line. In place of an empty universe, there was a flood of information: text, web, email, sounds and videos. Their online library, which had become barren and tired, sprang to life like a desert after a tropical storm.

To most of them it was a welcome escape from their troubles, with even Mei-Li enjoying the sounds and sights of faraway Earth. It was almost a drug that they couldn't get enough of, a reward for their persistence in survival.

It was not all good news. While they had known things were bad for them to be left on their own for so long, they hadn't guessed about the scale of the devastation, of the famines that had killed by the hundreds of millions. Nor had they heard of the Food Wars and the economic collapse that had followed, which had left their communications hubs, their ground stations, without power and then empty, doors locked and rusting.

Despite that, the others couldn't keep away from the comms room and the stream of human contact from the home planet. But not so for Tom, who refused point-blank to see any of the sights that the others spoke so warmly of. It was not for him, he felt; it was wrong to benefit from his lethal mistake. The approaching spacecraft was like a reproof. All they had had to do was wait.

Tom pushed away the efforts of JT and his mum to bring him back into the group. He knew she was hurting too and wanted his company, but he only wanted to be left alone.

They seemed to have split into six separate lives, meeting just once a day, where Victor relished his new authority and four of them had to say "sir". Only Mei-Li's life didn't change, though she was quieter and had stopped dancing.

Apart from the new commander, the only one that seemed stronger than before was José, who used the gym to brew beer and vodka as well as pump weights. He sucked power from the base to make the room warm and humid, allowing the Venezuelan to forget the present and imagine himself on a Caribbean beach, while Victor turned a blind eye.

After the wormery and the human waste system, Tom was sent to clean the showers and wash area. He supposed it was a slight improvement on human waste and worms, and he had to acknowledge that his mood did lift a bit. The showers were a treat they all enjoyed, an opportunity to wash away the grime of Martian dust.

It was while he was cleaning the showerheads that he was interrupted by his mother.

"Tom?" she began.

"What?" He looked round but didn't stop.

"How do you feel?"

"Fine."

He wasn't fine, but he still wanted to be left alone. He knew it must be as bad for her, but he couldn't see what he could do: another of his failures.

"You should see the videos from Earth – they're scary but wonderful. It's amazing what's changed in the last ten years."

"Another time. I'm busy."

"The spacecraft is coming, Tom. We'll soon be going home to Earth."

"It's not my home. I've never been there. I don't know anyone there." Angrily, he scrubbed a spot that he had already cleaned.

"Someone sent a message for you by name – for Tom."

At that he stopped and looked round, puzzled. "But I don't know anyone there. Who's it from?"

"There's only one way to find out. Please, Tom, just this one message. You can't keep running away and just working."

He paused. It seemed ridiculous, a mistake. *Is it worth it?* he wondered.

"Ok."

He followed Elena to the comms room. It felt alien, the domain of Victor Dubois, where he was an interloper. Elena had almost to push him into the room, even though he was considerably taller than her.

Victor sniffed. "This doesn't mean you escape cleaning the washrooms."

"Victor, please," said Elena. "Let's leave him be to listen to his message."

Victor stared at her, as if calculating something. His head half twitched. "So, again, you want me to do something for you, don't you, Elena?"

Tom was suddenly furiously angry and leapt forward, but his mum pulled him back.

"Yes, *sir,*" she said.

"Elena..." he began.

"Isn't it good that we will soon be going home, *sir?*"

Victor narrowed his eyes and looked up at Tom.

"Ok. You can make me a tea," he said, and then left them.

Tom's mother pressed him down into the chair and then smiled; while lopsided, it was the first he had seen since the accident.

"We'll leave you alone," she said, and left.

They had both seen it, whatever it was, he was sure.

He looked at the controls: like everything on the base, he had studied them and learnt how they worked in one of the lessons that had filled his early years. He pressed play and turned to look at the screen.

"Hi, Tom."

It was a girl: about his age, he guessed, long dark hair, dark eyes, rather serious but with a friendly smile.

"You don't know me, but my father's in charge of the spacecraft that's coming to rescue you, and they asked me to blip something to say how sorry we all are to hear about your dad. Oh, sorry, my name is Sophia, forgot that bit. It's hard to remember how different things must be up there for you. We've got so used to blips, qIDs and c-agents that do all of that, and from what they said you don't have that. But then living on Mars sounds real auth. You must tell me about it."

She paused, as if wondering what to say. Behind her, Tom could see an apartment with windows that showed the sun setting into a golden sea.

"I know what will interest you: I was at the launch of the actual lander that will be with you in a couple of months. It was amazing, the take-off – I wish you could have seen it for yourself, but I've attached a c-vid of it."

There was the sound of a voice just outside the camera's field of view. "Not now, Nina," said Sophia. "Sorry about that; my sister. Maybe you'll meet her when you get here? 'Here' is a place called Justinian, by the way, built on three artificial islands. Anyhow, if you get a chance, send me a message. We can be like blip-buddies – what they used to call pen-pals. My mother actually has a real pen, totally auth, it has a little pump which sucks in ink and then a nib which you write with. Oh, and can you say something we can release blipverse global? Just something simple, like you saying 'Hello, world.' There's been all these crazy rumours down here about your non-appearance. Sorry again, hope things improve. Bye now."

Then it stopped. There was an option to play the attached vid of the launch, which Tom looked at once before playing the message again.

Enough of this, he thought, and went back to work.

But when he scrubbed and wiped, he no longer saw in his mind's eye pictures of a suited figure flying through the air, but a pair of dark eyes and a sunset.

Is she thinking of me? he wondered.

23: Sophia

Sophia did think of Tom, sometimes, but not often: she was too busy and finding life far too interesting.

Things seem to be going ok with Alejandro, though sometimes she wondered how well she really knew him. She had been trying to get to know him better, to see what made him tick, but what she found were red lines. His mother and father were off-limits, not to be discussed at any time, and even approaching them obliquely could end up with him heading off with Pepe to C Island to do who knew what. Similarly, when they were close to Cloud Heights, he grew nervous, and then angry when she hinted she understood his feelings. But she could sort of see where that could be coming from, and had learnt to avoid those topics.

However, she didn't see at all why Mars was on the list, and why even the slightest mention of her father's work made Alejandro angry. She had mentioned the blip to Tom on Mars the once, and that had been enough. It was one of the unmentionables.

It was the one that really bugged her: not just not knowing the reasons, but also because she needed someone to talk to about all the craziness of meeting Cita Stone in the construct. He had been there, meeting her just outside that off-blipverse room, so surely he couldn't pretend it didn't involve him? Why couldn't he talk to her about it?

But that didn't change how she felt about him, about being with him, to dream of those blue eyes locked on hers and her hands in his curly hair.

Why her? she sometimes wondered. He was Felix Fernadez's son; he could have been with anyone. But she realised that half the girls were scared of BCC and the other half wanted something for themselves from it, usually a starring role on one of the blip-soaps.

Once she had the strength to ask directly – after both of them had had a few drinks.

"I don't have to pretend when I'm with you," he'd said. "You understand me, Soph."

But if she was honest with herself, she felt that she didn't really know what went on deep inside him.

And then there were his friends. She and Pepe had ended up in some form of competitive battle for Alejandro's time. She disapproved of where he took him, though to be truthful she didn't really know where it was, just that it was somewhere on C Island – just that he was embarrassed about it and often came back either smelling of drink or with a hangover. In return, Pepe pretty much straight-up accused her of being a stuck-up Londoner who'd only be there a few months before flying off somewhere else.

She'd managed to impress him just the once, when Alejandro had wickedly got Pepe to challenge her to a race at an illegal speed-bike rally being held on C Island. She'd pretended to be horrified but game and then thrashed him soundly, ending up third in the race. He'd got his own back in the drone races, which she found vertigo-inducing.

Most worrying was the day that Alejandro had vanished, returning as if from a haunting. He'd said he was with Pepe, but Sophia had seen Pepe on his own. After subtle enquiries through Yeliz, she discovered that Pepe had thought Alejandro was with her, which raised a whole host of questions. How many times had this happened before? How often had he been away, doing something he didn't want to reveal to either of them?

So what had he been doing, and with whom?

But then he'd sweep her off her feet, taking her out to the most auth clubs where she could dance under the stars, and he would tell her how beautiful she was until she felt she could melt. They would laugh together at the new kids at school, just arrived from what had been part of the old US, the southern states. The lemming kids, they called them, who spoke as if quoting from a book.

Which was the real Alejandro? Were relationships meant to be like this? Was it meant to be hard? But she was involved and had even opened up about him with her old friends in London, who seemed so far away, in a place that was no longer home.

Luckily, she'd seen nothing of Cita Stone, but one evening Mr Bevan came for dinner and what Artur called a bit of schmoozing. He reminded them that he was firmly against further spaceflight missions into deep space – a point which seemed to infuriate Sophia's mother, who battled long and hard to change his mind. Artur seemed more resigned to Mr Bevan's opposition and kept his peace, as if holding fire for a more opportune moment.

But the evening had one result; it prompted Sophia to respond to Tom's message, something she had been putting off. It had come back soon after hers, and she was rather thrilled by being able to say "my friend on Mars", even if only when Alejandro wasn't around.

"Hi, Sophia," it began, and Sophia saw a boy about her age, or maybe a little older. Wide face, short brown hair (shockingly short, compared to Alejandro's luxurious curls) and brown eyes that were filled with pain, though she felt she could also sense intelligence and a hint of eagerness. "Thanks a lot for the message; it's great to hear from someone outside the bubble here on Mars. It's also good to know someone on Earth and be assured that the spacecraft is really on its way. You can imagine how much we're looking forward to finally escaping, though I know so little about Earth – maybe you can tell me a bit about it?"

He paused, and then seemed about to add something, before changing his mind.

"We've been trying to keep busy; there are always tasks that have to be done. How do you spend your time? Er..." Tom paused again and stared at the camera, then looked sideways as if at someone just out of view. "That's about it for now – say hi to your family, and thanks again for the message. Oh, and 'Hello, world' – you can quote me on that."

He'd had to wait a week for a reply, even with Sophia getting her c-agent to remind her; it was the World Fair week on A Island's central park and the Carnival of National Animals, all on top of school, projects, Alejandro and everything else.

Sophia decided to tell Tom a bit about Justinian.

"This place is slicing-epic and I'm still exploring it, as we've only been here six or seven weeks. Yesterday I went with my friend Alejandro to C Island, which is where all the support services are – things like wind farms, solar plants, hydroponics, monorail repair, and docks. To be honest it's not visitor-friendly, but it felt real.

"After the famines of '54 and global warming, feedback kicked in; there was this big debate about how to respond. The old UN way of talk talk talk, blah blah blah, and do nothing was one of the reasons we're in this mess, and so when the UN building was burnt down in the riots during the USA split, it was decided to start again, and so here we all are.

"Of course, all the countries were against too much pooled sovereignty, so the GC was only given powers over real global issues, like climate and of course space travel, such as the mission to rescue you up there on Mars. And there wasn't agreement on how to tackle them. Then there was this *huge* row about AIs, which led to this big split between basically the low-tech Earthies and high-tech Technos, and who'd want to go all low-tech, right? To be off-blipverse, all the time?

"Anyhow, that's enough history for today. I've got to go; Alejandro and I are off to this endo-rag gig in the B Island Irish sector. Blip you later – and take care!"

For some reason Tom didn't respond so quickly to that message, but Sophia didn't notice, for she was sixteen now and there was so much more to do.

24: Tom

The days slipped by for Tom, merging together to become indistinct, lost. He gave up counting down to when the lander would arrive, and the weeks passed, filled with work and loss, time measured by the depth of the lines on his mother's face.

He wasn't the only one working hard: Victor wanted everything on the base checked and double-checked, ready for when they could finally go home. Busiest of all was JT, who had to audit the garden, check the gas-management systems, clean out the tanks and hydroponic beds, build reserves of gases, document what they had learnt, prepare stores of fresh products for the flight back, and configure the garden to be self-sufficient without humans to manage it.

It was clearly an impossible load, which seemed to amuse Victor, not bothering to hide his contempt for the older man, or José, happy to follow in the base commander's slipstream. But Tom helped out, quietly, when he could, despite the fact that – or maybe because – he knew he wasn't meant to, that his mum wanted or needed his company while Victor wanted JT to struggle by himself. It made Tom feel better to be working in the garden quietly with JT, a solid, reassuring presence.

"You're a good lad," said JT when Tom volunteered to dive into the shrimp pool to change the filters. "Any more messages from that young lass of yours?"

"None," said Tom shortly, climbing into the pool in his boxers and grabbing a lungful of air before disappearing beneath its waters.

When he surfaced he heard voices, and cautiously hid behind the rim of the pond to listen.

"You're late," said José.

"I'll come when it's done," said JT. "If you like, you could give me a hand."

"Do I look like a farmer? Do these hands look like those of the peasants on my father's estate?"

"There's nowt wrong with being a farmer. Nor a fisherman. Both honest trades. Like messenger boy."

José walked over to a rack of hydroponic beds and kicked it over in a flood of water and nutrients.

"Oops. Looks like the farmer's got some cleaning to do – but not now; you're late."

"You've already said that," said JT, calling after him as he left.

"What's got into him?" Tom asked, slipping out of the pond and stepping into the shadows to change.

"The thought of home, that's what," said JT.

Victor Dubois was not pleased with Tom and JT when they finally arrived.

"Where were you?" asked José of Tom.

"Nowhere," he replied.

"Enough," said Victor. "Reports: status."

They all gave updates, even Tom, whose tasks had included maintenance of the surface suits and checking the airlock's pumps.

Last was José, reporting on the state of the sample collection. "By the time the lander gets here, I'll have prepared a dataset of over a thousand ice cores and tagged rocks."

"There's an update on that," said Victor. "Earth says no samples to be returned. None."

"What?" asked Elena. "That's just crazy. Isn't that the whole point of us being here, of Mei-Li's research – to bring back what we've learnt to Earth?"

"That's what they say, so no arguments."

"Then you'll have time to give me a hand," said JT to José.

"No – Victor, tell him, tell our worker."

"Mr Trevelyn, you will do your job."

Tom looked over at JT and gave a minute nod.

"That is all; on your way," said Victor, and the meeting was over.

"Tom, stay for a moment, let's have a chat," said Elena. "We haven't talked for ages."

"Not now, Mum, I'm busy," said Tom, escaping into the base, leaving his mum looking after him sadly and nursing a cold tea.

It was another layer of guilt, more than he wanted, so much that it seemed to threaten to bury him as the sands covered his father's body. He felt he should do more to help her in her grief, but it dredged up memories he was trying to avoid. After midnight, in the thirty-nine extra minutes they had each day above the twenty-four hours of Earth, he asked himself whether he was a coward, but there was no answer except the ticks and hisses of the aged base.

Focus on Earth, that's what he kept thinking. All would be well; they would be free of Victor, and his vow would be kept when they got to Earth.

He almost relented one day, heading for the central kitchen area mid-morning when he knew she'd likely be there. He did find her there, but she was talking to Victor over cups of tea, sharing some recollection of Michael in the early days of the mission before they had known they were marooned.

"He was an exceptional commander. Exceptional," said Victor. The words seemed to be dragged out of him like a dentist pulling a bad tooth, but Elena welcomed them.

"Tom?" She'd spotted him watching them, but he turned and ran, his blood boiling. The thought pounded through his head – *how could she?*

After that he avoided the kitchen, and the days passed as the *Odyssey* got closer. One of these was his sixteenth birthday, but unlike it had been under Michael's regime, it was a footnote on a day much like any other.

Each day they could see the graphic of the spacecraft's position, and each time it was that bit closer, eating up the kilometres by the million.

***

The *Odyssey's* arrival at their planet was as a burning comet streaking across the sky as it used the planet's thin atmosphere to aerobrake, a giant shield slowing the craft down from interplanetary speeds to enter Mars orbit.

Under Michael that would have been a moment for celebration, but with Victor it meant more work, the final preparations. Tom wanted to say he was sorry to Elena, but she seemed angry with him too, so he brooded on his own.

Finally came the time for the lander *Boreas* to split from the main spacecraft and descend to the surface. On this day no one worked, and no one complained or could even sit still. Tom tried to burn off his excitement on the running machine, but José was on it all morning, so he ran round the garden as an ad-hoc track and did press-ups between the beds. Mei-Li smiled, though she didn't know what was happening.

It felt like sixteen years of Christmases and birthdays all rolled into one.

"*Boreas* will land early afternoon your time," said the voice from Earth, a Dr Khujandi, over an animation of the procedure, landing legs opening out like a spider's. The home planet was so far away that messages sent by radio across the interplanetary network took a full fifteen minutes to reach them, making conversations impossible.

After a lunch, for once shared and full of laughter, they crowded round the main screen in the comms room, glasses of home-brewed vodka to hand.

Earth had prepared a vid for them that was synchronised with the landing timetable. Usually Victor had the blinds on the window closed so the room felt like a metal cave, but today he opened them. Through its sand-scarred glass, they could look across the barren Martian landscape, rock after countless rock until the far horizon, and imagine the gleaming spacecraft from Earth descending from the sky on a pillar of fire to rescue them.

"Soon," whispered Elena, her arm around Tom. "Soon it will be here."

He smiled back; for a moment he felt content, forgiven. It was going to be all right. Earth was within reach.

"In orbit burn," said the voice from Earth, and in the sky there was a light, a spark that travelled from west to east. It slowed, then began to glow as it entered the atmosphere.

"That is it!" said Victor, and they rejoiced, clinking glasses.

It began to descend slowly, just a spot of light.

"Cross-track manoeuvre, heading towards your site," said Dr Khujandi.

The light dimmed slightly, barely noticeably at first, and then a bit more as it fell towards the horizon.

There was a muttering in the room, a wondering as to why it didn't look closer.

"Probably want to protect us and not land on our heads," said JT, but no one replied, for the dot was getting fainter and lower till it vanished on the horizon, a falling star that they had wished on for so long.

There was a silence.

The video continued, the animation showed *Boreas* firing its engines to cushion the landing, throwing up clouds of virtual dust as its silvery legs touched upon virtual Martian soil.

"We have predicted touchdown – please update us with status from your end," said Dr Khujandi from Earth.

For a moment no one said anything. Then Victor leaned towards the console and said, "We saw the in-orbit burn but the lander is not within visual range. Repeat, we do not have visual on the lander; it appeared to descend towards the south of the base."

Tom imagined the message heading out into space across the millions of kilometres. There would be no reply for thirty minutes at least; there was nothing they could do but wait. Some drank. José and Victor refilled and emptied their glasses. Elena held Tom tight, but Tom said nothing, just stared at the screen, willing for it to wake.

Thirty minutes came and went, then forty-five, then an hour, and José had to go get another bottle.

Come on, thought Tom, feeling Earth slip away from him, a cold knot of lead filling his stomach and the dark weight settling back on his head.

"Mars, this is Earth; we have identified the *Boreas* from observation satellites. We can only assume there has been a guidance computer error, as it has landed at the right latitude and longitude apart from one discrepancy."

There was a pause, as if the voice from Earth was unable to find the words.

"It had the right latitude but wrong sign. *Boreas* landed in the southern hemisphere, not the northern hemisphere."

There was another silence, and one that no one dared break, either on Earth or on Mars. The rescue mission had failed; it had landed on the wrong side of the equator, and they were still the castaways.

They were stuck on Mars and stuck with each other.

Part 4

25: Tom

There was a long silence.

"So that's it," said José, voice thick with drink. "We're never going to be rescued; we're going to die here."

"Fatalistic nonsense," said JT. "Bear up and take it like a man."

"Who are you to talk, peasant?!"

"You're drunk, you idiot."

"Why, you—" José's wrist shot out, smashing into JT's chin, knocking him off his feet and against a rack of equipment. As the older man crashed to the floor, José began to kick him, hard blows against the legs, groin, chest.

Tom broke away from his mother and pushed José away, hard, then stood in front of JT. "Let him be!"

"What the f—"

"Leave him alone!" Tom shouted.

JT raised his head and sneered at Victor. "In seventeen years under Michael, we had not a single fight. Great base commander you turned out to be."

"Stop it – stop it, all of you!" cried Elena. She burst into tears and gave a moan of pain.

Victor's head twitched – a twitch that expanded as his shoulders jerked in rage; then he turned to Elena with open arms, and she, after a moment's hesitation, fell into their comforting embrace.

"Not everyone thinks I'm a bad commander, Mr Trevelyn, so be careful what you say."

Without thinking, Tom flung himself on the nearest available target – José – knocking him over, and they ended on the floor locked in a rage of blows.

Mei-Li started screaming, then ran out of the room, wailing. Elena extracted herself from Victor and, with a guilty half-glance towards Tom, followed her, head low.

"Get up, both of you," said Victor.

He directed a kick at Tom, who reluctantly backed off and stood to help JT up.

"None of that. It's time for discipline." Victor twitched again, eyes scrunching closed for a moment, shoulders buckling in. "Discipline," he repeated.

They stood for a moment in silence, Tom and José panting slightly.

"We must find out where we stand."

"We know where we stand – we're stuck here," said José.

"The lander could have fuel enough to get here; there might be a second lander; they could send another mission," said Victor.

"And how long will that be? It took them seventeen years for this one to get to us."

"Well, you might give up, but I don't intend to die on this planet," said JT.

"Who said anything about giving up, peasant?"

"Enough!" roared Victor. He twitched and then said it again, more quietly.

Then he stopped, as if drained.

"We should ask Earth whether they've any suggestions," said Tom.

Victor nodded. "I'll do that. You three, get back to work."

"What for?" asked José. "There's nothing to do." He took a swig from the bottle full of vodka. "Unless you know how to grow us wings so we can fly all the way home."

JT started, looking as if he was about to say something, then seemed to change his mind.

"Like some angel of death," he said.

"What's that nonsense?" asked Victor.

"Poetry, Mr Base Commander Sir."

Victor sniffed. "Useless. Go on, out of here."

"Glad to."

"I'll help," said Tom.

"You could tidy the garden: I've got to work outside on the gas storage pumps."

At that José laughed. "See – the farmer wants to get his hands dirty, in the Martian soil."

JT ignored him, as Tom ignored his mother, who called out to him as he went through the kitchen on his way to the garden.

How could she? How could she turn to *Victor*?

Tom tidied up the tables that José had pushed over and wondered about the spacecraft up above their heads; it was only a few miles, but they were all straight up and against the gravity that pinned them to the planet. JT was out all afternoon, working on whatever he had to do, so Tom was on his own. He snacked on what he could pick from the hydroponic beds, unable to bear going into the kitchen.

Later he heard voices from inside the base core, and rather than join them he listened in to the conversation, hidden just outside the door. Victor was there with his mother and José.

"It's not good," said Victor. "Earth says that the spacecraft had just the one lander, which had fuel for only one landing and take-off."

"Then it can't help us," said Elena.

"No, and they don't know when they can send another. Sounds complicated – political."

"Oh no," she said, and then there was quiet, broken by a sob.

"Elena?" asked Victor.

Tom couldn't listen any more. He fled back to the garden. Again, he asked himself: *How could she?*

He couldn't think of anything else to do, so he sat in a corner, arms around his knees, brooding on the day's events. They were stuck here, he'd never get to Earth, he'd never keep his vow, and his father had died for nothing. *Nothing.* The hours went slowly, and as the sun sank his thoughts got blacker. Once his mother came to the door and called his name, but he didn't reply, shrinking further into the shadows.

As darkness fell, JT returned from his tasks outside. He was tired, breathing like one who had worked hard for a long period, longer than the body was ready for.

"It is done; time for some food and then rest."

"What were you doing?"

"Another time," said JT. "Now I must eat."

As JT went to the kitchen, Tom headed to his bunk, switching the light off and just lying there looking at the ceiling.

***

He must have dozed. When he woke it was the witching time of night, the minutes after midnight that counted as neither one day nor the next, and he could hear shouting.

Tom leapt up and headed out to find JT and José at the intersection between the garden and the tunnel that led to the water mines. José was still drunk.

"Go on, farmer, kneel down; clean my shoes."

"No," said JT.

"Aren't you afraid of another round, peasant?"

"Not afraid of someone as stupid as a dog."

"You—!" José flung himself on JT, pounding him with his fists.

Tom jumped forward to drag José away; he spat at JT.

"Get off me! Let me at him!"

"What's this racket?" Victor had joined them.

"Where've you been?" asked Tom of Victor, letting go of José. "Where's my mother?"

José started to laugh. "Tom, little Tom, oh so worried."

"Never you mind."

"Two fights in one day. Michael would spin in his grave," said JT.

Victor twitched. It seemed to be spreading, reaching past his shoulders to his arms. "Shut it."

But the words continued to flood out from JT, as if a dam that had held for years had finally broken.

"You were always the second in command, always the runner-up."

"Shut up!"

"Michael called you 'unstable' – did you know that?"

With that Victor broke, and flung himself at JT too, punching hard. Tom grabbed one arm to pull him back but was thumped by José, who with his greater strength grabbed one of Tom's arms, twisting it behind him until he screamed in pain. José kicked his legs under him so that Tom crashed to the ground. He struggled against the weight, the arm-lock and the pain, smelling the alcohol and sweat from José after a day of drinking. He could hear thumps and groans as Victor took out his frustrations on JT, pounding him again and again, gasps of breath interspaced by the thuds of fists hitting flesh.

Finally, the groans went quiet.

Tom struggled to turn his head until he could see JT's unconscious body against the wall, blood seeping from the wounds on his face, breathing slow.

Victor stood up straight and took a few deep breaths.

"What do we do with this one?" asked José.

Victor stood over Tom, then crouched down to whisper in his ear.

"Now, now, Tom, you don't want to make a noise that might wake Elena, do you?"

At that Tom made a huge effort to dislodge José, pushing up with his free arm from the floor, crying out. But José pushed harder, his weight greater than Tom's, and he crashed back down again. His face was pressed against the cold metal floor.

"Silence him," said Victor, and José put a scrap of dirty cloth in Tom's mouth and then held both his hands behind his back. "Get him up."

Tom could see Victor staring at him, face expressionless, deep shadows of tiredness beneath his eyes.

"We can't harm him; *she* wouldn't like it."

As the pain from the twisted arm mounted, sweat trickled down the side of Tom's face.

"How about the ice mine?" said José.

Victor twitched again, but less, as if the aggression had leached some anger from his body.

"Yes – it's time the boy wonder cooled down a bit." He stood so close that Tom could feel his breath on his cheek. "Why so sad, so angry? All that lives must die."

He opened the airlock into the tunnel that led into the hill. José dragged Tom through the door into the cave, then Victor picked up a rock from the ground and used it to smash the controls for the light and the door on that side.

"There. He'll be stuck in here until we let him out."

Tom was thrust into the tunnel. Then they slammed the door shut, leaving him alone in the dark and the freezing cold, deep within Mars.

26: Sophia

Sophia caught rumbles from the storm that engulfed Justinian after the news broke of the Mars lander's navigation error.

She arranged to meet Alejandro under the statue of Athena in the entrance hall to the GC. All around her delegates rushed past, the usual gentle muttering turned to a roar of disquiet. Out of the racket she recognised some voices, and turned to see a cluster of people including her father.

"No, no, no," he said, both hands in the air. "Of course we're as appalled as you, Mr Bevan. This is the last thing we wanted – but there are those on your side who are not unhappy. Sabotage, some are saying."

"Dr Kasparov, you do us a disservice. Such an action would be ethically unacceptable."

"Then stop this nonsense, and let's discuss a follow-up mission."

"Ah, I thought you'd come to that," came a woman's voice which Sophia knew all too well. Cita Stone was back in Justinian. She was accompanied by a man in a military uniform.

Sophia was tempted to move away, but made herself sit still and listen.

"You!" said Sophia's father.

"Oh yes, Kasparov, and you remember my advisor Mark – now Captain – Vaughan? Bevan is right: this is suspicious, and who knows what other schemes that artificial intelligence of yours has cooked up. How can we trust it when it's thinking faster and quicker than you or me?"

"That's nonsense. We had nothing to do with *Boreas*'s guidance system – it was done by Bangalore Systems. Ask Bina here what went wrong."

Sophia saw the usually confident Indian woman looking a lot less cheerful than before; miserable, even. "We can't understand it; everything looked fine in our tests. But one thing I would like to make clear: that we didn't use any AIs, just our own Cores."

"There you go," said her father. "Human error. Let's agree a new motion for another mission."

"No," said Mr Bevan.

"Never, you mean, Bevan. Not a single other mission into deep space, ever," said Cita.

At that Mr Bevan looked like a bishop who had to apologise for the faults of his church. "We can't leave them up there; we have to be merciful."

"Exactly," said Artur.

"It would be criminal to launch another mission without approval," said Captain Vaughan.

"Exactly," said Cita with a smile. "No more launches."

"How can you say that?" raged Artur, his hands clenched in anger.

"Wait – please wait, let's not be reckless," said Bina. "Let's at least give time for an enquiry into what went wrong."

"Time-wasting," snorted Artur.

"I can see no reason why, after waiting fifteen – or is it sixteen years now? – we can't wait a few weeks," said Mr Bevan.

"Ridiculous."

"Oh no, Kasparov, not ridiculous; not to us, at least," said Cita. "For now, no resolutions?" she asked of Bina, who nodded.

"How sweet of you," Cita said, moving away. Captain Vaughan nodded at Bevan before following her.

"I'm sorry," said Mr Bevan in a low voice. "You must understand she is making my position very difficult. She made Bina give her a place in the Space

Reception group. Her supporters are growing fast in the Southern Confederacy – scarily fast."

"Of course we understand; don't we, Artur?" asked Bina.

Artur shook his head. "Ridiculous," he said again, and then he saw Sophia. "I must go. Hello, Soph. Waiting for Alejandro?"

She nodded. "Did you hear about Nina?"

Her father sighed. "What has she done now?"

"She tried to abseil down the apartment block, getting out through my bedroom window. But Mum stopped her in time."

"Oh, heavens; I'd better blip her," he said, and then vanished into the crowd.

Sophia was left alone again, pondering what she had seen and heard. Cita Stone was back, talking about Mars and space missions, along with Mark Vaughan. Sophia recognised the name: he'd been the one left on the beach with the boats when the *Prometheus* had exploded.

Then she spotted Alejandro. Did he know anything about this?

"Hi, gorgeous," he said, and kissed her – long and passionately, holding her tight, making her heart beat faster.

"Hi to you too."

"Let's go," he said. "Quick!"

He took her hand and ran towards the moving walkways that whisked them into the centre of A Island.

A few minutes later, they arrived rather breathlessly at the Planet Park located in the middle of the island. It was circular, and at its centre there was the One Earth sculpture – a one-hundred-metre globe programmed to display what the satellites observed, the planet in real time: its clouds, seas, deserts, and forests all illuminated from within to make the globe seem alive.

Wrapped around the sphere's vertical axis were two helixes to represent DNA, along which rose and fell platforms, ferrying visitors between the ground and the observation platform at the top where the North Pole would have been.

From the top, the park was at Sophia's feet, radiating out in all directions.

"Can you see the standing stones?" said Alejandro.

Sophia followed his pointing hand and could see a couple of them dotted round the edge of the park.

"What are they meant to be?"

"You know how these conceptual artists like to connect up the past and the present? Makes their work sound deep and them clever."

Sophia nodded, laughing.

"Well, they're partly to reflect those ancient stone monuments used to measure time, but also they've been positioned at the same scale of distance from this Earth as the geostationary satellites would be from us."

"Ha, yes, sounds typical. How many are there?"

"A hundred and twenty, I think, but hey, who's counting? Especially when the sunset looks so good."

It was indeed a lovely sunset, though they missed much of it.

As the light faded and the stars came out, Alejandro suggested they hunt for the final part of the park, which was a scale model of the moon that followed a track around the edge of the six-kilometre wide island. North represented full and south new. Looking into the sky, Sophia could see that the real moon was half full and waning, which meant its replica would be on the western side of the island.

They found it just where she had predicted it would be, which left her feeling rather pleased with herself. They decided to stay there a while, moving to one of Alejandro's magic spots where they'd be free from the blipverse's sensors. They could lie together on the sweet-smelling grass, listening to the lapping of the water and looking up at the stars high above, admiring the colours of dusk in the western sky.

Sophia felt so happy; to lie close to Alejandro on such an evening made her forget the sorrow of

Tom and his being stuck on Mars, and even Nina's annoyances. She eagerly kissed him back, running her hands through his hair.

"This is just heavenly," she murmured.

Then she remembered the meeting earlier, twisting round to lie on her side, resting on one arm.

"Alejandro," she began, "have you ever heard of anything about why the *Prometheus*—"

"No, no, don't bring that up!" He leapt up, agitated. "Let's not discuss boring, grown-up things. My dad is so anti-space now, after your dad turned him down."

His hands were shaking, she noticed.

"Come on, sit down with me. Do you want to talk about it?"

"No – don't you understand? You don't get it, you don't get me!" he was babbling, back down, on his knees now.

"It's ok, it's ok. We don't have to talk about it," she said, but even as she did she realised she now really wanted to, had to.

"Thanks, Soph, you're the best," he said, and he was on her, kissing her, holding her, touching her. It was unlike him: hurried, unthinking, selfish.

"This is better – right?" he asked, stopping for a moment.

She nodded, unsure.

"How about keeping this memory for ever?" he asked.

"What do you mean?"

Alejandro brought out two small vials of grey liquid. "We could take this, and then we'd never forget this evening, truly, for ever."

She sat up and took the one he handed her, curious. "What is it?"

"It's called Memory. It's the latest thing in nanobiotics. Just drink this, and in the next half-hour all your experiences become long-term memories straight away. They're burnt into your brain. Think of it: this moment, you and me, together, remembered forever, by both of us."

Sophia was unsure. It had been a wonderful moment – or at least it had been until she'd ruined the mood – and he seemed to want to so much.

"Go on," he coaxed.

"You've done this before?"

"Yes, with Pepe; it was fine. It's not like it's Belief."

"Belief?"

"You can add this silver powder to Memory and it makes you believe whatever you're told. Freaky stuff. It's what the lemming kids take – you know, the ones at school who come from the Southern Confederacy, the ones that think Cita Stone is some sort of holy woman."

"They scare me: their eyes are just dead."

"But this is Memory; it's auth. Ok then?"

"Ok," she said. But she regretted it straight away: was it really ok? And what else had he done with Pepe?

Alejandro opened his vial and drank its contents, but Sophia just sat there looking at hers.

"Go on," he said again.

"Can't this moment just be romantic as it is? I'm sure I won't ever forget it."

"But it's so much more intense using Memory! It's a bit like the difference between seeing something in a vid and real life. It's like you get photographic memory, but all the senses – just wild."

Sophia paused, realising she was feeling a very strong reluctance.

"Go on, for us, for me – you do trust me, don't you?" he asked.

"Yes, but…"

"You must now: I've taken mine. For me, Soph, please?"

Sophia's resistance was weakening. She did want to be a good girlfriend.

She uncorked her vial and slowly lifted it to her mouth. As she did, a memory drifted into her head: her mother saying "no sockets, no embeds and no nanobiotics" – when had it been? Just a few weeks ago?

Dead eyes! Robots!

Suddenly she threw the vial aside. "No!"

"What? Why not?"

"It's just, have you seen those lemming kids?"

"It won't be like that, promise."

She didn't want to become like them!

"I'm sorry."

"But I'll be stuck with this memory, forever – you saying no!"

Sophia jumped up.

"Sorry," she said again, tears appearing in her eyes as she ran, fleeing.

"Screw you, Sophia!" he shouted after her.

I'm a failure, she thought. *I've failed Alejandro. I'm a coward. I'm useless.*

When she got to the monorail station, she could see her reflection in its glass doors, her face red and dotted with tears.

How did it go so wrong? she asked herself. *What did I do wrong?*

She dried her tears and made herself ask another question. *How could he?* And then she wondered how well she really knew him.

But it was no good; she kept coming back again to the same thought.

What did I do wrong?

27: Tom

After the door closed, Tom's eyes adjusted to the absence of any light by creating fake images. But they faded when he was unable to detect even the slightest glimmer. There was nothing for his ears either but the sounds Tom made himself: his breathing, laboured after the fight, the faint heartbeat, the rustle of his clothes and the sound of shoes on sand and rock when he moved.

It was as if the world had disappeared, as if even his body had vanished, leaving him a disembodied intelligence floating in its own universe, alone in the darkness.

Tom felt his way, trying to find the door. For a while he was disorientated, and it was with panic gently rising that he stumbled around, hands outstretched to feel for the stony walls. Was this what death was like? he wondered, then pinched himself so he'd know he was still there.

It was with relief that he found the door, and his cage materialised in his mind; he could envisage the space with his inner eye, even if the outer was blind.

Tom banged and shouted, but without much hope. The door was thick, and those that could hear wouldn't respond. And if those like JT – who would respond if he could – didn't, then that was bad in its own way.

He decided to explore, if only to do something, to convince himself the world really did exist. There was half a hope that someone like José on their last visit had left something behind that could give light or warmth. For the cold was beginning to bite, remorselessly stripping his clothes of their protection till they too were enemies of warmth, frozen layers of flax.

"Keep moving," he said to himself, the words echoing around the chamber.

With his eyes useless, Tom's other senses improved as he focussed on every bit of information he could exact. His ears became attuned to the echoes like a bat, and he learnt how to understand what they told him: where walls were close and when there was space to move freely.

"Keep moving, Tom," he said.

"*Moving, Tom,*" said the cave.

He stumbled around, reaching for anything that might be there, but again and again it was just rocks, hard lumps of the planet left from the burrowing. The cold was beginning to hurt, and he began to shiver. He kept stopping to rub his hands together to generate some heat.

Run, Tom, run, he thought. But the walls were too close, too unknown and hard for that.

For a while he jumped, doing exercises on the spot to try to burn off energy, to get his temperature up and circulation going. Soon he had lost track of time. Had one hour passed or ten minutes? He could hardly tell.

"Time it, Tom," he told himself.

So he created a route he could walk, starting at the door: twenty paces forward, twenty paces back, and if he did that right he should end up at that one, known location.

"How long is that?" he wondered, out loud. "Maybe thirty seconds?"

He counted each time he did his track, twenty paces forward and back.

"One," he said, and then made the track again and again.

"One hundred" came round. Did that really mean he had been there fifty minutes, plus maybe an hour before he had started counting?

The cold! It kept biting and reaching for Tom's body, to take it over with its frozen embrace.

"Faster – we must go faster."

"*Faster, faster,*" said the echoes.

The walking became jogging, till the tiredness pushed Tom off the course, crashing into a wall.

"No, no, no! Mustn't stop."

His head and body ached, inviting Tom to close his eyes and rest, but he knew that siren's call, while tempting, was potentially lethal. And with the tiredness and the cold came the hunger and thirst.

Then Tom became unsure what number he had got to – was it one hundred and fifty? He gave up counting, instead building a cairn of stones, one for each journey there and back. To walk and keep upright with no visual clues was hard and getting tougher. Figures seemed to appear, memories from his inner eye leaking into his exhausted brain. His father, like a ghost, working at the controls of the blimp: "Remember me," he said.

And then two lovely dark eyes shone towards Tom, like those of a radiant angel with a friendly smile, who then turned away to look at another, standing next to Tom.

When he reached out there was no one there.

"No more, no more!" he cried.

"*More, more.*"

But no one heard, and he forced himself to stamp on the ground and use his fists to punch holes in the air, to use anger to fight the cold.

Eventually he collapsed by the door and felt for the cairn of rocks. One by one he threw them deeper into the cave, where they sometimes hit a wall with a dead thud. When they were all gone he didn't know what to do, and part of his brain didn't care anymore. Tom wrapped his arms around his legs, keeping as tight a ball as possible, and sat there, shivering. He'd lost everything and was alone. Time had mutated into his enemy, ticking slowly by, reality a lesson in endurance.

Suddenly there was an explosion of light, blinding him.

"You don't look too good, lad," he heard a voice say.

It was JT, he realised, standing at the open door.

"You… ou…" shivered Tom, "Nei… nei… ther."

JT had indeed looked better. His face was bruised and purple, one eye nearly closed by a bruise, and he was moving slowly, limping.

"Pretty pair we are," he said, helping Tom walk to the garden. "Would have let you out earlier, but only just come round."

In the garden, JT wrapped Tom in blankets, then went to the kitchen, returning with two steaming mugs of sweet tea, together with some welcome oatcake bars.

The base was silent, as if empty, and as warmth flowed into Tom's body and his energy returned, he asked about the time.

"Just after five," said JT. "How do you feel?" He looked at Tom closely, measuring him up.

Tom nodded. "Ok, now. So what next?"

JT took a deep breath. "Come; I have something to show you."

Tom followed him into the airlock, where JT began to suit up.

"Outside?" asked Tom.

"Yes, and keep the noise down."

As quietly as they could, they put on the surface suits, then cycled the air to open the outer door, revealing the world outside.

It was the time just before dawn, a time that Tom remembered, when everything was disguised, shadows in the dark. He looked into the sky and could see Earth. It was higher in the sky than before but dimmer, further away.

Tom went over to JT so their helmets touched and they could talk.

"What are we looking for?"

"Wait – soon," said JT.

Tom waited the few minutes before the sun reached the eastern horizon, turning the sky from the dark of night to a luminous blue, catching the glass top of the garden, showing the edges of the ruined dome under which Tom's father was buried.

"Now," said JT, "look away from the sun."

Tom turned and then gasped. Behind the base, lit gently by the morning sun, was the blimp, fully inflated, ready to go.

"No," said Tom. "No way: you're crazy."

"Listen! We can do it. The lander is at the right longitude, just four degrees south, not north; that's eight degrees of latitude, or five hundred kilometres. The blimp will get us there."

"But JT, there'd be no way back – we'd be stuck."

"We wouldn't need to get back. We'd be at the lander; it could support us."

"If we miss it we're dead."

At this, JT grabbed Tom by the shoulders.

"Listen, Tom, I am not going to die on this planet: understand that. Whatever it takes, I am going to get home. And you made a promise – no, a vow. Don't you go yellow on me, lad; this is the time to decide."

Tom was silent, heart beating, trying to square the impossible circle.

"But what about my mother – you're mad! I'd never leave her with Victor. I can't decide this now, just like that."

"You can and you must. I know Elena and her strengths; you only know her as your mother. Trust her. She'll understand: I left a note explaining everything." JT gave Tom another shake. "Listen, Tom, it's only a matter of time before one of the others thinks of this, and if Victor decides to go, he's not going to take you or me, is he? But you have no choice; you swore an oath. I can't fly it with this black eye, and I'm not going to be stuck here, and neither are you. Think of yourself for a change – and Earth, Tom, think of it: Earth!"

Tom took a step back. He needed a moment to think, a moment on his own, not centimetres from JT's face. Close to the other's wounds and purple bruises, the dried blood was all too real. Yesterday, when JT had been outside, that was when he'd done this.

But what was he to do? What was he to choose? It seemed simple, either to go or to stay, but each path led somewhere very different.

He had made a promise; he remembered it, here on the surface on a dawn just like this one. But did he have to keep it? Would he be damned for breaking his oath, or damned for abandoning his mother, who loved him? But what was love worth when it led to death, filling him with grief?

Whatever the price – that was what he had sworn to, bound by his blood, blood that he remembered dropping down onto the Martian rocks.

Tom turned to look at the base, and his stomach tightened. He didn't want to go back into that prison, to face the quarrels of the last day and to see Elena with Victor. The thought of flying across the plains of Mars intoxicated him, the realisation of a dream he'd had ever since he and his father had worked on the blimp.

And Earth: he'd get to Earth!

He nodded at JT, and then together they made their way to the blimp to prepare it for take-off.

It was decided. Tom would keep true to his vow, whatever the price.

28: Tom

The blimp was secured by hemp ropes to an instrument platform halfway between the base and the black cube of the thermonuclear plant. Their power station had been placed a hundred metres away for safety, though the reality was that if it were to fail, they would have been as dead from cold as they would have been from radiation.

JT untied the rope that held the blimp down and indicated to Tom to help. Together they used a bracket on the platform to take the strain as they pulled in the slack until the blimp was directly above them, as if the sky were squeezing them into the ground, forcing them to kneel.

Tom held the slack fast as JT tied the loose end of the rope around a jury-rigged bamboo cage. He turned to Tom and pressed their helmets together. "Doubling up, that is. I used to do this when mooring my little Cornish Crabber. We can let go from on board this way."

"Let's go."

"No – first we must give the blimp a name," said JT.

"A name? We didn't need one..." Tom struggled to find the words. "...last time," he said finally.

"All craft need a name: it makes them real, defines their character. And I name you *Endurance*, after Shackleton's ship."

Tom stood, feeling awkward, waiting for JT to complete those words with some ceremony, but the old sailor just reached out and gently stroked the vessel.

"Ok," he said, "now we are ready to cast off."

He climbed into the bamboo frame and Tom followed, taking the pilot's position on the left with the controls. He swallowed, trying to remember everything he had learnt when helping his father build the blimp.

"System check," he said, and JT nodded. Tom flicked the power on and experimentally spun up each engine, first forward and then back. The *Endurance* surged around, as if itching to be off. Then he tested the vents, first dumping gas so the blimp sank down, pinning them to the platform, before inflating it so it rose again, waving gently from side to side.

JT looked up at the three tanks, a large one for hydrogen and two smaller containing oxygen.

"All tanks full," he said.

"Ok," said Tom.

JT leant over to the knot in front of him, loosening it.

"Give the word, skipper."

Tom could see his lips mouth the words, and faintly heard the sounds. He took a deep breath. Was this how his father had felt on the blimp's last flight? *No,* he told himself, *don't think of that; think of our destination. Concentrate on that and remember that this is the start of the long road to Earth.*

"Let go."

With that the rope coiled down through the platform and then the *Endurance* was airborne, shooting up, released from its tether, free at last.

Tom struggled to control it, trying to manage the bobbing effect as its nose rose and sank. He tried power on, power off, more gas, less.

"Easy, lad, let her settle first."

Her? Tom thought, but he followed JT's advice, letting the oscillations dampen. For a moment he watched the base decrease in size below them, but it made him worry about what might be happening inside. All his life had been within those cramped spaces and enclosing walls.

No, I mustn't look back, and before the nodding had completely stopped, he powered up both engines, driving them forward.

The controls took a bit of getting used to. Everything seemed to happen in slow motion, and the *Endurance* seemed to have a mind of its own, not wanting to turn but drifting sideways as if in revolt.

"Which way?" Tom asked.

"South, always south," JT said. "In the morning, we just keep the sun to our left. Follow the Maja Valles south, passing Stege Crater and into Chia Crater. Then, in the afternoon, keep the sun to our right. If it's where I calculated it is, the lander will be in the Juventae Chasma, and we can't miss that canyon – it's huge."

The afternoon seemed far away to Tom, but he was focussing on flying the craft, knowing how little margin they had in fuel or air. Slowly his confidence grew, and he was able to make smaller and smaller adjustments, correcting their heading, altering their height, smoothly flying in the direction they had to go. He couldn't change what had happened in the past in the base, and he didn't know what would happen when they got to the Juventae Chasma, so he concentrated on the present, on flying the blimp, on enjoying the freedom of the skies.

Initially their path south took them along the dried-up riverbed on which the base had been built. Millions of years ago water had flowed there, and Tom would have been travelling towards its source. The cliffs on the left, the east, were slightly higher than those to the west, though occasionally the banks were broken by craters.

They headed further upriver until it turned to the right and branched, the left channel dotted with hills that once had been islands, the right rising gradually. Tom leant forward and dumped some water, so the blimp rose slightly to climb out of the river bed and over the plains of Mars.

The sun rose slowly, heating the landscape below and the *Endurance*. The shadows shortened, pointing west, giving a clear indication of which way to fly.

Tom found he was enjoying himself. It was his, this great blimp, his to command, and it responded eagerly.

It – he couldn't quite get round to calling it a her – vibrated gently, the reassuring hum of the propellers spinning. He could sense the breeze that followed the morning sun gently buffeting the envelope, sometimes to the left, sometimes to the right. But the engines were running smoothly, and by moving the power levers a few millimetres, he could adjust and keep them on track, heading the direction that he wanted to go. If he saw something of interest on the ground, he could vent hydrogen and they would drift lower, but then if a crater or hill appeared, he could turn the other valve to inflate the envelope and they'd rise up again, higher into the sky.

He felt he was seeing Mars for the first time. Sure, they had images on the tablets, but that was abstract, as if in a game. This was real, seen directly with his two eyes, and there was nothing else that could give the feeling of scale and size. JT, with only one working eye, had no way of judging the distances accurately.

But Tom could. He could see the river channel and imagine a raging torrent, full of blue water in Mars's youth. He could see the craters and imagine flaming rocks falling from the sky, exploding into the surface. He could see the dunes of sand, blown and crafted by the wind over aeons of empty time.

The Maja Valles led them into the Chia Crater, where they flew through one of the breaks in its kilometre-high walls, edges rimmed with frost. In the middle of the gap was a hill worn by ancient floods into the shape of a teardrop.

Time seemed to go slowly. JT fell asleep, and Tom wished he could do the same, but was left alone with his thoughts. He tried not to think of the base, of his mother and Victor, pushing those memories away, focussing on the lander, and the long journey across space to Earth. And, he admitted to himself, the girl with dark eyes – Sophia. He began to feel hungry, to feel thirsty, and his muscles were beginning to complain, but he ignored all these cries for attention and flew on. Below him the shadows on the rocks grew shorter and shorter, and *Endurance's* shadow joined them, nearly underneath Tom and JT. It was approaching noon, when they couldn't use the sun to navigate.

So Tom had to fly by picking a point to aim for that was on the horizon and on their route. Before the *Endurance* reached it, he had to choose another target, lined up with the first, like standing stones in a row. It was hard work, needing concentration, all too easy to get disoriented and be lost forever.

But some faraway features were becoming visible on the far side of the Chia Crater. Cliffs, shining bright in the noontime sun, could be seen slightly to the left of their course, helping Tom picture in his head where they were and which way they should go.

The heart of the Chia Crater was flat and featureless, only a handful of craters to give a sense of motion. Later the soil colour changed from the familiar rusty red to an ominous dark purple. Flying became tedious, draining, having to be endlessly alert while the blimp seemed to be making no progress. Sometimes he felt they were pinned to the sky.

He was tired, and his brain was refusing to think, shutting down, asking again and again when there would be a chance to sleep, to rest, to close his eyes. He gave in to the blessed relief, just for a moment...

Tom woke in a panic. There was a rock face directly in front of them.

29: Tom

"No!" Tom cried, leaping at the controls to dump water, fully opening that valve, while putting both engines in reverse before opening the hydrogen inflation valve. The *Endurance* reacted with a jerk, which woke JT.

"Come on, come on, come on!" shouted Tom, furious with himself, too busy to be scared, putting all his weight on the power levers, trying to open the valves just that little bit more.

The blimp rose, jerking backwards, but its momentum carried them forward, closer and closer to the rocks – sharp, jagged layers, approaching like knives to open them or their blimp, slicing through its envelope. All they could see in front of them were rocks, closing in, blocking out the sky.

The front of the envelope smashed into the cliff edge, flinging Tom and JT forward.

JT raised a hand to grab the gas bottles and, with the other, the bamboo cage, to hold their craft together. Tom held his breath. Would the envelope tear?

The *Endurance* ground to a halt and bounced back, the cage rattling, the engines screaming, blades now working with the direction of motion rather than against it. Then, finally, it began to climb as the water dropped out of its tanks, lightening so it could rise again.

Tom set the engines to neutral, his hands shaking, heart pumping.

"I'm sorry," he said. "I must have dozed off."

JT looked around at the craft, taking stock. "She's ok," he said, "so don't you worry. We all go aground once in our lives – all sailors do."

"This isn't sailing, JT."

"I know, lad, I know," and then he laughed, and Tom joined in. "You shouldn't have let me sleep; it was dangerous. Should always be two on watch, so you can keep each other awake with stories."

So, as they flew south over the hills of Mars, leaving the Chia Crater far behind, JT told Tom about his youth on his father's farm in Cornwall, and how his father had wanted him to follow in his steps. But JT had preferred the sea, first fishing and sailing as a child, then when grown as a biologist, understanding how all the plants and creatures worked together as a system without realising it, creating their environment.

Afterwards he told Tom the story of the original *Endurance* and its mission to the icy heart of Antarctica, and how it too had been trapped, but the crew had against all the odds made their way home safely.

There came a time, later in the afternoon, where they climbed a hill that seemed to go on and on. And when they finally flew over its top they could see cliffs ahead of them. Far, far away they were, but Tom and JT could tell they must be huge – kilometres high.

"The Juventae Chasma!" shouted Tom. The fear of the crash flew from his mind in his delight.

"Aye, it certainly looks like it – you've done it, Tom, you've done it."

The land beneath them slowly dropped away. On this, the north side, there were no cliffs; just hills that rolled ever lower, down to the depths of the canyon. It was huge, over a hundred kilometres across and about five kilometres deep: the mind had difficulty understanding the scale.

"How do we find the lander in here?" Tom asked.

"It should be somewhere at the south end, roughly in the middle. Let's head over there and spiral down."

It was an amazing, magnificent sight, though slightly scary. As the land dropped away, Tom felt a moment of vertigo; they seemed to be climbing, though the weight of his stomach didn't increase as it did when the blimp rose. His instinct was to follow the land down, but then they wouldn't see so far, and it would take fuel to climb back up.

He looked up at the tanks above him, checking each of the dials. He was shocked to see that all were approaching empty; the long day and recovery from the earlier crash had taken a lot of reserves.

The sun was sinking towards the west, and shadows were beginning to lengthen: already the cliffs to Tom's right were lost in shade.

Then Tom noticed the *Endurance* was drifting slowly down into the chasm, even when all valves were closed. With horror, he realised that the envelope must have sprung a leak, probably during the crash. It was to be a race between them finding the lander and what now felt like a host of demons: the leaking envelope, the empty tanks, the exhausted crew and the setting sun.

"Where is it, JT, where shall we look?" he asked urgently.

"I dunno; could be anywhere, maybe over by those hillocks, over there at the base of the southern cliffs. Hard to see with just the one eye, and my eyesight isn't what it used to be."

Tom's eyes flashed over the landscape far below. All he could see were reds and browns, darkening in the sunset.

"We'll never spot it from up here. I'll spiral down, while it's still light."

What would they do in the dark? he wondered. Their air would not last through the night, and the suits could only protect for so long against the cold.

Tom flew the blimp close to the cliffs on the far side and then turned, starting the spiral. As they descended the cliffs seemed to rise higher, a trap from which there would be no escape. With evening coming, temperatures began to fall, fastest in the shadows hidden from the sun, and with it came gusts of wind, thermals pushing upwards while katabatic winds flowed down the cliffs. Tom found himself again and again battling the controls to keep the spiral under control, struggling to fly and search at the same time.

Halfway round the spiral Tom could look back to where they had come from, a jumble of hills stretching to the horizon, beyond which was the base, hundreds of kilometres away.

Don't think of it, he told himself. *Only look, search for that speck of silver amongst the endless red.*

As they sank, the hills that had seemed so small began to grow into mountains, the sort that they had flown over on the way there. But all they could see were rocks and more rocks. A gust of wind blew Tom off track, and he struggled with the controls. He had grown fond of his command, but he had to admit to himself that *Endurance* wasn't that good at circling.

Not circles, squares, he decided, and that worked better and gave more time to look. Fly for a bit, then turn and fly again; keep going and keep descending. Tom checked the tanks above them: almost empty.

A panic began to rise inside. The canyon was so vast, and it appeared empty apart from sand dunes and rocks. The lander could be anywhere, lost behind some boulder or in a shadow, and they'd never find it before their air ran out. Already the air felt wrong, breathing that bit more difficult. And Tom's head felt like it was made of lead. It ached for a rest, projecting mental pictures, imagining his comfy bed back at the base. His mouth was dry, until the thought of food flooded it with saliva. *No, no,* he thought, *got to forget both and keep searching.*

But the canyon was enormous, and Tom had to concentrate so hard on flying and hunting. He wished he could have a break, to get out of the cage and stretch his legs, which itched with an eagerness to be exercised. He tried bending and unbending his knees, stretching his legs to get the blood circulating.

Another loop, another nothing. Round again Tom flew. What would they do if they couldn't find it?

Come on, come on, where is it? He tried to will himself to see it.

Nothing.

Panic battled with anger within him. Where was it? His vision blurred as his tired eyes strained, darting from one side to the other. A cloud of sand, picked up by the wind, drifted across a crater, then twisted into a column. *Not a dust devil, not now, please not now.*

"What's the plan now, JT?" he demanded.

"Keep looking."

"What do you think I've been doing?"

"It's in here somewhere."

"But where, JT? Where? We could spend days hunting for it, and we've an hour, max, before the sun sets."

"Did you know this used to be a great sea? Imagine that: waves crashing against the cliffs and that mountain down there an island."

"JT, we have to find that lander, now! This is not the time to blather away about what happened millions of years ago."

"More like a billion..."

Tom thumped the bamboo frame hard. "Damn it, JT, forget the history lesson. This is not the time! We're going to die, here, soon, if we don't find that lander."

"Hey, that attitude's not going to help."

"So what is, JT?"

There was a pause.

"We keep looking."

Round again Tom flew the craft, sinking gradually into the canyon which he knew it would never escape. His head ached from the effort to concentrate and stay awake. His eyes stung and his vision was blurred.

"We're not going to find it, JT."

"Don't give in, Tom; we can't give in, not now."

"No," said Tom. "We have no choices now."

"No," agreed JT. "None."

One last push, thought Tom, banging the side of his head against the glass face of his surface suit, trying to shock his system into alertness.

Suddenly – "What's that?" he asked, pointing ahead and downwards.

JT followed the line and saw too a spark of light, the sun's reflection dancing in the dusk.

"It's the lander – it's there, just there: we've found it!"

Tom grinned and steered the *Endurance* towards the dot. It was going to be ok; they were going to make it. He looked across at the far wall of the Juventae Chasma, where the gullies were becoming hazy.

"That's funny; I can't see the cliffs anymore."

"Don't worry about that. Keep heading down."

Tom kept watching. "It's getting closer."

"Don't be a fool. Cliffs don't move."

Then horror hit Tom. "It's not a cliff, it's a sandstorm!"

A wall of sand was rushing at them across the canyon: a thick curtain, dark reds and purples, wrapping itself around and around, angry fingers of dust. It moved like a snake, coiling, two kilometres high and a hundred across, bearing down on them like a train.

"Get down! Get us down right now!" cried JT. "If that storm hits us we'll never find the lander again."

"We'd probably hit those cliffs first," shouted Tom. He powered the engines up to max, aiming towards the lander, and then opened up the hydrogen vent valve. As the gas streamed out they began to sink, faster and faster.

But the cloud was on them, grabbing the *Endurance*, throwing it from side to side, dragging it along in its wake.

They were blind. In the storm it was near pitch black, and Tom had no way of knowing where they were or how fast they were travelling. He could only guess from the direction of the wind, and he struggled to fly into it to hold his position.

Through the swirling black clouds, there was a glimpse of land, rocks rushing by, terrifyingly close.

"Watch those rocks!"

"I know, I know!" Tom fought with the controls.

Suddenly he realised that they were in a crater and its far wall was fast approaching. This time the crash would not be gentle.

The blimp slammed into the rock wall, stopping almost dead. The bamboo cage split, flinging Tom and JT out. Tom turned as he flew in the air, so he was looking back at the *Endurance*. The last thing he saw was it lifting off by itself, now free of their weight, and vanishing into the night.

Then he smashed into rocks and knew no more.

30: Tom

Tom came round hearing JT call his name.

"Come on, Tom, come on – please answer, Tom, please."

Tom groaned and sat up. "I'm ok," he said. At least, he thought he was.

They were alone in a crater: all they could see of the *Endurance* were some splintered fragments of the bamboo cage. The storm was passing, and the dust was thinning. The sand cloud was pink, faintly lit from the last remnants of the sun, before it disappeared behind the canyon walls.

"Where's the *Endurance*?" Tom asked.

"She's gone – blown away. We'll have to walk the rest."

Tom nodded and stood up. Nothing seemed broken, though he could feel that the suit had a new dent behind his head and he had a cracker of a headache. "It'll be dark soon – is your head light working?"

In answer JT lit his, and its cone showed them a jumble of rocks.

"Could be anywhere."

"Let's get out of this crater first," said Tom.

They stumbled towards the nearest side, then began to climb its edge. First there were sand drifts, which were hard work to wade through, each footstep a struggle. Then it got steeper, and they had to climb from rock to rock.

The light faded rapidly, and the stars came out in the sky above. One was brighter by far, dominating the sky.

"Earth?" JT asked.

"No," said Tom, "it must be Phobos – look, you can see it moving slowly."

At the rim of the crater they stopped for breath and looked around. All was dark, cold and silent... dead.

"Do you remember which way it was?"

Tom looked around at the rocks and low hills, and the deep shadow in the distance which was the canyon walls.

"West, I think, towards the setting sun."

They began to trudge in that direction. Tom had never felt this tired, and he could tell by the ache in his chest that the air was running low. In his stomach the hunger grew and grew, as if sharp stones were grinding against each other inside him. Without the power from the blimp, their suits' batteries were struggling to keep them warm, and the cold was beginning to seep in, chilling the fingers and toes first.

Beside him, JT stumbled and staggered from side to side, before falling back to sit on the sandy soil. Tom looked at him through the glass of his suit. He looked older than Tom had ever seen him, creases deeper, eyes deader, with dark blue patches under them. He gasped for breath, which froze as a mist inside his helmet.

"I'll be fine, you'll see," he gasped. "Just give me a moment."

"No," said Tom. "We can't stay; we have to push on, now."

JT tried to rise, and then fell back. He shook his head. "No," he said, "you go on, I'll follow if I can."

"Come on," said Tom, trying to pull him up, but his grip slipped, and JT fell back.

"No, Tom, I'm sorry. It's too big, this canyon." JT gave a half-hearted wave around at the land hidden in the dark. "We'll never find the *Boreas*; we've failed. We might as well rest here and enjoy the night's sky while we can, before the air runs out. It won't be a bad way to go."

A wave of despair washed over Tom. It would be so easy to agree, to surrender to his tiredness. Would it be so bad to join his father?

He sat down next to JT, who put his arm around Tom's shoulders. "I'm sorry, Tom. I thought we could do this. I just wanted us two to get to Earth."

"I know, JT, I know. I wanted it too."

They looked up the stars, connecting them together into the constellations that had been unchanged for millennia. Tom thought of those thousands of years during which humans had struggled and battled against the odds to cross the planet and now head out into space. Countless millions must have died, but their ancestors had been the ones that survived. The ones that had made it were those that hadn't given up, and they had bequeathed their victories to their children and children's children.

Tom turned to JT. "We have to try, JT. While we have air, we must go on."

"You go, lad. I'll rest here."

"No, JT, both of us."

Tom shrugged off JT's arm and put his own around the old man's shoulder, pulling him to his feet. The pain in his chest was getting stronger as the air got thinner. Next to him JT staggered, and Tom needed all his energy to pull him up again. He let himself rest for a breath or two, then they started off again.

Was it his imagination, or were they going upwards? Tom turned off his head light for a moment and let his eyes get used to the dark. Under the faint light from Phobos, he could just make out the circle of cliffs they were stuck within and the rim of the hill somewhere ahead. In the dark there was no sense of distance: it could have been one hundred metres or a kilometre.

"Only one way to find out," he said.

"Whass tha?" slurred JT.

Just one more step, then another. Limbs ached from being forced to be motionless all day and now being asked to carry another, almost dragging the old man's legs across the freezing deserts of Mars. *Earth*,

Tom kept telling himself. *Keep walking, you can make it.* A blue planet, a warm planet, a planet with life-giving air, a planet where lived a girl named Sophia, the girl with dark eyes.

"A rest," he said, and they collapsed on the ground, back to some rocks.

Tom checked the gauge on his tanks: empty. He then turned to JT's: empty too.

"We don't need these," he said, and removed them, flinging them aside with fingers stiff from cold.

"Make do," Tom gasped, "with what in suits – weigh less."

JT nodded. Lightened, they were able to stand up and begin to move on again. Whatever happened, it would happen soon: the air wouldn't last much longer. He could smell the staleness above the stink of his sweat.

Left leg forward, drag JT, right leg forward, repeat. Always repeat. Each breath was rasping, empty, grasping for more, the lungs always disappointed.

Suddenly Tom realised they had reached the crest of the hill and could see the view on the other side. Halfway down its flank he could see a flashing red light.

He felt like crying. They were safe; the lander, the *Boreas*, was there.

"Come on, JT. It's there, can you see it?"

"Wassit?"

"Come on – don't give up now."

Tom dragged the old man, pulling him with all his might, staggering down the slope towards the dark shadow within which were reflected the stars, a machine the colour of the night sky.

One, two, four, seven... Tom counted each step but counting was too hard, so he just walked, one step at a time.

Suddenly it was there. A few more steps, and then he was at the legs of the lander.

JT collapsed, and under the glare of his head light Tom could see he was unconscious. He shone the light at *Boreas*, hunting for the way in. The lander squatted on the ground, cylindrical base and conical nose. The spot of light traced out a hatch, an airlock, and followed it down to the ground. There was a ladder, one they would have to climb.

His chest ached intolerably, as if bolts were tightening around his body, crushing his lungs together. He put his arm under JT's shoulder and dragged him to the ladder. For a moment he leant against it, and then he began to climb, step by step. With each rung upwards he lifted JT and then wedged his feet into a step so he could climb one himself.

"We're halfway there, JT, halfway," Tom said, but there was no reply.

Then Tom's grasp on the slippery suit faltered and JT clunked back down the steps beneath him, all the way back to the soil of Mars. The suit and unconscious occupant lay there unmoving, arms and legs sprayed out in all directions.

"No!" Tom cried. "No!"

It was too much; why was life so unfair? Tom felt totally alone, deserted in the midst of Mars, one human in the vast silent expanse of the canyon.

He rested his head against the step, looking at the surface of the lander just inches away from his face. To his amazement, on the side of the ladder he saw a mark. Sand blown in the wind had stuck to something greasy on its side. The Martian dust made the shape of a pair of lips, of a kiss.

Suddenly Tom felt warmer: he didn't feel alone, and he knew he could do it.

He stepped gingerly back down the ladder to where JT was lying.

"Come on, JT, off we go."

Tom lifted him and climbed back up the steps with renewed energy until he reached a flat surface by the airlock. At the centre of its door was a metal bar that Tom tested and found he could rotate anti-clockwise. As he did so lights from above switched on, blinding him.

When his eyes returned to normal, he could see the door had swung outwards. The lander was open in front of him and he staggered across the doorway into the airlock. After he closed the door behind him, air flooded the chamber – warm, life-giving air – and he had just enough energy to open JT's helmet and then his own before collapsing to the floor.

Part 5

31: Tom

Tom woke slowly from a deep sleep. Why should he stir when he was warm and safe? But there was something constraining his body like a cage. He could tell this wasn't his bunk, even when half asleep.

With a jerk he opened his eyes and sat up, images flooding into his mind. They had made it; they had flown hundreds of kilometres across the empty wastes of Mars from the base to the lander.

He struggled out of his surface suit, which clung tightly to his body, and then looked around with interest at this, the first new place he'd seen in his sixteen years. He was struck by the lack of scratches on its shiny surfaces and how it smelt new – or was it the absence of aromas, the base's smell of old socks and Mars dust? The only sand was that scattered around where he and JT had collapsed on the floor the previous night. The lander was circular in cross-section, and the open-plan cabin occupied all of the mid-deck. On one side was the airlock through which they had entered, while on the other was a window that stretched over a quarter of the way round, with panoramic views over the Juventae Chasma.

Tom noticed that just below the base of the wide window was a short sheet of glass, like a shelf, that followed its curve round and inclined downwards towards the floor. By the window were three padded seats, and behind them in the centre of the craft were four more. Seven seats, for seven of them, he thought. He touched one of the ones by the window: would this have been his father's if all had worked out as planned?

He sat in the central one and looked out at the landscape outside. It was a stunning sight: of rocks and dunes, rolling hills in the near distance and, far away, the cliffs at the edge of the canyon. Tom grinned and stretched. He had no idea how to fly this craft – indeed, there were no controls visible – but first things first: a wash, then breakfast.

Ten minutes later, a refreshed Tom was struggling with the ship's kitchen, trying to get a cup of tea; instead, the machine produced a cup of some other liquid. He sniffed, took a sip, and then made a face. It was hot but very bitter.

"Coffee," said JT, waking at last. "I smell coffee."

"Morning, JT. Was wondering how long you'd be slumbering away."

"Easy, lad, I'm not as young as I was – and pass me that cup. It's been way on twenty years since I've tasted coffee."

He blew on the cup to cool it, then took a few mouthfuls. "It isn't an Italian-blend cappuccino, but I ain't going to complain. Suppose I'd better get out of this suit too."

Tom helped him out, and they looked around for somewhere to store the suits.

"Strange sort of craft," said JT. "There're no controls. How do we fly whatever it is? *Boreas*?"

"Yes," said an expressionless voice. "*Boreas* lander, awaiting your instructions."

JT and Tom searched for the source of the voice, but it seemed to come from all around.

"Who are you? What are you?" said JT.

"I'm the semi-aware entity in control of this craft. As such, I have been given the names of either *Ship* or *Boreas* and will respond accordingly."

"Respond? To what?" said Tom.

"I can act as your c-agent to interface to the blipverse or any of the ship's features. In addition, I can read standard gestures and communicate via touch surfaces. I also have a blipcom for you from Earth."

"Didn't get a word of that," muttered JT.

"Ok," said Tom, "better go through that again, explaining what you mean by c-agent, blipverse and blipcom. And tell us how to avoid making control gestures by mistake."

"You can activate almost any surface as a touch interface by double-tapping on it, and again to close the interface. Gesture control is the same, but in mid-air."

"Like this?" asked Tom, double-tapping in mid-air.

"Exactly."

"Or this?" he said, and tapped on the curving plate of glass, which awoke with a flood of colours and shapes. He could see a keyboard, a red globe, clearly Mars, hanging in space, an icon of the lander, a map of the canyon, and a representation of their cabin rotating in 3D.

"Wow," Tom said. He noticed the cabin representation was live: there was a 3D version of himself, small but accurate in every detail, which moved as he moved.

"That's like television, but it's in 3D and it's from all angles," JT marvelled.

"That is for blipverse interactions, where individuals can join in virtual environments that can include live events."

"And by blipverse you mean the cloud?" asked Tom.

"The blip universe or blipverse is the aggregation of services available using the communication capability of all Earth networks, including what was called the cloud. The 'blip' is a complete message that includes all formats so that it can be received in the preferred form, whether textural, voice, image, video or space interaction, as you see here. It also supports archival services, security, privacy management, c-agent to c-agent communication, and AI-generated material."

"And c-agent?"

"Given the complexity of the blipverse, it has become essential for humans to use a communicating agent, or c-agent, as intermediary: that is, artificial entities such as myself. We can interface to the various services, undertake routine tasks, act as your representative for blips when you are busy, and handle archival, security and privacy management."

Tom looked at the image of him and JT, standing there talking into the air.

"And is this – what was it? – *blipverse interaction* available to others on Earth?"

"No. The default privacy settings prevent that, unless you modify them."

"Thank God for that," said JT.

Tom double-tapped on the plate again, and the graphics disappeared.

"What do you think: message first, or breakfast?"

"Breakfast! I haven't eaten in twenty-four hours, and that message can keep – can't it?" JT asked.

"Yes," said *Boreas*. "The next time constraint is the first launch window, which is in one hundred and seven minutes."

With a bit of help from *Boreas,* they made themselves first one, then a second breakfast. With their stomachs full and a mug of tea (Tom) and coffee (JT) to hand, they could relax and look out over the canyon, talking over the events of the day before, and idly double-tapping on the glass to alternately switch it on and off.

"See," said JT. "I can just about open this eye."

"Oh yes, a regular pirate you are, one-eyed and all."

"The Pirate of Mars – great title. I like that, I like that."

"Wonder what this message is?" said Tom. In fact, he'd been thinking of little else, and in particular whether it was from his mother.

"Only one way to find out. *Boreas*, play the message, please."

The window became partly opaque, and in place of the rolling landscape was a man wearing a white long shirt who seemed vaguely familiar.

"Greetings, Jim Trevelyn—"

"JT," he muttered automatically.

"—and Tom Tesla, and welcome to the *Boreas*. My name is Dr Khujandi and I am – indeed we all are – very glad that at least some of you were able to reach the lander. I can only say again how sorry we are that something seemed to go wrong with its guidance system. But now we can at least ensure that you two are able to dock with the *Odyssey* and return to the Earth.

"The *Boreas* is only designed for a short stay, so we suggest you launch the next time there is an orbital window. The ship can determine when that is and control the ascent automatically, so there is no need to fly it directly, though you can ask it to display relevant data overlays if you so wish.

"Of course, you're wondering how I know your names. We received a communication from the base explaining you were missing and that you had left a message saying you were attempting to reach the lander. You can use the ship's systems to send them an update of your status.

"You can also blip us, and we look forward to hearing from you direct." At this he broke off and smiled. "I must say, it is a relief to be able to communicate with something blip-aware and capable, rather than primitive like the base."

"Huh," said JT.

"Well, that is sufficient for now. Let us know what you flight plans are – when '*the bird is on the wing*', as the saying goes."

The figure vanished from the window, which became transparent again. There was a silence as both looked over the landscape outside.

Eventually JT said, "We should send them a message."

"I know."

"She'll be worrying about you."

"I *know*."

"All you have to say is we're here, that everything went ok—"

"Ok? *Ok?* How is it ok when she's stuck there with… with… you know, *him?* When we're about to head back to Earth leaving her – and them, too – here?"

"Damn it, Tom, I am sorry for Elena but I'm *not* sorry we're here. There was a chance for two at most on that blimp, and I was not going to die on this planet. And you made an oath—"

"Don't talk about that."

There was another silence.

"*Boreas,*" said Tom. "Is there any way you can fly over to the base and then take everyone up to orbit?"

"This ship is designed for a single landing, so is unable to perform the manoeuvre you described."

"Huh," said Tom. He took a deep breath. "Ok, let's do it – now. *Boreas,* start recording a message."

He didn't know which way to look, so simply talked at the window where Dr Khujandi had appeared.

"Hi everyone, sorry to leave like that, wasn't my idea. Anyhow, we're here now, all safe – amazing journey, must tell you about it sometime. Yup, lots of stories next time we meet, so remember that."

He stopped, and JT took over. "We've been told the ship will be ready for launch in" – he looked at his watch – "fifteen minutes or so. Look after the garden for me, will you? I've left instructions about maintaining it. Take care, all of you – see you back on Earth."

"Yup," said Tom. "See you on Earth, Mum." He looked at JT for a moment, and then added, "Message end."

"Would you like to review it?"

"No – yes, play it back."

They watched a 3D projection in the window of themselves saying their short message. Tom noticed that the ship had trimmed the unwanted bits at the start and end without them having to ask. He experimented with the gestures, first double-tapping in the air and then, as he rotated a finger around, smoothly turning round the 3D projection of them. Despite himself, he laughed and then double-tapped again.

JT peered around the craft.

"Where are the cameras?" he asked. "They seem to follow us, but I can't see any."

"There are a number of electromagnetic sensors at fixed locations, and from them I can extrapolate to what the image would be like from any direction."

"That's fine; send it," said Tom. It was a relief to have done it, for the message to have gone.

The response came ten minutes later as they were strapping themselves in for the launch. It was in audio only, no video.

"Tom, why did you fly away like that, without telling me?" It was Elena. "You could have been killed, like Michael. Did you think about that – think about me?" There was a pause, a cut, then: "I'll be fine here, don't worry yourself about me. Take care of yourself and get to Earth safely and we'll meet… well, whenever. Lots of love, always."

That was it, and then they were silent.

"Why was there no video?" Tom asked.

"The data stream from the base included audio only. I have no information as to why that was," said *Boreas*.

There was another silence.

"She sounded fine," said JT. "She'll be ok."

"When is the launch window?" asked Tom. His voice sounded harsher, louder.

"We entered it a minute ago and it will remain open for a further seven-point-three minutes. I've already undertaken pre-flight preps, so after you give a clear launch command, I will only need two minutes to pressurise the fuel tanks and spin up the turbines."

"Do it," said Tom.

"Say 'raise ship' – go on, Tom, say it like they did in those old books."

"Raise ship, *Boreas*; take us into orbit." He took a deep breath. "We're done here."

They heard the whines of pumps starting, building the pressure in the tanks below them.

"All system checks complete. Ninety seconds prior to launch. Ensure seat straps secured and tight."

JT checked his, and then leant over to check those of Tom, who was staring unseeingly out at Mars. It all seemed to be happening very fast.

"Sixty seconds. Fuel tank pressurisation complete. Turbines activated. Thirty seconds. Launch overlay visualisation on."

Images appeared on the window and the glass ledge below, showing the launch corridor curving up to meet the *Odyssey*, steadily orbiting above the Martian equator.

"Twenty seconds. Committed resources to launch, final sequence started, log blip sent Earth-side, *Odyssey* informed of our imminent arrival."

Tom's heart began to pound, excitement building with the tank's pressure: he was finally about to leave Mars.

"Ten... nine... eight... seven... six... five... four... three... ignition..."

The craft began to vibrate, first gently, then stronger.

"One... And we have lift-off."

With that, the *Boreas's* engines powered up to maximum thrust, pushing Tom and JT firmly back in their seats. Around the ship, clouds of the Martian sand were flung up, for a moment obscuring the view until they were above it, climbing up into the sky.

The cliffs in the far distance, the five kilometres of rock face that had dwarfed them the day before, seemed to shrink as the ship rose skywards, higher than the blimp had ever flown, rising out of the wide bowl of the canyon, up into the sky, which turned from red to black.

Suddenly Tom's fears vanished and he felt estatic. *This is amazing!*

The *Boreas* began to level off as it headed towards orbit, accelerating to meet the *Odyssey*, waiting to take them to Earth.

32: Sophia

Sophia ate her dinner mechanically without a word; she was too tired to be polite. Her mother was giving her black looks, which Sophia ignored, but she knew what they meant and heard her mother's voice saying 'Behave yourself' echoing around inside her head.

She should really be more responsive. It was another big evening, with the guest of honour the chair of the Technocrats Conference – TechCon for short – Neil Bolden himself. He'd flown all the way from New York, the city state that was so great they had named it thrice, officially known as the capital of the New Republic.

But Sophia felt drained. After running back from the disastrous date with Alejandro, she hadn't slept a wink all night – or at least she felt as if she hadn't. In the long quiet hours in the middle of the night, her thoughts had gone round and round in circles.

"We must do something to stop these damn Earthies," barked Neil. "So the lander went off course – big deal! Just send another. Having to wait on approval is the real problem."

"How many times do we have to explain to them that the guidance system was developed by Bangalore Systems, not us?" said Artur.

"They see AIs under every bed," said Neil, waving his knife at Anna, "and still blame us for the *Prometheus,* which is just crazy."

"Maybe I could personally guarantee that I'm not under *any* bed?" said Humai, his twin spinning globe ident glowing on the wall.

"The trouble is," said Anna, "that they fear you, Humai. You're smarter than any human and your brain isn't wired like ours. They say they can't follow your thoughts or understand your motivations."

"Which is why I'm not allowed to move, reproduce or own property, yes, I know – isn't that enough?" asked their AI, prison bars appearing on the ident to lock both spheres in cages.

Sophia lost interest and dived back into her thoughts. Where was Alejandro now, and what was he thinking about her? Had he talked to the others at school about it, and what would they say? She felt guilty and ashamed of her failure. She had hurt him, betrayed him even, and failed to meet his expectations.

But she also knew she'd do the same again. That was the way she was wired – she could blame her parents, of course, for that.

The project. Could they still do that together? If not, it would look odd and her school friends would know something was up. She wished she could fly back to London to have a long chat with her friend Maria. She could blip, but she had been too embarrassed and distracted to keep her blips full spectrum and tell all the gory details, so it would get complicated. She'd have to admit to Maria how much she'd been holding back.

She wasn't the only one not listening in to the politics. Nina had been talking to Neil about his robotic legs before dinner. He had lost his real ones when the New Republic had been formed, and they had been replaced by nerve-spliced metal ones. He and Artur had been exchanging stories of desperate battles and bloody victories that her mother had tried to censor. So, instead, Neil had entertained Nina by telling his c-agent to map her hand gestures onto his leg control algorithms, so that when she clapped her hands he would bang his feet together. Then he had taken his shoes and socks off, so Nina could get his toes to drum a pattern on their wood floor by wiggling her fingers. Nina had loved that and had laughed and laughed. For a moment the gruff old man had melted.

It seemed the gesture-to-movement link was still partially active, and while trying to smother a gurgle Nina was seeing if she could get his knees to knock, to which Neil seemed oblivious.

"We should just launch a second mission; ignore the talking shop here in Justinian," he said.

Anna was shocked. "No, absolutely not! We worked hard to create the GC; it was our idea. We can't ride rough-shod over it."

"But they don't understand – they're too backward-looking. We know we're right, we have the means: we should just do it."

"No, Neil, no, that is all wrong. If we're right we can argue our case, convince them. Are you so lacking in confidence in your own ideas?"

"It's pointless. They'll never fully understand now BCC has come out against spaceflight, supporting Stone."

"You do them an injustice, and we must try."

Artur broke in. "Let's just follow the plan and see if it is enough," he said.

"What plan?" asked Sophia.

There was a silence.

"I hear you're something of a sailor, Sophia," said Neil. "Have you been out recently?"

Sophia muttered something about having been too busy, but she remembered the day with Alejandro sailing round B Island. She had loved it: the feel of the tiller in her hand, the wind and spray on her cheeks, the smell of the salty water, the pleasant ache in her limbs and being lost in the moment, everything forgotten but wave and wind. But Alejandro hadn't felt like her. He had only been there because she had asked him.

Should she talk to him? she wondered. It couldn't be left like this; anything would be better than this uncertainty without closure. Possibly they could be friends; she'd like to know more about him, to understand him better, for she realised her picture of him had been somehow lacking. Maybe she could help undo the hurt she had done him, somehow.

"If I can interrupt?" asked Humai, breaking into a heated discussion of which way the Indian voting block would go.

"What's up?" asked Artur.

"Dr Khujandi has just detected a signal from the *Boreas*. Some of them made the journey to the lander."

Sophia caught her father give a look of triumph at her mother. "See! See! Didn't I say let's wait? Didn't I say there were ways across – that some would make it?"

"But not all—" said Anna, and was about to say more, but she stopped, frowning at her husband.

"Hah!" said Neil, banging a fist hard on the table. "Let's bring them back here and they can convince the Space Access Committee of the foolishness of blinkered, limited resolutions. They will be our finest witnesses and work to our timing. How long will it take for *Odyssey* to return to Earth?"

"Theoretical earliest – three months. But it would be risky, needing an aerobrake way above safety margins. The safer option would be to wait eight," said Artur.

"Make it three. If they burn up they'll be our martyrs."

"Three months would also keep the next phase on track."

"Excellent. Time to organise a TechCon, get a strategy in place to ensure the delegates are lined up for the next vote, make it go our way. We should get even the dour Mr Bevan to see sense, though Cita Stone might make trouble."

"What about this rumour that she's building a base in your neighbour, the Southern Confederacy?" said Anna. "Cita's said to be creating an army that calls her their holy mother, her Defenders of the Planet."

Sophia looked up. Stone as holy mother – who had said that?

"Ignore them. Rabble. We in the New Republic are well rid of those southern states."

Sophia's mother seemed unsure about that, but was too polite to comment.

"It will be a good opportunity for another Forward Project meeting," said Artur.

Then Sophia was lost again in her thoughts, wondering who had made it to the lander and whether Tom was amongst them. And that look from her father to her mother had been – well, odd. There was a message there, something they were concealing from her and Nina. She wanted to talk about that too, but with whom and how? She thought of her old friend Maria and setting up a virtual meet blip session with her. But then the warning her father had given about the blipverse came back to her: to be careful about her footprint and what the other side's trawlers could dredge up. *Were* there ways of tracking what happened in the blipverse? She had always taken it for granted, from the early days with a school c-agent to her current one with youth settings.

She wasn't going to make a slip that could help Cita Stone harm her family, of that she was determined. So, no discussions about Mars or the *Prometheus* over the blipverse with Maria.

Suddenly something clicked. The lemming kids, the ones who thought Stone was their holy mother – they were the ones who took Memory and Belief. Until Alejandro had mentioned them, she hadn't heard of such drugs, but it was definitely not a parent-safe topic, so who was there she could talk to about it?

Never had she missed seeing her London friends in person so much. What with blipping them and spending all her face-time with Alejandro, she had probably come across to the others at the school here as a bit stand-offish. *Well,* she thought determinedly, *that's going to change.*

33: Tom

Tom could tell that JT was impressed.

"Quick launch, no checklist, constant acceleration trajectory, and all without any need to run any orbital mechanics programs; that's neat," he said.

Tom was trying to spot the base, somewhere to their north, but it was hard to know which way to look as the spacecraft pivoted and headed towards the east. Too late, he thought of asking the ship to overlay its position on the display.

"During launch I am limited to z-axis rotation, which means that the Mars base is not currently visible from your point of view. However, when we dock with the *Odyssey* there will be an opportunity after each orbit of the planet."

"How long till we dock?" asked Tom.

"Another thirty-two minutes," said *Boreas.* "Overlay updated."

Tom and JT watched on the display the curved line of their launch trajectory rise up to meet the *Odyssey.* The ship manoeuvred, rotating round so they were looking straight down at the Mars surface passing beneath them, now twenty kilometres below and dropping away slowly.

JT gulped, then suddenly slapped his hands on his seat's arm rests. "Music," he said, "that's what we need in a moment like this."

"I'm sure they didn't give you music when you left for Mars."

"No, but they should have. Ship, is there any music on board?"

"I am able to stream from the *Odyssey,* which has a copy of the standard Public Library. That is likely to contain every piece of music available prior to your launch."

JT laughed. "What do you think then, Tom – classical? Bit of rock? Dance? Hip-hop?"

"You choose."

"Feel like classical today. Maybe the Planets, but not Mars – we had that all the time during pre-launch PR. Ship, play us Jupiter."

As they listened to the music, the *Boreas* made a series of orbit changes, bursts of power followed by periods when they were weightless. They flew over a huge crater with a canyon entering from the north east.

"Wow."

"Orson Welles Crater," said JT. For some reason he was whispering.

Finally, the ship rotated around until they could see from the wide cabin window not straight down to the surface but a panoramic view of Mars and, flying alongside them, the *Odyssey.*

"We've arrived," said JT. "Not sure I recognise the design – must be since my day."

"*Boreas*, can you show us what we're looking at?" asked Tom.

The display lit up, and Tom was able to see labels overlaid on the image, identifying each of the components of the *Odyssey*.

At the core of the ship Tom could see a framework of carbon fibre criss-crossing bars like a 150-metre-long tower. At one end was the primary nuclear propulsion system, far removed from the rest of the spacecraft, hidden within black cooling fins. Further up the tower were ranks of storage tanks, about twenty metres long and five wide, stacked around the trellis. Tom had to peer hard to make out their shapes as one side, the one facing the sun, was a perfect mirror while the side facing away was as dark as the cooling fins.

At the end of the tower there were boxes labelled power storage, fuel processing, grapples and attachment legs, and then a cylinder about ten metres across – the living quarters. Tom was disappointed that there were no windows.

"We won't be able to see out," he said to JT, but it was *Boreas* that answered.

"The living quarters have to be shielded from radiation, which comes from the rocket's nuclear plant, cosmic rays and solar flares, so as well as the magnetic shield there are multiple layers of gold and tanks of water to protect the astronauts."

Astronauts, Tom thought. He liked the word, though to date he'd been nothing but a passenger.

Then there was the docking area, where they were headed, the recreation and laboratory module, more cooling fins and finally, at the other end, the aerobraking shield. A slightly squashed, rounded cone with three short fins to control the ship's orientation, it had a stained, burnt look from its arrival at Mars.

"Home till we get to Earth," said JT.

There was a final burst of manoeuvring rockets, then a conclusive clunk and the music was switched off. They must have come in backwards, because all they could see out of the window was the darkness of space, studded with stars.

"Docked at *Odyssey*; please exit via the airlock," said *Boreas*.

Tom wondered what he should say to the ship. He found the idea of a semi-aware ship slightly disconcerting. Did one say thank you? Would it care if he didn't?

"Thank you, *Boreas*," he said.

"You're welcome," it said.

Tom unstrapped himself from his seat and was about to stand up when he found himself floating upwards.

JT grinned. "I always loved this bit, weightlessness. Though there were those that got sick."

Tom grinned back; it was exhilarating. They competed to see who could do the most turns, crouching into a ball so they could spin round faster and faster, the more the better, before they touched the far wall, floor or ceiling – now there was no difference between them.

Then JT bashed his head on one of the chairs.

"Oh bugger," he said. "Best we were heading in, anyhow."

They opened the airlock's doors and found themselves in a short corridor before reaching a junction with openings in five directions.

"Hi – *Odyssey*?" asked Tom into the air.

"Welcome aboard. I suggest you make your way to living quarters; that's downwards, from your perspective." The ship sounded exactly the same as the *Boreas*. Tom wondered if it should have sounded different, given that the main spaceship was so unlike the lander.

Tom pushed off and glided down the tunnel as directed. It felt a bit like flying, but in a white-padded pipe. After about ten metres he entered the living quarters with a kitchen, table and seats.

"This would get crowded with all seven of us here," said JT.

It seemed a lot of room to Tom. There was another ladder heading down and, peering down, he could see another four levels beneath them.

"Might as well have a look around," suggested JT.

It didn't take them long to explore the ship. In the living quarters there were five levels: the living area, then below that sleeping, then further down two floors with racks to grow food on, and then at the bottom a huge storeroom.

Next, they made their way back up the ladder to where *Boreas* was docked. They found on either side two pods, one of which was a laboratory and the other a gym. Tom was pleased to note that both had windows, so they had views out over Mars. The final opening opposite the *Boreas* was another airlock with spacesuits.

They were interrupted by a blip from Dr Khujandi.

"Before *Odyssey* can leave orbit, it must refuel at Deimos: '*The better moon arose*', as they say. In the meantime, the chair of the Space Committee, Bina Thakur, will be contacting you at seventeen hundred hours to speak to you and ask some questions. Please note, this will be a blipverse global broadcast."

Tom shrank from the thought of eight billion people on a world he'd never walked on watching him and recording every word.

"Maybe I'd better try some of that coffee," he said.

JT watched him take a drinking tube and fill it from the coffee machine.

"It's not that bad," he said. "We did loads of interviews for the launch. Just remember to keep things neutral and simple all the time."

"Do I have to be there?"

JT shook his head. "These are the people that paid for all this, remember, and we want them to send another ship. Who knows how difficult that will be – how much they need us to speak up on their behalf."

Tom nodded slowly, eyes out of focus as he thought it through. "They will want to know about, you know, Dad, and why it was us two that left."

"But this Bina is likely to be sympathetic, as she's their choice. And with it taking twenty minutes for the questions to reach here, it won't exactly be a quick-fire session: they shouldn't notice if we take some time to answer."

Tom sighed, but told himself it couldn't be worse than the ice caves.

"And you ought to have a shave," said JT, with a smirk.

"I do not."

"Sorry, lad; time you accepted the hairs on your upper lip aren't just going to vanish."

Maybe it could be worse than the ice caves.

34: Alejandro

"My son!" boomed Felix. "My heir!"

Alejandro's father image loomed high over the ballroom, three times normal size, dominating the room, glowing like a genie. He raised a translucent glass filled with light.

"Raise your glasses for my birthday boy, Alejandro!"

All around Alejandro the guests followed his father's lead, toasted him and then drank champagne from the BCC's private vineyard. The ballroom was filled with the good, the great, the beautiful, the powerful the dangerous and the crazy: all those that Felix considered worth impressing or courting - and one day using.

Of course, his father wouldn't come in person, couldn't come, tied as he was to the BCC cores, the warehouse of the blipverse, his most precious prize.

At least he had thrown this, a seventeenth birthday party for his son. But Alejandro wasn't in the mood, hadn't been since that evening with Sophia.

What an idiot I was.

Now he had to give a speech in return.

Shit!

"Thank you all very much for coming," he started. It had been scripted for him, and the words appeared in his eyes, projected directly into his eyeballs by smart contact lenses, his voice amplified by hidden sensors.

"It's an honour and pleasure to see so many of you here tonight. Welcome one and all to Cloud Heights!"

He had done several circuits of the room, shaking hands, reciting the pre-programmed words that BCC needed to be said. Ambassadors, delegates, chairs, lobbyists, technologists, blip-crafters, his father's employees, agents, artists, dancers, actors... they all wanted to talk to him, to get something from him, following their own agenda.

Sophia hadn't been like that.

He'd flirted with one of the young actresses of his father's blip-soaps; her eyes had sparkled then glowed gold as her dress had tightened, squeezing the flesh within just enough to attract attention.

"Blip me," she'd breathed.

He'd been tempted, the animal within him growling as his brain admired her fashion tech.

"Special thanks to my father for organising this party and to BCC planners for making it totally auth-epic!" Alejandro continued.

His head ached, but there were more words to recite.

"There is nothing like a BCC party, trust me! Just as there's nothing as entertaining as our blip-soaps or as reliable as our blip-news feeds. For the latest about Martian plagues or the Dynastic League's policy towards the Global Council, there is only one voice worth listening to, BCC's Honeyed Semtex!"

On those words there was applause and the walls glowed with his father's favourite newscaster. Maybe some of them really clapped, but it had sounded just as loud in rehearsal when the ballroom had been empty. The phrase "Martian plagues" had been inserted at the request of Cita Stone, part of some deal. The women with tufts of hair the colour of mud and her team had been at Cloud Heights several times over the previous weeks.

Sophia would have snorted at such fear-mongering nonsense.

He felt a wave of despair: he'd have to take another of those NoWorries, the latest nanobiotic party pill that Pepe had introduced him to.

"It's been a long path since those early days in Barcelona," Alejandro said. "But BCC has grown and grown, a bit like me!"

There was laughter in the room. Maybe they were on NoWorries too.

The previous evening Pepe had taken Alejandro over to the docks on C Island, to introduce him to the source of the nanobiotics. Here machines smelled of oil and burnt electrics. They continually moved, sounds and lights breaking the darkness. Walking along a path that weaved between stacks of containers, they had reached a repair yard where robots arms dissected their cousins while humans used embeds to live in the blipverse, controlling cranes and ships. Beyond this was the manager's office: under an animated graphic of the port, a woman worked, hands sending instructions, eyes flowing with information. She looked up and scowled until she recognised Pepe.

"Another pick-up? Scan your qID here," she had said.

Pepe nodded and tapped: in exchange he had been given a cylinder packed with tiny glass flasks.

"Don't worry, this is just a small-scale operation, pocket money," he had smirked as they left.

Alejandro hadn't – or at least not enough to not try the NoWorries: he really needed a pick-me-up.

How can I get her back?

"Whether you have a good story to tell or just want to hear one, remember your friends here at BCC," Alejandro continued. His father was always greedy for more information and more influence, and there were agents or potential agents in the room, waiting to be used.

He hoped he wasn't one of them. Despite his father's instructions, he hadn't told him anything Sophia had said, and he'd tried to protect her where he could. He hadn't mentioned their row, how they'd split, only Pepe knew.

It was one of the few things that made him feel good.

"My father wishes he could be here in person to greet you - what can I say, but I wish it too!" said Alejandro.

Did he? He wasn't sure. Living with Pepe in the worker's quarters he'd learnt what they thought of his father from their reaction to the boss's son. They feared Felix and saw how he treated to the girls of host entertainment, how he used them like he used everyone, even Alejandro.

But Felix was his father, his connection to Barcelona, to his childhood and his mother. He'd done all this for him.

My father's a bastard, but I love him, for what could one do?

"So, I ask for you to raise your glasses to BCC, to its founder, to my father, who gave me so much including this party, the one and only Felix Fernandez!"

It was over, everyone drank from their glasses and then applauded. This one sounded more authentic, for everyone likes a party. There'd be more entertainment, for the evening was yet young.

He grinned at the flirty blip-soap actress who winked back and turned to find Pepe at his arm.

"I need another NoWorries," he whispered in the other's ear.

Pepe nodded and a tiny flask passed from palm to palm, invisible to the room.

"Your father wants to see you," he said.

"Now?" Alejandro asked.

The party was in full flow, could he really leave?

"Yes, it's urgent he said."

There was a guilty look in his friend's eye. He'd said something, he knew something.

Sophia: he'd told his father about Sophia, their argument.

Shit! How could he?

Suddenly, despite the crowds around him, Alejandro felt totally alone. There was no one he could trust, everyone wanted something.

What can I do to get her back?

With a shake of his hand, he woke the nanobiotics and poured the activated liquid into his champagne glass and downed it in one.

He'd need all the support he could get to face his father.

"Ok," he said, nodding at Pepe.

Pepe turned and led him down into the cores.

How will my father react? What would he do?

35: Tom

"Nice package."

"Shut up."

"I'm just saying, that suit doesn't hide anything. Not that you should be worried about that."

JT grinned as he watched Tom try on the spacesuit. Deliberately baggy, once worn its smart fabric contracted to expel all the air, leaving a very tight fit that left nothing to the imagination.

"Feels weird," said Tom, "as if someone was hugging me all over."

"Don't get distracted, now. Remember there are no girls to impress out there."

"Oh, yup, just in case I forget that there are no girls on Deimos."

After they had agreed to Dr Khujandi's plan, the *Odyssey* had powered up for the short hop to Mars's outer moon, Deimos. "'Only' twenty thousand kilometres," joked JT.

Here the ship had manoeuvred into the saddle that covered the south pole of Deimos. Drilling into the moon, it began to extract the water they needed for fuel. Tom had seen it as a great opportunity to taste freedom again and grabbed the chance to explore the moon.

He reached for the oversized-goldfish-bowl helmet, and JT helped him screw it on.

"See you later, lad," he said.

Tom entered the airlock, which closed behind him; then the outer door opened, revealing the red-rock landscape of the moon. Using the gesture controls described by *Odyssey,* he pressed his thumb against his palm as he pointed towards its rocky floor. Or was it above him, and therefore the sky?

He pointed the suit towards the ridge that his helmet's display said was the meridian line, accelerating until he hit eight metres per second, before switching off and drifting, weightless.

It was one of those moments when there was nothing to do but focus on the sights around him – something he knew he'd remember forever. Tom used his left hand to spin himself round to look at the ship rapidly retreating behind him. It had seemed so huge, but now it appeared as small as one of the shrimp in the pool in the base, lying at the bottom of a rocky valley, dwarfed by its surroundings.

Tom turned round again and was in time to see what he had come for. Rising out of the hollow, he could see Mars, the planet on which he had spent all his life, laid out in front of him. The glass of the helmet was forgotten, and the reds and blacks seemed to float just in front of him, as if he could reach out and touch it.

"Home," he said.

He stopped the suit and tried to fix the picture in his memory. For a few minutes he didn't move; he remained lost in his thoughts, staring at the planet beneath. Then, with a sigh, he turned and returned to the ship.

At seventeen hundred hours sharp the figure of Bina Thakur appeared projected in the *Odyssey*'s living space, cheerfully beaming at them.

"Tom, JT, great to have a chance to talk to you, and remember this is a blipverse global broadcast. Sorry again about the lander's navigation fault – we're still looking into that. Anyhow, here you are, safe and on your way back to Earth. So, the first question: what's the latest news on the re-fuelling and flight back?"

Tom relaxed at the question. "We're pretty sure we'll be fully fuelled later today and then we'll head back to Earth as fast as we can. I think the ship said it would be just over three months' flight time."

Tom noticed the figure nod in reply but realised there was no way the real Bina could be reacting this fast, and the image must be a ship-generated construct – one of those c-agents that could talk on her behalf, a product of this all-seeing technology. It unsettled him that he couldn't tell where the real woman ended and the generated image began.

"And, Tom, how do you feel? It must have been a tough time for you, with the sad news about your father."

JT saw the confusion on Tom's face and answered. "He was upset, as you can imagine – that's all you need to know."

"You know there's been a lot of talk here about his death, along with the earlier loss of Amina and Mei-Li's sickness. Can you confirm they weren't victims of a Martian plague?"

"That's total rubbish," said Tom brusquely. "None of us have had as much as a cold."

"What have you learnt about humans living on Mars?"

JT got there first. "We showed it *is* possible, not just for a short time but for years, and not only for explorers but families too. It is home for us."

Tom thought that missed out a lot of what it had felt like, condemned to live in a prison.

Easier questions were about the flight of the blimp, though both ducked the one about the decision to leave the others behind. Harder ones were about Tom, and most JT helped deflect, apart from whether he'd missed having friends his own age.

"I don't know… I've never known that, so don't know what I'm missing. I'd imagine it must be a lot."

"Though he has a blip-buddy on Earth now," said JT.

Tom glared in reply, but said nothing. He felt oppressed by the thought of all those billions of watchers, and had not forgotten that Sophia might be one of them.

"Very interesting," said the avatar of Bina, beaming with pleasure. "Tom, do tell us more about your friend."

"There's nothing to say. No, that's not true; there is something I want to say. There are still those stuck down there on Mars, including my mother. We need another mission to be arranged to get them back too, as soon as possible."

For once, the smile on Bina's face faded. "Well, that's certainly going to be a hot topic: we shall see, we shall see."

Eventually she was satisfied, and the interview ended. Tom was relieved. This wasn't a task he felt naturally good at; while he guessed he'd get better with practice, it wasn't a skill he wanted.

Later that evening, the ship announced its tanks were full. Tom and JT watched from an observation window as the *Odyssey* uncoupled from Deimos. Tom had one last look at the moon, which from this angle reminded him of a lump of kneaded dough.

When they were clear, the main rockets fired. Water extracted from the moon was pumped into the nuclear reactor until it became super-heated. At first the acceleration of the *Odyssey* was slow, a fraction of the Earth's gravity. It was pointing down towards Mars, and soon they were skimming past the planet only a few tens of kilometres above its thin atmosphere. To Tom it felt like a great wall a few inches in front of him, a stunning landscape of canyons, craters, volcanoes and river valleys the size of countries. Sites made familiar from childhood lessons slid by their window, places such as Olympus Mons and the Valles Marineris.

But the *Odyssey* didn't stop, continuing to power on and on, minute after minute and then hour after hour. As Tom lay in his bunk he could feel the faint vibration of the engines pushing them faster and faster into the darkness, away from Mars and everything he'd ever known.

36: Sophia

Sophia was off to the beach, Justinian style.

Together with her new friend, Ling Chan, she'd headed off after school to the Sky Beach's desert island: a circle of land surrounded by sand, then a sea like pool that stretched to the horizon.

"Not bad," said Ling. "Given there's only water for the first fifty metres and the rest is projection."

"And all this is quarter of a kilometre up in the sky," said Sophia.

They walked along a wooden plank pier that connected the arrival stairwell to the beach. She could see swimmers dive down to the glass plates at the bottom of the pool with the view two hundred and fifty metres down to Justinian or playing in the surf generated by the Sky Beach's rim plates. Ahead was a shack apparently made from driftwood. Behind the bar stood a large jukebox, its colours glowing from a flickering light within, in front of which a dozen robot arms poured drinks and handed out bottles.

They took a pair of seats and ordered: juices with insect nibbles.

Sophia's new friend had been like making a new start at Justinian, someone to shop with and chat to over coffee, though she was a bit too quiet and studious for Sophia. Ling's family came from the closed China Dynastic League, which had refused to fully join the Global Council but stood aloof, sending out observers as if to a barbarian court.

"Was it you or Alejandro that came up with 'lemming kids'?"

"It was probably him; he seemed to know more about them," said Sophia.

"They freak me out, the way they just parrot what they've been told."

It was nice to have someone she could talk to about this.

"Have you heard anything about a nano-drug called Memory?" Sophia hadn't planned it: the question just burst out.

"Memory? No, but I can ask."

"Best play this one carefully."

They exchanged smiles.

"Trust me: I can be discreet," said Ling.

They drank and gossiped while the sun set, before splitting up to head home.

On the way back, Sophia was interrupted.

"Blip received from Pepe," said her c-agent.

"Play," said Sophia.

"Hi, Sophia," said Pepe. "Look, I'm worried about Alejandro – can you come over right now? We're in Cloud Heights. The guards know you're coming."

She played it again, wondering what to do.

Alejandro, back at Cloud Heights? But he hated it there – so he had said, hadn't he? Things must be bad. And why her? She sighed, wanting to go home, wanting this to be over, but knowing she couldn't turn her back on him. He might know something; he might help her; he might have got into trouble.

He might – or it might be one of his games.

But what if something horrid had happened and she didn't go: how would she feel then?

Ok, ok, this time she'd go.

Sophia waved down a robocab and gave it directions to Cloud Heights.

On the way she watched the gleaming lights of Justinian though the cab's windows. Tower after tower, filled with representatives and their families from all the planet's countries, safe in their homes. What secrets and stories must be in all those heads, each one a life on its own?

When the robocab arrived, she looked up at the pencil-thin tower. Unlike last time, when she had visited for the party, it was dark – just a handful of nav-lights blinking, brooding in the dusk, waiting for her, dense, black, heavy with information. She shivered.

The guards at the base of Cloud Heights nodded to her, expectant, pointing her towards the vertical monorail.

"Where's Pepe?" she asked.

"At the top."

She wished the ascent wasn't as quick as Felix's experts had engineered it to be. *I don't want to be here. I don't want to arrive. The view is just amazing.* She began to feel sick. What had happened?

At the top she was met by Pepe.

"What's going on? Where is he?"

"Come with me," he said. "Let him explain."

She followed down wide spiral steps to double doors, big enough for a concert hall, which opened as they approached. Inside were dark shadows with indistinct swirling clouds of light.

"In there, the BCC off-cloud room."

She walked in, alone. She turned to see Pepe watching her as the doors closed.

"So good of you to come, Sophia Kasparov," said Felix Fernandez. His voice came from the darkest of the shadows. "Congratulations on making a new friend – that must be nice after my son was such a disappointment. He generally is a disappointment, I've found."

Around her the lights showed scene after scene, just quick enough for her eyes to catch icons and idents spilling from Felix's head. Pepe, her father, Alejandro, the *Phoenix* launch, Cita Stone, a man running from the *Prometheus* explosion, Justinian, her meeting with Ling Chan...

"Where is he? Pepe said something was wrong."

"I told Pepe to blip you that message. I wanted to meet you."

"Why me?"

"In my simulations your name keeps coming up. You have connections, between your father and Tom Tesla, between Cita Stone and my son. You could be a problem. Or we could help each other. I could tell you something about Memory."

"You've heard of Memory?"

"I hear many things, but not enough about some. What does Kasparov know about the *Prometheus* explosion?"

Sophia was suddenly scared. This was like the blipverse construct disaster with Cita Stone, but worse. She wasn't at home, able to simply take off the data glasses, but trapped in Felix's tower. No one knew she was there.

Felix walked closer to her, out of the dark. She hadn't realised how large he was, how engineered his body was. His eyes ran up and down her body, slowly, and she wondered what he was seeing, what overlays his systems were displaying.

"I can see why my son was so keen on you, Sophia," he said, softly.

She wanted to leave, immediately, but the doors were closed, hidden in a sea of images and datasets.

"My father will stop you."

"I have facilities of which Kasparov knows nothing."

Behind him, two black diamonds swooped across the data fields, and he took a step closer.

Desperately, without thinking, she said, "Humai could: it has ways and means *you* know nothing of."

He paused, and the black diamonds turned in circles. Then for a moment Sophia was sure she could see two globes, rotating and spinning around each other, one blue and the other red. The diamonds dissolved into dust.

Sophia felt her pendant grow warm, then hot, against her skin. She looked down and its surface glowed with blue filaments, flickering like the aurora.

"What?" said Felix.

The images halted, then strobed. There was a deep thunder which increased in pitch and volume until it became a piercing warning tone, beeping on and off. A giant "U" appeared, surrounded by # symbols, which then shattered into glass splinters. Sophia ducked, but they were all virtual.

"What have you done?" he cried. "Unverified boot! Unverified boot!"

Sophia stepped back, unsure.

"Go!" he shouted. "Go now!"

The doors flung themselves open and she ran through, then rushed up the stairs, panting, until she reached the monorail going down.

"Is everything ok?" asked Pepe.

"You lied to me!"

He shrugged. "I do what Felix asks; don't we all?"

"Not me," said Sophia.

On the way down her pulse began to return to normal and the pendant faded. What was it? What had happened in there? Could she tell her father about it?

He'd freak if he knew, she decided. It would have to be another secret to add to her collection.

37: Tom

In the space between planets, Tom dreamt he was back on Deimos.

He was showing the moon to his mother, who was in her own suit, floating next to him above its surface.

"I want to see Mars, Tom," she said, "one last time before we leave for Earth."

"Follow me," he said, flying up the ridge towards the horizon.

"Wait!" she cried, and he paused and turned. She smiled at him as she drifted past, until the glass of her helmet began to scatter reflections of light from the hidden planet.

"It's beautiful," said Elena, and Tom turned to see the red planet that was engraved in his memory: his home.

"Soon we will see Earth," he said.

Suddenly she started to move, pulled upwards towards Mars. And then the scene flipped in his head and she was falling downwards.

"Tom!" she cried.

"Mum!" he said, but she accelerated ever faster away until she was little more than a dot tumbling out of the sky.

Then there was a beep from the comms system in his ear and a familiar voice.

"When something goes, it's gone forever.'"

"Dad?"

But there was nothing more, and Deimos too vanished, leaving Tom alone in space, stationary at the centre of a sphere of stars.

With a jerk, Tom awoke. Over the last three months he'd had similar dreams, with Elena falling out of the blimp, being left behind on Deimos, and falling from *Boreas* onto Mars.

He looked around and saw that JT had already got up. Not for the first time, Tom had overslept.

Earth was close now.

During the flight Tom had become accustomed to weightless living, his body no longer alarmed by waking floating in his bunk. His days gained a rhythm: getting up late, breakfast, gym, study, gym again, dinner with JT, then watching the universe spin round while exploring the ship's apparently limitless music library until it was time for bed.

The universe didn't spin round, of course, it was the ship. After the long burn to escape Mars, it had extended an arm out from *Odyssey*'s axis. At the end of this arm was a pod, where, when the *Odyssey* was spun up, there was an artificial gravity similar to Mars's. So the sky seemed to spin round and round, a day passing by every twenty-five seconds.

It was hypnotic, particularly when the pod was flooded with repetitive music, like minimalism or dance tracks.

Both Tom and JT kept themselves to themselves, falling into their own routines, agreeing without discussion to always eat their evening meal together. A stream of messages and interview requests came their way from Earth, but Tom couldn't face them, always making sure he was elsewhere at the time. JT seemed content to take over, as if it were a way of making amends for something he had done.

Neither seemed eager to message the base, though both knew they should. A week away from Mars, JT had suggested that "Maybe we could ask what's happening there?", to which Tom had agreed, but without enthusiasm.

In the end JT had made a call, but there had been no reply. Later Tom worked out that on Mars it would have been the early hours of their morning, for time on the *Odyssey* was locked to Earth's 24 hours per day and so drifted thirty-nine minutes every day away from that on Mars. Had JT planned it that way?

Neither of them wanted to talk about how they had left the others. JT distracted himself by pottering around the *Odyssey*'s mini-garden, and Tom in studying the ship's design. For Tom it was a relief to lose himself in technicalities. If he thought about Earth, he worried about what they'd all make of him. A freak, he could hear them say, eight billion people all crying at once.

Mars wasn't much better, his mind picturing his father frozen under a pile of Martian dust, his mother stuck in the base with Victor, the endless dark and cold of the ice caves and poor lost Mei-Li Wu wandering around the base's corridors.

Odyssey's neutrality was a comfort as it explained the ship's NERVA class engine, the water fuel energy equations, and the aerobraking system they'd use through the thick atmosphere of Earth.

For a couple of days Tom and JT were forced together when a solar flare made the gravity pod too dangerous, even with the magnetic shield on max. They bunkered down in the heart of the ship in the habitation core, surrounded by thick layers of shielding and metres of water.

"Wear these," JT had said, giving Tom a pair of shorts threaded with lead.

Tom had laughed. "You're kidding."

JT shook his head grimly. "I'm too old to have kids, but you're not. Wear them."

So Tom wore the lead shorts, and afterwards, even when the flare had gone, JT had made him wear them anytime he left the habitation core.

"I've done some things I'm not proud of, but I'm going to look after you, Tom. No one's going to say I didn't do my bit for you. No one."

It made Tom's weight in the gravity pod all the more draining, and the gym's exercises harder; but that made it more like Earth, the planet that was getting ever closer. But it felt as though they were stationary, while Mars sank away into the dark and the Earth glided towards them.

Only in the last days before arrival did Tom start to study Earth, the panic in his chest beginning to overwhelm him. He read up about the famines and the Collapse, studied the re-arranged map of countries and technologies created since his parents had left, nearly twenty years earlier.

He had summoned the courage to blip Sophia a couple of times but had just got the one reply that simply thanked him for wishing her happy birthday. *She's not interested in me,* he thought, *or at least only as a celebrity, not as a person.*

Tom felt barriers growing up in his mind as his connections to others seemed to weaken. They were far away from anyone: those they knew well on Mars and also the billion unknowns on Earth. Looking out at the emptiness without end, Tom felt he needed to be strong inside, toughened and independent.

On the last day before planet-fall, Tom was in the gravity pod, gently rotating around and around the *Odyssey.* From here he could see the Earth, a blue pebble hanging in nothing with a faint silvery dot to one side – the moon.

Tom stretched out his arm and extended his thumb: he could just cover the Earth. Hidden behind it were all eight billion people on the planet that had been humanity's home for all its existence, but never his. What was he?

As the *Odyssey* rotated, its axis centred on the Earth; around it spun the universe. To one side was the brilliant dot of Jupiter, and to the other the constellation Orion. Straight ahead were the Pleiades, and with his thumb blocking out the glare from Earth, Tom could count six of its stars. He knew that with the help of the ship he could augment the pod to see many more, but he preferred the naked eye.

The Earth had grown noticeably larger since he had first checked it that morning, but it was hard to believe they were moving. Everything was so peaceful and quiet, yet he knew they were rushing at incredible speeds, dangerous even, towards their destination.

"All systems off," said Tom, and the pod went dark and completely quiet. No, there was a sound – the gentle double drumbeat of his pulse.

Tom stared, transfixed, at the Earth. *Drum-drum* he heard, then shortly after another *drum-drum.* Yet in that short period between heartbeats, he had travelled thirty kilometres.

Drum-drum: another thirty had flashed by, invisible in the emptiness of space.

Drum-drum: and he was another thirty kilometres closer to Sophia.

Drum-drum: and thirty fewer kilometres stood between him and – what?

Drum-drum.

Part 6

38: Tom

Like a falling star, Tom blazed an incandescent line across the Earth's sky, announcing his arrival at the planet they called his home.

An hour earlier the *Odyssey* had been broken in two. The forward section with the heat shield and *Boreas* lander had detached from the rest of the craft; what was left was lighter and built to withstand the shock of hitting the Earth's atmosphere at high speed.

A long burn of the *Boreas*'s rockets separated them from the core of the *Odyssey*, which was to fly by the Earth and head out into dark empty space, alone, leaving them falling ever faster towards the sun's third rock.

It was, according to the emotionless voice of the ship, risky.

They were lying in the couches in *Boreas*'s cabin, where a few weeks earlier they had said goodbye to the surface of Mars. To mask the knot in his stomach, Tom racked his brains to think of something to say to JT, but the long flight seemed to have drained the words from him.

Almost there, he told himself, *just another step on the path to Earth.* But he couldn't stop wondering what the ship had meant by 'risky'.

JT seemed to guess what was going through Tom's head.

"It'll be fine, Tom," he said. "I've done this dozens of times."

Tom wasn't in the mood for soothing words. "No, you haven't," he snapped. "Not this fast, not pulling these Gs. Not with an adaptive shaped shield. No one has. And there were accidents, weren't there?"

There was a moment's silence.

"At least it will be quick," JT almost pleaded.

"So?"

"When you get to my age, you begin to wonder how it will end, whether it will be a good way to go."

"You're pretty hopeless at reassuring, aren't you, JT?"

JT laughed. "I guess so, but it distracted you for a bit. Anyway, it works for me. You must find your own way to come to terms with life and death."

"Any more pearls of wisdom?"

JT didn't laugh, but thought about it carefully.

"Two minutes to entry into Earth's atmosphere," said the ship.

"Life is short, Tom, and what matters is *how* you live it and what choices you make."

"Is that it?"

"Yup, that's all there is to it."

"Er – thanks, I guess."

Tom wondered about that and what they'd find when they arrived. He felt tired out from all the many hours of thinking, guessing and imagining without conclusion.

"One minute to entry into Earth's atmosphere," said the ship.

"I'm sorry, Tom," said JT suddenly.

"For what?"

"For forcing you to choose. That was unfair."

Tom knew what he meant, but not what to say; this sort of conversation made him uncomfortable.

"It's ok," he said, gruffly.

"I just wanted it said, if things go wrong."

"Huh?"

"But they won't, of course."

They shared a nervous laugh.

"Thirty seconds."

In Tom, excitement at closing in on Earth battled with fear. They had no controls, none of the banks of switches he'd seen in old movies. The ship managed everything, and all they could do was lie back in the seats and hope it did its job.

"Fifteen seconds."

Tom leant his head back to try to look out of the window, but they were covered by shields to protect against the raging heat.

Suddenly he laughed.

"It will be a real Viking burial," he said.

"Aye, lad, that it will," said JT.

Then he felt the first tremors.

"Contact with thermosphere," said the ship.

Gently Tom felt himself being pushed back into his seat, the feeling of weightlessness fading away like a dream on wakening. The ship began to shake, gently at first, like a tremble, accompanied by a rattle of fittings and rumble of far-off noise.

"Easy-peasy," said JT.

Then they were thrust back into their seats, hard.

"Entry into mesosphere," said the ship.

The roar began to grow along with the pressure.

Tom's vision began to blur as the seat shook him back and forth. Even tightly strapped in, he felt himself trying to grab the armrests to hold tight. Teeth banged against teeth and it felt like someone was sitting on him, someone heavy.

"Eight g," said the ship.

Tom tried to focus on the visualisation the ship projected in front of him. It showed what they looked like, the shield drilling a hole through the planet's protective covering, a trail of red turning yellow, then white, as the temperature rose.

"Ten g," said the ship. "Shield reshaping to create negative lift."

The graphic showed the shield changing shape, from a symmetric stubby cone to a lopsided one, creating the force to pull them down to the planet and keep them from bouncing out into space.

Tom looked sideways at JT; it was hard to see through the water that was squeezed from his eyes like juice from an orange, but he could see that his eyes were open, open and afraid. The old man's skin rippled like the waves of an old flag in the wind.

Then it got worse – much worse.

The ship said something; Tom couldn't tell what, though on the graphics he could just see the message *Control fin failure* flashing in yellow. The noise was deafening, and he was choking as the air turned oven hot. He wondered about the sweat, his sweat, and whether he'd slide out of the seat to fall crashing to the floor, breaking something, maybe everything.

The roar increased in pitch to a scream, the shaking so bad he couldn't focus on JT, who became a blur of impressions. The cabin lights flickered and then cut out completely, dropping Tom into total darkness, where nothing seemed to exist apart from the noise and heat.

Emergency lights, dim and red, came on, illuminating the cabin as if it were hell. Tom struggled to breathe, fighting the heat and the weight on his chest. It was as if an enormous monster were sitting on him: a monster that shook him in its teeth, a monster with fiery breath and a roar as primal as life.

He turned his head to look towards JT, but his vision was going, closing in like a tunnel towards the old man. Tom was just able to make out that his eyes were closed, his limbs were slack and there were lines of blood flowing from his nose, before all went black.

39: Tom

Tom woke suddenly. It did not feel good.

"God," he said, thickly.

His face felt wet and warm, and when he wiped it with his hand he found it was red with his blood.

Tom took a long breath and then thought of something.

"JT?" he cried, and looked over to the other. There was no reply.

He tried to sit up, but found himself constrained by seat straps. As he did so, drops of blood and sweat were dislodged, a rain of clear and red drops drifting upwards from him: they were weightless again. He could see that his body was covered in bruises, and every movement was painful.

"JT!" he cried again, but again there was no response. Tom clawed at the straps holding him down, struggling with buckles until he was free. He grabbed JT's arm to pull himself over the old man.

The face was a mask of drying blood, colours stark against the tired face, full of lines, its features slack and empty. Tom shook him. In the weightlessness that made him move back and forth, head flopping forwards and back, eyes staring empty at nothing.

Tom remembered the day his father had died. He too had had empty eyes; he too had had limbs that felt like dead weights.

"Ship, do something!" he cried.

"No actions suggested," it said.

"What the hell does that mean?"

"At present my medical information suggests the recommended course of action is observation."

Suddenly JT twitched, then started to cough. The eyes stopped staring and moved together, focussing on Tom.

"I feel like shit," he whispered, but Tom didn't care, a grin splitting his face from one side to the other.

"You had me worried then."

"Me too."

"You were unconscious."

"Less lip, lad, and help me get cleaned up."

Floating in the weightlessness, they hosed themselves down and wiped away the worst of the mess from their faces.

"Ship, can we look out?" Tom asked.

"Yes," it said, and as it removed the shield plates, they were blinded by the light that poured from the great window. Gradually Tom's vision adjusted; the blues and whites came into focus and he gasped.

Earth, the planet he had dreamed of for so long, struggled so hard to reach, was there in front of him. It glowed with a welcoming gentleness, so different from the harsh colours of Mars.

At first he struggled to understand what he was seeing: were the white bits clouds, mountains or ice? But then it snapped into place; they were clouds, and below them the blue of the sea. He was looking down at a great ocean, thousands of kilometres of water across which weather systems travelled, structures with fronts, massed blocks of cloud, interspersed with gaps and dots of solitary white clumps.

It felt warm and alive even from high up above; even if individual life could not be seen, the difference from the dead world he came from was stark.

Then Tom could see dots in the endless blue, brown-green islands, and around them the clouds curled, oscillating to one side and then the other. Another stretch of water and then land to his right, first a black line and then a rolling landscape of red and brown.

For a moment he was disappointed – it seemed too like Mars – then more land came from the left and nearly joined, a gap between two pillars of rock.

"Gibraltar," said JT quietly. "That's Spain on one side and Morocco on the other: the pillars of Hercules."

They flew in silence along the straits and then above the Mediterranean.

Every now and then JT would give a commentary as to what they could see. Corsica, Italy, Greece, then on to Turkey. In the sea by Istanbul they could make out three identical islands – dots in the blue, connected together by grey lines to make a triangle.

JT gasped. "That's new – what is it?"

"We are currently above Justinian," said the ship. "Home of the Global Council."

JT shook his head. "How much else will have changed?" he wondered.

But to Tom it was all new, all amazing, and he would have been happy to gaze for hours, nose against the window, relishing the range and complexity: the river valleys, deltas, wrinkly coastlines, jagged mountains, ribbons of wind-blown sand, straight lines of human structures, and the ever-present but always-changing clouds. It was everything he had hoped for, struggled for.

"Incoming blip, global public," said the ship.

For both of them it was an unwelcome interruption, but they pushed themselves back from the window to the seats and waited for the figures to appear in the window display.

Tom wondered who it could be – would it be the familiar face of Dr Khujandi or even (his heart gave a thump at the thought) Sophia? But it was neither. Three figures, only one of whom he recognised.

"On behalf of the Space Access Committee, may we welcome you to Earth," said Bina Thakur.

"Hello, Earth," said Tom. He felt good, despite his slight disappointment.

"May I introduce my colleagues, Dr Kasparov and Ms Stone of the Space Reception group," said Bina.

Both of them spoke at once, a jumble of words of welcome and greeting, an angry look between the pair, and a corresponding frown on Bina's face.

"Er, yes, indeed," she said. "Your arrival was rather spectacular, watched by half of the blipverse."

And how many were watching now? wondered Tom. In the rush of images and thoughts, he tried to place where he had heard the name Kasparov before.

"It was pretty impressive from inside here," said JT.

"We're looking forward to hearing all your stories, and would like to arrange a welcome for you," said Bina. "Have you any preference as to location?"

"Cape Canaveral," said JT. "Isn't that right, Tom?"

"Yes," said Tom, "Kennedy Space Centre, Cape Canaveral." All his life that was what his father had talked of: the one place to return to.

"We would be delighted to welcome you," said the woman – Ms Stone.

"Excellent," said Bina.

"Listen, Bina," said Dr Kasparov, turning to her. "This is a really bad idea."

"Sorry, Artur, I think it's clear that it's to be Kennedy," said Bina.

"We'll start making arrangements."

"Thank you, Cita. So you'll arrange a spaceplane to bring them down, right, Artur?"

Artur nodded, his head dipping by no more than a few millimetres.

"Good; that's agreed. We look forward to meeting you in person," said Bina.

"We look forward to it too," said Tom.

"Until then, blip end," said Bina, and they were alone again.

Unthinkingly, Tom stared at the planet below and fiddled with his pendant as he thought through the short conversation. Suddenly a connection fell into place: Dr Kasparov was Sophia's father, and he was the one who had objected to Cape Canaveral.

The confidence began to leak out of him to be replaced again by fear, this time for the unknown. What was it about the Kennedy Space Centre that made it a 'really bad idea'?

40: Sophia

Why, thought Sophia, did her father have to ruin everything?

The last weeks had been pretty good, at least for her. Thankfully all that crazy stuff with her parents, that mad attacking woman Cita Stone and the creep Felix Fernandez, had gone quiet, leaving her to enjoy life in Justinian. Nina had been an above-normal pain but that made her appreciate Ling all the more, so when it was time for her friend's seventeenth birthday, Sophia had planned a weekend stay-over party. Sophia was at home in her glam clothes, hemline as high as she dared, her weekend bag packed ready for her to head off, when her father stormed in.

"That damn woman," he said, "she's threatening to grab the two castaways that made it to Earth."

BCC coming out against spaceflight had not improved his mood.

"What's up?" asked Sophia.

"Didn't you see the blip?" asked Nina. "It was blipverse global."

"Cita Stone's twisted them around her little finger, and they're going to land at the Kennedy Space Centre," said Artur.

"What's wrong with that?" Sophia asked.

"What's wrong?" he exploded at her. "What's wrong? Have you understood nothing of what's been going on the last six months?"

"Easy, Artur," said Anna.

"You of all people should know what a piece of work Cita is! I even took you to see *Phoenix* launch the Mars lander!"

"So what if they land in Florida?"

Her father had swung a chair around so he could sit with its back facing Sophia.

"Do you really want to know?"

"Yes" she said, and then regretted it, for she saw a gleam of triumph in his eye that meant she'd fallen for one of his verbal traps.

"Our projections are that Stone and BCC are going to use them as pawns, to set them up to say things that make spaceflight look bad, to limit any future flights to just the minimum to get the rest of the castaways back."

"Your projections?" asked Nina. "Or is that one of Humai's?"

Artur ignored her.

"If we let them get away with this we could lose everything. And you owe us – again."

"Eh? For what?"

"We pay your robocab account, remember? Just as well, as it turned out, but it wasn't easy to get you out of Felix Fernandez's clutches."

Damn. Were there no secrets in Justinian?

"You'll back me up, won't you, Anna?" said Artur.

Sophia's mother paused, as if unsure of what she was agreeing to.

"It would be better if Tom and JT were here with us, for sure."

"There you go," he said, as if in conclusion. "Your mother agrees with me."

There was a pause.

"So what?" asked Sophia.

"If they land at the Kennedy Space Centre, we've got to get them out, back here where they'd be safe."

Suddenly one word jumped out.

"We?" she asked. "What's this 'we'?"

"You know the boy, Tom; he knows no one on Earth but you. If you asked him to return with us, he'd follow."

"But I hardly know him! Surely a blip would be enough."

"Canaveral's blipcoms free, so there's no guarantee we'd get that through. And nothing beats being there in person."

"Artur, what is this?" asked Sophia's mother.

"Sophia and I fly out there to attend the welcome ceremony, and she invites him back here – simple. After all, she saw the take-off; now she can see the landing."

"Mum, I can't do that! You see, don't you?"

Artur swung round and stared hard at his wife.

"Humai says this is the best way, and if we don't everything could be ruined."

Anna turned to look out of the window as she thought that through.

"We can't live our lives by what that machine thinks," she said after a moment, turning back.

"You know the stakes. You know the plan. Do you remember those days in uni where we dreamed of making a difference? Remember the London Revolution? That was just one city, this is where we can change *everything*."

"Could it be dangerous?"

"No. We just fly in, attend the ceremony and then fly out with them. It'll be simple."

"It doesn't matter. I won't go," said Sophia.

"You must," said Artur, then to his wife, "Mustn't she?"

Anna sighed. "Just that: fly in, ask, then fly out? No more stratagems and tricks from Humai?"

"Just that."

"What about me? Don't I get a say in it?" Sophia was indignant.

Her mother looked at her, eyes locked on hers; Sophia saw resolve, but thought there was a warning there too, somewhere, one she couldn't decode.

"It might be best if you postpone your weekend, Sophia."

"No. I won't go."

"Maybe I should blip Ling's parents myself to cancel for you?" Anna threatened.

Huh? The only thing worse than having to cancel on Ling would be their parents discussing them and making arrangements behind their backs.

"Ok," she said in a quiet voice.

"Good," said her father. "And you've even packed a bag; we can leave right away."

"Can I come too?" asked Nina

"You're too young," said her mother, and there was finality in her voice.

"This is so unfair."

For once Sophia agreed with her sister. *Damn him,* she thought. *Damn this oh-so-secret project.* And damn Humai for dragging her into it, again.

41: Daniel

Daniel peered into the sky, hunting for the aircraft, grinning to himself. He'd escaped Miami into the world outside. The Canaveral airport! He'd got all the way to Canaveral! Life was good.

"It won't be here for an hour," said Judith, and he nodded.

Judith was the woman who had handed him his holy water at the initiation and was now his friend in the Defenders' special training. For the last three months, he'd been learning all about the water's preparation and use: in particular, how to prepare the initiates. He had to make sure they only heard true voices after they had drunk, those that spoke for the Defenders of the Planet. He learnt how long the spirit was within them and had been studying what doctrines were approved so that one day he too could speak to the new recruits and guide the lesser Defenders.

They were waiting for the next delivery, packages labelled BCC that came from somewhere overseas and contained the holy water and the angel dust, to be mixed only at the last moment. It was better than the military training the others had had. Daniel didn't like the stories he'd heard of how they toughened up recruits – the bullying and the violence.

"It's noisy today," said Judith.

She meant the Geiger counter, whose amplified clicks echoed across the weed-covered runway like a mutant bush cricket, drowning the real ones, even though they were twice the size of the ones he remembered from Miami.

"The wind's from the east," he said. From the ruins of the *Prometheus*, he meant.

"In that case, I'm going back inside."

Daniel was happy to stay outside in the open. Planes from all sorts of romantic faraway places sometimes visited, and if they didn't come, well, he could imagine it.

"London... Justinian... Nairobi... Caracas..."

The names were enough by themselves, even if they were rare. This wasn't a busy airport; that was why it had been chosen – or so he had been told.

His dreaming was interrupted by the sound of a plane. They watched it approach, expecting a freight aircraft containing those BCC packages, but instead saw an executive jet from which a passenger appeared, Cita Stone herself. She was followed by a man and woman, grey-clad technicians who assisted her in making the final little jump down to the tarmac.

"Daniel, how nice to see you waiting for me," she said. "But where are Vaughan and his men?"

Daniel turned and spotted squads of Defenders approaching, the men and women marching alongside some rugged off-road cars. He recognised Captain Vaughan in one.

"Stone," the captain said, getting out of the vehicle.

"Join me in the plane," she said. "We need to make some plans."

The man at the head of the squad of Defenders spotted Daniel.

"What do we have here? Don't I remember you?" he said.

Daniel saw a face with a great scar on the chin and with the lobe of one ear missing. He wanted to shake his head or think of an excuse to leave, but nothing came.

"Yes, I know you. But do you remember me, little Daniel? You do, don't you?" said Nails. "It's been a long time since Gladys hit Miami."

He grabbed Daniel's arms and twisted them behind his back, locking them together, close enough for Daniel to smell whisky on the other's breath.

"Look at this, little Daniel," he said. "Look at my lovely new nails."

Daniel looked at them: gleaming white. They seemed to blur, then he heard a faint hum.

"See?" said Nails. "These are nails to be proud of. Nanotech, polycarbonate saw edge, thought-controlled, powered by blood sugars. Would you like me to tickle you?"

"No," said Daniel.

"No? What could you fear about a little tickle under the arm?" Daniel could hear the pleasure in his voice and struggled to break free, but the grip on his arms tightened as the other hand reached into his armpit.

"No, don't!" Daniel cried, but it was too late; Nails cut through his shirt and drove into his flesh.

"Tickle, tickle!"

Daniel screamed.

"None of that," said Nails, clamping his hand over the other's mouth, fingertips gleaming red. But at least that meant the sawing had ended.

"There are demons coming," he whispered. "We must be ready for them, mustn't we, little Daniel?"

He was interrupted by two bangs. Echoes rumbled their way around the sky, like the thunder of a breaking storm, and they saw two black diamonds flash between the clouds.

"That will be the Wolf Bats," said Stone, reappearing. "We should prepare."

"What's happening?" asked Daniel, escaping Nails while he could.

"We have visitors – visitors from space," she said. "And you must be there too, Daniel: you can be a friend for Tom. But make sure you have your holy water. We must make Tom drink some so he can be convinced to join us."

Daniel managed a smile. Making people drink the holy water was what he was good at.

"Kasparov killed my son," said Stone. "We will make him remember what he did."

"What happened?" asked Daniel.

"Demons killed him," said Nails. "Demons from the sky."

Demons.

"And Kasparov is coming here, flying into our trap," said Stone. "He will drink too, and victory will be ours."

Death.

42: Sophia

Sophia fumed ten kilometres high.

There was nothing she could do, press-ganged into a flight she didn't want, away from a birthday party she'd been planning for weeks. So she'd sulked at the back, listening to music and even – she couldn't quite believe it – catching up on her studies. It was, after all, a long flight, uninterrupted time with no distractions.

She was flicking through some of her old projects when she spotted something in her *Prometheus* file.

"That's odd…"

She replayed the construct of the launch pad, and there wasn't anyone running away from the rocket. But in the off-cloud room with Felix Fernandez, there'd been a clip that had definitely shown a man, just before the explosion, running as if for his life. She tried to remember what he looked like; he had seemed familiar somehow.

"Dad…" she started, but then she heard a change in the growl of the engines and felt the plane pitch up and accelerate, pushing her into her seat.

Sophia looked over to her father, deep in conversation with Humai, gesturing at the display, flicking away at icons. Looking over his shoulder, she could just see two black diamonds.

"What's up?"

"We must fly at the airframe's limit to keep the schedule."

Sophia was puzzled. "Why?"

"Safety."

She pondered that, suspicion building. "From what? You told Mum it was safe."

"It will be, now we've rendezvoused with additional assets."

"Assets?"

"Another aircraft: you can see it on our starboard."

Sophia flicked a virtual window open and looked out at the stratosphere, where she was closer to the dark blue sky above than the white of clouds far below.

"There's nothing out there."

"Keep watching," said Artur. "It's in max-stealth mode – now, look again…"

She saw a shadow form in the empty sky alongside them, which became an aircraft, smooth curves, a matt texture like shark's skin, its wings little more than sharp-edged fins. It was covered in lumps and modules that could be sensors or weapons. There were no windows, but she could see markings of an entry door at its back. Then it faded away again.

"That's a SpecOp craft! Why do we need that?"

"Precaution, that's all."

"Oh, come on, don't treat me like an idiot – I'll blip Mum."

"I'm sorry to say communications must be restricted," said Humai, breaking in.

"What?" Sophia stuttered with anger. "But you're in contact."

"As an AI I can hide my tracks from everything in the blipverse except another AI, but a human blip is easy to trawl. They'd spot our new route and company immediately."

"But – what do you mean 'they'? Who? Why should we hide our tracks?"

"Just a precaution, Soph, honest. Might be nothing. But you know how that Cita Stone woman is. And now she seems to have the anti-space BCC behind her."

He keeps throwing that woman in my face, thought Sophia. But what should she do? Funnily enough, school had never covered what to do when your dad decides to take you halfway round the world on some allegedly safe mission that suddenly needs SpecOp backup.

"Trust me, Soph, the plan is to just fly in, pick up the two from Mars, head back – that's it."

"If they want to come."

"Yes," he said, patiently, "if they want to come."

"Hmmm."

Taking that for agreement, Artur turned back to the display and Humai, talking in a low voice. She leant back in her seat and turned up the music in her hairband while she wondered what she should do.

Then the engine noise increased till it filled the world, and the thrust pushed her back again.

Artur grinned at her. "This craft has a little more legs than we advertised."

He looked different to her. Tension and energy seemed to flow from him as if he were twenty years younger. His eyes gleamed with a determination she had never seen, a scary resolution to do whatever he had to do to achieve his goals.

What was driving him, and what was so important to him?

Looking ahead at the display, she could see maps and navigational marks, lines and dots, arrays of numbers and strings of letters: complexity, organisation, plans.

And in one corner she spotted the rotating twin globes, the ident of Humai.

Huh.

43: Tom

Tom floated, watching the blue and white world turn beneath him. Earth, he thought, he had reached Earth. Would the reality live up to the dream?

Boreas had brought them this close but could take them no further, and they waited for transport for the final leg down.

It was close enough to Tom, for whom it was all new. The colours were alive after the dead reds of Mars: blue waters, white, grey and black clouds, yellow and brown deserts, green vegetation, and everywhere signs of life. Lights glowed in the shadows, towns and cities, millions of people – no, billions of people. He tried to imagine them all, but the scale of the numbers defeated him, and his attention was caught by details, like the dividing line between browns and blues, a coastline.

Tom for once was at peace, happy to simply watch the planet flow beneath them as they orbited around and around.

JT was looking in another direction.

"That's the old station: we left from there," he said.

"What?"

"Over there, see. I don't see why we don't just go inside. I spent six months in there working on closed-cycle ecosystems."

"Hmmm…"

"*Boreas*, why didn't we dock with the station?"

"The space station is currently mothballed, without a functioning life-support system," said the ship.

"What's that new structure being built beyond it?"

"Beyond the station is an operational workshop developing an automated deep space facility. The spaceplane *Phoenix* is currently approaching from a lower orbit to deliver its payload of additional components."

"See that, Tom? I can see the spaceplane! It's coming, it's coming!"

"I saw it – but look at those islands."

"Oh boy, soon to be home, soon home, eh – how good is that, Tom?"

"Home," said Tom, trying out the word.

They watched the *Phoenix* approach, its swept wings a shadow against the blue world. With the elegance of a flower opening at dawn, its cargo bay opened, exposing its contents to waiting robots. The watchers saw a stack of thick coils, maybe ten metres across, loops as smooth as poured concrete but with the texture of oiled metal, in its core a bundle of carbon trusses. The robots darted in with claws open, locking on and pulling it slowly away to the workshop.

"Don't recognise what that is," said JT. "Come on, let's get ready."

But Tom was reluctant to leave, content to hang by the window forever.

"It'll be fine, Tom, honest," said JT, quietly. "I'll show you round."

"Starting in Cornwall?"

"Of course."

"Deal," said Tom.

He took one last, long look through the window: the *Phoenix* was approaching *Boreas*, its dark, wide wings blotting out his view of the planet. It was time to go. With a sigh, Tom turned and reluctantly followed JT as he headed for the docking port.

The spaceplane's quarters were cramped; it was clear that they were not expected to remain on the *Phoenix* for long. Inside all they found were seven seats, and the sight of the empty five quietened even JT's enthusiasm.

The ship talked them through the procedure.

"In five minutes we enter the prime re-entry window and will undock from *Boreas*, execute the de-orbit burn, and enter sub-orbital flight. When we reach the entry interface, we start a series of s-curves until at sufficiently low speed for powered flight and Kennedy final approach."

"Ken-ned-dy Space Cen-tre," said JT, stretching each word, grinning at Tom.

Tom said nothing. What would he find down there? What would it be like?

They watched the separation from *Boreas* on the displays.

"Bye-bye, *Boreas*, again," said JT.

Phoenix rotated round and powered up for the de-orbit burn. Suddenly the *Boreas*, the old station and the workshop seemed to accelerate away from them.

"And down we go," said JT. "You know, that's the thing about gravity wells: much easier to go down than up, eh, Tom?"

Tom stared at the display, saying nothing.

"Soon good old Earth gravity again. I wonder if an astronaut knows the feeling of weight in the same way as sailors know their home waters? Guess there's only one way to find out."

On the display the view was obscured by the glowing pinks and reds of the plasma: they were starting the re-entry.

"No choices now," said Tom, breaking his silence.

"No," said JT, looking over, hoping for more, but Tom had returned to his thoughts. "It was worth it – wasn't it, eh, Tom? All those struggles, just think: the *Endeavour*, that storm, the flight, that aerobrake – wasn't that something, eh?"

Tom looked over at JT, saw his eyes bright with anticipation, and wanted to join him; the longed-for

Earth was just minutes away. But then he thought of the empty seats and his mother back on Mars. He opened his mouth to reply, but no words came out. Instead he turned to the display to watch the world beneath him.

"Come on, Tom," said JT. "Don't be like that – we made it, against all the odds, like we said we would, like we swore we would."

"Yes," said Tom, finally. "We did it."

Below he could see the sea, the wide expanse of the Pacific as the craft swung in broad zigzags down through the atmosphere.

Then there was a line, the blue waters cut off by a transition to green-brown – land.

"You're right, though, your father would have loved to see that sight, to see the old country beneath him again."

Tom said nothing to that. His new toughened self seemed able to throw off the emotional load of the other's reminder.

"We'll remember him when we get down: he'd have liked that," said JT, and Tom nodded.

The *Phoenix* ended its breaking curves and its nose dropped, heading purposefully downwards, seeking their goal.

"Warning," began the ship. For a moment their stomachs tightened. "Blipverse public domain access to all ship's audio-visual sensors in ten seconds."

"Just leave the talking to me," said JT.

"Not all," said Tom, though he was already beginning to feel self-conscious.

"Ok," said JT.

"Public live," said the ship.

On the displays Tom could see the runway ahead of them, with an inset box showing him and JT in a rotating 3D view. He tried to imagine the millions upon millions watching them, but soon gave up.

The sensed audience or the sight of the runway silenced JT too, so for the final moments they just watched, overwhelmed by the moment. Both without realising it held their breaths as they listened for the touch of the wheels, and let them out when they heard the roll and felt the craft vibrate softly.

"Feel that?" said JT, lifting up his arm and letting it fall down on the arm rest. "That's what you should feel like: that's your true weight."

Tom held up his arm, duplicating the action.

"Home," said JT. "I'm home," and Tom, looking over, saw the old man's face was wet with tears.

"It's ok, JT, it's ok."

"We're home."

But Tom, instead of euphoria as he'd expected, felt leaden, constrained by the downward pull of a planet he'd never known. So much was wrong; so many people who should be there too weren't.

"Instructions requested," said the ship.

"What?" ask Tom.

"I have not received the terminal park coordinates, and there are no disembarkment facilities."

"There was meant to be a reception for us." But many things had been meant.

"There are a group of humans at one end of the runway."

"Let us out by them."

It seemed rather shambolic compared to the hi-tech spaceplane.

There was a pause while the ship taxied to the group, and then a strange quiet as the engines spun down.

"You will leave out of the port hatch and down the emergency steps," the ship said.

Tom expected some quip about port and boats from JT, but there was none: for once he was silent.

"I'll go first," said Tom.

The *Phoenix* opened up the hatch and bright sunlight seemed to blast its way in, blinding them. Tom was hit by a rush of smells – rich, warm, decaying and alive, the edible and inedible. It made him feel giddy, and for a moment he just held his place, breathing it all in. But the call of the hatchway was too strong, and Tom peered outside where he could experience planet Earth for himself for the first time.

Part 7

44: Tom

Tom's head was spinning with the rush of experiences.

Standing outside with no surface suit was scary but exhilarating. At every moment he subconsciously expected the air to vanish from his lungs, and he more gasped than breathed. The sky was so high and big, echoes lost in the emptiness.

The plane was on a concrete runway. On either side were fields of green and yellow, long grasses that waved in a breeze that was warm on his cheek. Towards the west, the sky was red from the setting sun. Clouds of mist drifted towards them, clouds that smelled of salt; somewhere a seagull called.

Small dots swarmed around his face, stinging slightly – programmed, he realised, to eat him alive. Suddenly he looked at the greenery around him and saw not lushness but the alien. Creepers had spread over a nearby building, taking it over, making it their own, but then both were swallowed by the rolling mist. Gravity felt wrong, far too strong, dragging him, pulling him downwards to the ground.

He looked at his arm and saw an insect land. Its mouthpart stretched down to his skin and pierced it: he could feel the bite and watched as it sucked his blood.

This wasn't Mars; here, life killed, not the planet.

"Demons," said a voice.

Tom focussed for the first time on the people. There was a large crowd at the foot of the steps, and the nearest was a young man with a scar down his face.

"Now, now, Nails," said the woman from the blip-con, Cita Stone. "Welcome our guests."

He turned and climbed down the steps. Close up, Tom's eyes were drawn to the bulging growths on her neck.

"Do you want to know how I got these?" she asked.

Embarrassed, he shook his head and looked around him. There were hundreds in a green and black uniform, armed... an army. They had been met by an army.

"I will tell you, later," she said.

JT climbed down to join them. He looked around at their faces and at the ranks behind her silently watching them. "Where're the old agency people? I thought they'd be here."

"Much has changed since you left, Jim Trevelyn—"

"JT."

"JT, then. The Everglades were hit hard by global warming and the Collapse."

JT shook his head. "It doesn't feel right without the old crowd. And there are weeds, everywhere there are weeds. It's all wrong." Suddenly his legs gave way and he had to grab on to Tom's arm. "Sorry – should have spent more time in the gravity pod."

"Of course; you'll want to sit down. We have transport ready for you," said Cita, directing them towards a fleet of aged vehicles, paint worn, rust showing.

"What about Dr Kasparov?" asked Tom.

"He'll be here later," said Cita, a smile appearing and disappearing so quickly that Tom might have imagined it.

"Why isn't he here now?"

"Later, Tom, just get in. We'll take you to meet him."

"Who are these?" asked Tom of the army.

"This is Captain Vaughan," said Cita, indicating the man standing at the front wearing a military uniform. "And these are his Defenders of the Planet; they're trying to protect the planet from anything that might threaten it."

"I have these," said the scar-faced one, Nails. He raised his hand palm-inwards so they could see his fingernails. They were silver, ridged like a saw, sharp as needles, and without warning they began to move back and forth, faster and faster into a blur.

"I can give you a tickle," said Nails. "I've been practicing on this one, but he's too soft."

He indicated a boy about Tom's age, quieter, younger, standing behind him and holding a bottle of grey liquid.

"Would you like a drink?" the boy asked.

Tom and JT looked at the bottle, in which flecks of silver seemed to rise and fall. Tom shook his head and looked around, trying to see a way out, but in every direction there was the green and black of the Defenders. He caught JT's eyes and could sense the fear and uncertainty in them as well. JT made a show of staggering, and Tom caught him.

"I don't trust this lot," he whispered.

"Me neither," said Tom. He nervously reached for his pendant, seeking reassurance.

"What's that around your neck?" asked Cita.

"This?" asked Tom. "It was a present from my father: it's a sample from the Origin Stone."

There were cries from the Defenders.

"You brought back a Martian rock? Even though you knew that was banned?" There was triumph in Cita's voice. "You have broken the quarantine of Earth," she said. "Those Technocrats lied, as they always will. You must be detained for the safety of this planet."

"That's rubbish," said JT.

"Yes," said Tom, "this is all total rubbish. There's nothing to fear: we're fine and we've both breathed in Martian dust. I've even got some in my blood."

There were screams from the Defenders, drawing backwards like excited molecules.

"Contaminated!" shouted one, then "Red Plague!"

"Demons," cried Nails.

"See – they don't want your infections. What was it? Two deaths and one so sick she can't think straight?"

"That was nothing to do with Mars!" said Tom. "Amina Sissoko killed herself, Mei-Li Wu was buried in a sand avalanche, and my father, he… It wasn't a sickness."

"So you say, but do we know that for sure? All we have is your word."

Where was Kasparov? he wondered. They had to get to Sophia's father.

"Come," said Cita, indicating the first two vehicles. "Bring the prisoners."

"Where are we going?" asked Tom.

"Would you like a drink?" the boy asked again.

Tom shook his head. "What's your name?" he asked.

"Daniel. Would you like a drink?"

"Where are we going?"

"The holy mother is returning to her son. Would you like a drink?"

"Why do you keep asking me that?"

"Mother Stone told me to. Would you like a drink?"

Tom looked into Daniel's eyes and saw in them total certainty; but without uncertainty there seemed to be no life, either. He was thirsty, but shook his head and climbed into one of the vehicles.

Where was Kasparov?

45: Sophia

The aircraft nose dipped sharply; its engines cut out, and then they were falling. Sophia grabbed the seat's arms tight.

"It's ok, Soph. We're diving below their sensors before landing at the Air Force base, just south of Canaveral," said Artur.

"I thought the Earth Firsters didn't use that sort of tech?"

"Nor did we, but we received intel that Cita has gained access via an unknown ally—"

"Though we suspect BCC," interrupted Humai.

"—to two now-gen Wolf Bat semi-smart fighters, which is why we have backup."

"So where are they?"

"I can't detect them, which is ominous," said Humai. "Just a couple of SkyWhales and long-line observation kites."

On the display Sophia could see a layout of the Canaveral site – once a cape, now an island – the spaceplane on its runway to the north, the old Air Force runway to the south. Dotted over the site were icons for vehicles, aircraft and Earth Firster units, lots of them. Out of the window all she could see was the grey-white of clouds flying by.

"I don't know how she got so strong, how she got this army, without us finding out," said Artur.

"She's using nano-drugs," said Sophia. "There's this thing called Memory that blats the brain and another called Belief that makes them turn into lemmings and do what they're told."

"What? How do you know?"

"Kids at school from the southern states – we call them the lemming kids."

"Warning, high-g stealth glide parachute deploy imminent," said Humai.

Her seat swivelled back beneath her, so she was horizontal. For a moment nothing changed, and then it was as if she were buried under a building; the pressure pushed her back into the seat, which absorbed her like dough. Her vision shrank to a dot and then expanded again, and she could hear the roll of wheels on a runway. They were down, and Sophia's seat rotated upright so fast she was flung onto her feet. The doors snapped open and she jumped out of the plane, glad to be free.

It hadn't been an Air Force base for decades and was deserted, with weeds sprouting from cracks between concrete slabs. Clouds of fog rolled across the runway, out of which another aircraft could be heard, and a dark shadowy smudge could be seen, landing close by: the SpecOps plane. It taxied up to them, steaming slightly, looking much larger to Sophia than it had in the sky. The rear door opened, and a ramp extended from the frame onto the ground, down which drove first one power bike and then a second, electric, silent and fast, auto-stabilised, auto-standing.

"What the hell is going on?"

"I can't say, not now – there's no time. All our plans were thrown out by the castaways landing at Kennedy and Cita getting Wolf Bats. And if she has an army programmed with nano-drugs, then we're running out of time and options. I have to go."

"Go? Just like that?" She wondered how desperate he must be.

"It'll be dangerous, but we'll have Humai."

As if on cue, a swarm of drones popped out of the SpecOps aircraft, sensors focussing in on her. "Hi, Sophia," came the voice of Humai. Half sped off into the distance, while the rest hovered, including one the size of a small aircraft.

"The flight that left was surveillance and offence, the ones that stayed are support and defence. You can stay with the plane or bike in with me: I won't force you."

"Why should I do anything for you?"

"Do you really think I'm crazy? Do you think your mother is? Or Cita?"

"Could you be any more manipulative?" she said, but she remembered back to an angry face of scars and growths, the untidy tufts of mud-coloured hair, a face that hardened, then changed, with a dead gleam to the eyes.

"Look, if she gets those castaways, it'll be bad, believe me, for all of us."

"For your plans."

"Yes, but why do we do this? Why does your mother do this?"

"She wouldn't do *this*."

He was silent at that. Then, "No, she didn't."

"Didn't?"

"In the fight for London's independence – did you think it was all pretty speeches?"

"Oh my God, what did you do back then?"

"What I'm doing now – making things change, making things better. Look, I really have to go – the *Phoenix* has landed; the castaways are already on Earth."

"We've missed it." All of a sudden she found herself disappointed. She'd envisaged herself at the centre of it, blipverse global. "So it was all for nothing?"

"No. Cita's announced a blip-con; BCC will no doubt be covering it. That's our best chance, but we have to go now."

"*That's* our best chance?"

"We're getting drone-feed," interrupted Humai. "Stone's taken Tom and JT prisoner and is about to force nano-drugs on them."

"Memory and Belief?" asked Sophia.

"It seems so."

"Then we have no choice," said Artur. "We have to act. You too, Sophia."

He kept taking her for granted.

"No way. It was your plans that screwed up like this, not me."

"We need you, Sophia."

"Tough. Enough is enough."

"You've seen Stone and BCC up close; do you want them to win?"

"Your problem, not mine."

"Do you want Tom to become one of those lemmings?" asked Humai.

Sophia found that harder to answer.

"He thought you were a friend," it said.

Bastards, bastards.

"Maybe – but only if I'm in control, not bossed about by you two."

"Ok, ok, whatever."

"I want to be in the loop and see whatever it is that Humai's telling you."

Artur reached into the locker under the nearest bike's seat and pulled out milspec goggles and earplugs.

"Take these, then: your pendant isn't enough protection."

"Isn't what?"

"Hi, Sophia," said her pendant with Humai's voice.

"What the—? You've been spying on me through this?"

"This is only the second time my c-agent's been activated via the pendant. The first was when you were in Felix Fernandez's cores, and weren't you glad about that then?

"And how could we trust you after you let Cita Stone into your *Prometheus* construct? And then walked straight into Felix Fernandez's trap?" said Artur.

"How many times do I have to tell you, I didn't let her into the construct!"

"Penetrating BCC's AI defences was a challenge and required intrusion vectors only available to a local node, which you were kind enough to provide us," said Humai.

Smug bastard.

"So, do you want to save Tom, then?" her father asked with a smile.

Another smug bastard.

Deep breath, earplugs in, goggles over the eyes. Layers of information appeared in front of her, signing directions, maps and views from the drones.

"Let's do this."

46: Tom

It was a car, or so JT said. Something called a four-by-four, a vehicle for rough terrain.

"I used to have something like this," JT said. "A Land Rover, back in the day."

"Get in," said Nails.

"Easy, lad," said JT. "Got to go slow in this gravity. Tom, can you lend a hand?"

Tom got out to help JT into the driver's seat.

"Not there," said Nails. "In the back."

"Listen," said Captain Vaughan. "Can you hear that? A faint whine?"

They stood still, heads turning from side to side to pick up the faint noise. *Yes,* thought Tom. Out there in the mist there was something mechanical, something moving.

"Kasparov," said Cita.

Suddenly from the mist there were screams. "Alligators! Alligators everywhere!"

"They're crawling outta the Gator Hole! Hundreds of them!"

"Run – run for your life!"

The cries were followed by Defenders, apparitions that came from the fog and were lost into it seconds later, escaping their fears.

"What did you see?" asked Cita of one, who paused for a moment.

The Defender shook his head. "Nothin', but don't wanna to get me legs eat'n," he said, before vanishing into the mist.

"Don't worry, Tom," said JT. "Alligator attacks were really rare; no one took them seriously."

"That's true," said Cita. "It's most likely a ruse. Kasparov's machines are here, so we can't wait. Bring the boy here and give me the water."

Nails and Captain Vaughan grabbed Tom and dragged him roughly to Cita.

"Now, you, drink this," she said, taking the bottle from Daniel.

"No!" said Tom, but they were holding his arms and Cita was putting the bottle to his lips.

"Drink!" she commanded.

A boy's voice came from the mist.

"Mother, help me."

Cita seemed to freeze, then her eyes closed, just for a moment. She staggered slightly.

"That is not my son," she said, her voice as cold as ice. "That is not Ben."

"Please, mother, I'm wounded."

"The spirit of the holy mother's son walks with us!" said Daniel, his face alight.

"I will always remember his voice, and that is *not* him. He is dead, killed by those technocrats and their AIs."

"Mother, why don't you remember me?"

"It sounds just like him," said Vaughan, fear on his face.

"It's a lie; AIs can generate anything, anyone. I want Kasparov for this! Take out their plane."

Vaughan raised the command bracelet on his arm to his mouth and whispered into it.

"I remember that day, when Ben died in my arms," said Cita. "I always will."

Vaughan looked unsure, as if about to say something, but he decided not to.

Then out of the mist screamed drones – literally screaming, like humans tortured on a rack, painful on the ear, building fear in the chest. Vaughan and Nails let go of Tom, and he flung himself aside, away from them, crawling on the ground.

More drones followed, waves of them screaming in arcs between Tom and the Defenders. Carrier drones exploded into clouds of bee-sized microdrones that darted into the faces of the Defenders, biting and distracting. Some waved their hands to keep the microdrones away, only to have them cut and bloodied.

Captain Vaughan and Nails pulled out their guns and fired at the drones, bullets ricocheting off the larger ones, knocking out a few of the microdrones. One lucky hit damaged a carrier, which exploded, showering molten metal over the Defenders, slicing one's hand off. Other drones let off smoke bombs, and from within the clouds Tom could hear explosions and make out off-road cars blown over on their side, wheels spinning off, Defenders diving for cover.

One drone stopped in front of Tom, a fat torus with sensors protruding from it. The curved surface nearest him turned into a display and he could recognise a face: Sophia's.

"You have to get away, quick – we're coming!"

He crawled, then got up and ran away, but was spotted by Nails.

"No you don't!" Nails leapt at Tom, pulling him down again, but Sophia's drone rammed itself into Nails, knocking him away.

"You have to go! Use the car!" she said.

Tom looked around for it: JT had started it up and was driving towards him.

"I'll stop you!" cried Nails, pointing his gun at Sophia's drone.

He fired, and it wobbled, then fell on the ground, sparks flying, but Tom had time to run towards the car.

"Get in," yelled JT.

Tom leapt into the back and then pulled himself into the passenger seat.

"Stop them!" yelled Cita.

Vaughan pointed his gun at Tom, about to shoot.

"Aim at the car, not them – we need them alive!" Cita shrieked.

Vaughan fired, but drones had moved in to protect the car, absorbing the shot, then accelerating towards him. He dropped the weapon and ducked.

"Let's get out of here," cried Tom.

JT put his foot down and they accelerated into the fog, away from the battle.

47: Sophia

Sophia took off her goggles. Looking with her own eyes, she realised it was now dusk, the fog lifting. Above her, the first stars could be seen.

"What were you playing at?" she asked. "You could have killed someone!"

Artur shrugged. "They were about to brainwash the only two to escape Mars and get to Earth. We had no choice."

"Just get them out, that's what you said, nothing about starting a war."

"We used non-lethal methods; any injuries they had were self-inflicted."

"Then count me out; I'll get Tom my own way, with my share of those drones."

She ran over to one of the bikes, put the goggles back on and prepared to kick off.

Suddenly the SpecOp plane jerked into life, moving, beeping alerts.

"Warning! High-g emergency take-off enabled. Warning!"

"What the—?" Sophia began to ask.

"Get out of there!" said Humai. "Hostiles incoming: move!"

The SpecOp plane was already speeding down the runway, rear door closing as it moved, its camouflage blending it into the remaining clouds.

A black, bat-like aircraft flew out of the sky above them, spitting fire. Drones fired flares and deployed countermeasures, aiming lasers upwards to blind its sensors. Sophia powered up the bike but over-revved the engine, and the back wheel spun out of control.

"Shit."

She tried again, slower, and this time she got traction and began to move.

"Warning; second Wolf Bat incoming," said Humai in her earplugs.

Sophia accelerated away and had just hit 100 when an aircraft tore across the sky and she heard an explosion behind her. In her goggles she could see the scene she was leaving: the TAC aircraft they had come in was now a burning wreck, pieces blown across the runway.

What a total screw-up.

"Wait!" cried Artur.

But she'd had enough of them and their plans that had led to this mess. She would do it her own way: rescue Tom and escape.

Somehow.

Her drones were tracking Tom and JT's vehicle, and her goggles showed her a route to rendezvous with them.

First up, get to them. After that – well, she'd have to work that out later, by herself.

48: Tom

The sky glowed a dark blue; the ground was black apart from two cones of white from the headlights.

JT drove through the dusk, following the map in his head, away from the Defenders. Tom held on tight and watched behind: they were being followed.

"It's our lights," he said. "They're tracking our headlights."

"I need them to see," said JT.

Tom looked back again; the Defenders were closing in.

"Try it without," said Tom.

JT switched off the headlights, and the vehicle bounced through the dark.

"If we can get to the coastal path we can head south to the old Air Force base," said JT. Tom could just make out his face, lit by the sky, on it a smile.

"Seriously – we're driving in the dark, on the run from a crazy army, and you're enjoying this?"

JT laughed and sped up.

"You're right. Feels good to be driving again, back on ol' Earth, where we left all those years ago."

Tom shook his head. "Just focus on not smashing us up."

Ahead, he could see silhouetted against the sky four towers, bent outwards.

"What's that?"

"It's the old *Prometheus* launch site," said JT. "Those are the lightning towers, or at least were, before the explosion. There'll be a track all round; it will be easy driving."

They bounced off the concrete onto grasslands.

"Shit," said JT. "The track goes to the right here – forgot that. Might need those lights."

"Keep them off!" said Tom. "They're close; they'll spot us!"

The vehicle bounced again, and then the ride smoothed off.

"That's the track again," said JT.

"See," said Tom, "didn't need those lights."

A shadow flew past on their left.

"That's the old liquid oxygen tank," said JT. "If we keep that lightning tower to our right and the far one to our left, we can go straight through the launch site."

He drove fast, the wrecked tower flying past them.

Another lurch.

"JT, there's debris; the path's not clear."

"It will be fine, just like before."

"Slow down! Slow down!"

Suddenly they were in free-fall, the car heading down into the deepest black. It smashed into concrete, throwing JT and Tom forward over the bonnet. There was the screech of steel on steel, sparks flying, and the sound of humans in pain. Tom flung his hands up to protect his head and felt the bruises build up over his body. There was a final jolt and then he found himself still, the taste of blood on his lips.

"JT! JT!"

"Here…"

The voice was faint. Tom scrambled over the wreck of the off-road vehicle towards the sound. He felt the warmth of JT's arm before he could see him.

"Are you ok?"

"Been better."

"Can you move?"

JT struggled to his feet, then swore, loudly.

"My right arm hurts like hell."

"Where are we? What happened?"

"This trench is the flame pit – I forgot it was here. Thought it was the other side of the site. Sorry."

"Maybe if we hide here they won't find us."

"Maybe."

They crouched by the car, listening, looking up at the sky, a rectangle of dark blue.

"Can you hear them?" Tom dropped his voice to a whisper.

"No, nothing," whispered JT.

Then Tom caught a faint whining sound.

"Hear that?"

"Hear what?"

It was getting closer – louder.

"Now I do!" said JT.

"Shh…"

A vehicle was approaching along the flame pit, slowly, quietly. JT stiffened and grabbed at Tom's arm with his working left hand.

The vehicle stopped, and the whining sound ended.

For a moment all was silent; then they heard footsteps heading towards them. Suddenly a spotlight shone out, blinding them.

"Hello, Tom."

It was a girl's voice.

"Who's there?"

"It's me, Sophia."

49: Sophia

She could see the shadow answering to Tom hold up a hand against the light.

"Sophia?"

"Yup, it's me."

She smiled to herself. She'd done it, reached them first, without her father.

Sophia got off her bike and angled its light to one side so it lit up a wall of the trench, patterned by lichen slowly colonising surfaces blackened by rocket flames. Walking closer, she could finally see Tom clearly. He was taller than Sophia had expected and thinner, looking tired but determined.

"How did you find us?" he asked.

"These drones," she said. Out of the dark drifted a pair of drones, humming slightly. "They can see in the dark, and I can see what they see with these." She spun her goggles round in her hand. "Cool, eh?"

"Yes," he said. She hoped he really was impressed; for a moment she searched his eyes, looking for a reaction, only to realise he was staring back into hers and a beat had passed.

"So how do we get out of here?"

"We have a plane, not far – we just have to get you to it."

"That won't be easy," said Tom. "The crash was pretty bad, and JT's broken his arm."

Sophia spotted the wreck of the off-road car and gasped.

"You were lucky to escape," she told them, walking over to JT.

"Hello, Sophia," said JT, wincing. He was leaning against the wrecked vehicle, the hand of his broken arm facing backwards. "Hope it's not too far."

Two able-bodied and one wounded, with just the one bike for transport. Hmmm…

Then her earplugs beeped a warning and the two drones repositioned themselves, standing guard between her and an approaching noise. Something was heading their way, unlit, stealthy, hiding in the dark, from the same direction she had come. She snapped the goggles over her eyes: in their virtual viewpoint, she could see an electric bike heading towards her with overlays indicating *Friendly* and *Command*. In other words, it was her father.

"Don't do that," she called out. "Don't sneak up on us like that!"

He had tracked her down. Bother – she wanted to do this by herself. But, Sophia admitted, she could do with a second bike to get them out.

"You idiot, Sophia," he said. "Why didn't you wait for me?"

Well, she hadn't expected praise, but that was a bit much.

"Hey, you were slow! Anyhow, this is your mess, and look, here they are. I found them."

Ha!

Artur took off his goggles.

"Hello, Tom," he said. "And JT – glad to see you've made it."

Artur looked around, appraising the situation: the wrecked car, two electric bikes, the three figures and four drones. Underfoot, the trench floor was littered with rubbish and leaves, the mulch soft underfoot, stinking of rotting vegetation.

"It's simple," said Sophia. "We'll have to double up per bike. But first someone will have to have a look at JT's arm." She meant her father.

He nodded and turned to his bike. "I have a medi-kit; we can use that."

Then her earplugs screeched and warbled.

"Danger!" said Humai. "I've detected intrusions and subversions in our drone network – AI-grade!"

Sophia's father spun round.

"Countermeasures," he commanded.

"They're local to you!" said Humai. "Network integrity breached – evac immediately!"

"Who's behind it?" asked Sophia.

"It's unverified!" said Humai. "It's—" The earplugs screeched again and then went silent.

The drones flashed red then fell to the ground, motionless. All of a sudden Sophia was blinded as the trench drowned in light.

"Don't move," said an amplified voice. Sophia recognised it, remembered it all too well from Justinian. "We have Defenders at either end of the trench," said Cita. "Vaughan, get them."

A figure came running down the trench toward them, into the patch of light – a man. Something about his movement reminded Sophia of being trapped inside BCC's off-cloud room. Vaughan was followed by a troop of Defenders, too many, well-armed. Sophia instinctively turned the other way down the trench, looking for an escape route, but another troop was approaching from that way too.

Trapped.

She looked at Tom, wondering what to do, how he would react. He seemed calm. She shrugged at him, as if to say 'we tried', and he gave a lopsided half smile, half grimace back at her.

Some of the Defenders had poles taller than themselves which glowed, lights flickering in waves, as if an angry blue aurora had been imprisoned within.

"Photoluminescent nets," said Artur. "How did they get that?"

"What is it?"

"AI base-layer, next-gen tech, as used by Humai and, I'm guessing, BCC's in-house AI that they call Unverified. We can't do anything while they're active."

This was not good; Mum was going to kill him. Though, Sophia realised, that was the least of their worries.

Seriously not good.

50: Sophia

Vaughan dragged them out of the trench into the dusk, a gun poking into Sophia's back. She hated the touch; not just the physical intrusion into her space, actually touching her, but a reminder of how helpless she was, they were.

Tom helped JT walk, the old man's good arm around the younger's shoulder. A boy with a bottle came up to them.

"Do you want a drink?" he asked.

"No thank you, Daniel," Tom said.

"The holy mother is returning to her son; there you will drink."

The boy seemed to be in a state of ecstasy, eyes burning. JT's face was white and damp; every now and then he moaned in pain.

They were led to Cita, who had created a circle of the blue glowing poles. Further out was a ring of Defenders with lit torches, surrounding them. Cita stood at the centre, kneeling, caressing the concrete gently. She looked up at Artur.

"He died here, on Canaveral Island. Ben died here when your rocket exploded."

There were grass blades growing between cracks in the slab, and she pulled them out, then with her hand swept dust and gravel away.

"This" – she indicated the devastated site – "this wreckage – is his memorial."

Vaughan pushed Sophia, Tom and JT in towards Artur and Cita.

"I want this recorded, streamed. Activate the cloud sticks," said Cita.

Vaughan spoke into his command bracelet, which beeped an acknowledgement. The poles flickered in unison, and then each emitted a light which scanned the people as if via laser, a quick once-over. Then the light switched off and each cloud stick pulsed slowly.

"Ready," said Vaughan.

Cita stood up and walked towards Artur.

"Hold him," she ordered Vaughan, then spoke to Artur directly. "I want you to know how defeated you are," she said. "I have you, your daughter and both of the Martians. My cloud sticks have disabled your drones, while your AI is irrelevant, uncontactable. I have my Defenders, and you have lost."

Sophia's father said nothing.

"In a moment you will all drink the water and join us, but first you must pay your respects. Kneel."

Artur looked at Cita, his shoulders slumped: for once, he was empty of plans.

"You want this on record?" he asked, shrugging one shoulder in the direction of the cloud sticks.

"Records can be edited; BCC is rather good at that," said Cita. "But I want a copy for myself. Artur Kasparov, kneeling and kissing the ground where my Ben died."

Artur didn't move.

"You can't be serious."

"Go on," she screamed. "Kiss the ground, now!"

She kicked his legs under him and thrust his head down.

"Kiss it! Kiss the Earth!" she shrieked.

Still Artur paused.

"Guns out!" cried Cita. "Point at the others! If he doesn't kiss the ground, shoot them, starting with his daughter. If you see or feel anything wrong, shoot them!"

"Shooting's too quick," said a young man.

As he approached Sophia, she could see a long scar on his face and that part of his ear was missing.

He grinned and raised his hand; from each fingernail she saw blades emerge, gleaming in the blue light. With a whine, they blurred into life.

"Hello, Sophia," the man said. "Let me show you why they call me Nails."

He grabbed her arm, pulling it behind her until she winced in pain. He was close enough that she could smell him: sweat, unwashed clothes and alcohol.

"This job has its benefits," he leched at her.

Cita nodded. "So that's your choice: do as I say, or I'll let Nails have his fun."

Artur slowly bowed his head down to the ground, paused, then gave it a soft kiss.

"There. Are you happy now?"

Cita's face flushed, her face transformed from hate into joy. "If Ben could have seen that... The head of the Technocrats humbled at last."

She indicated to Daniel, who approached with the bottle of Memory and Belief.

"Now you will drink," she said. "Now you will join us."

"No!" said Sophia, unable to keep quiet any more. "I've seen what that does to people: it turns them into lemmings."

"If I drink it, will you spare the others?" asked Tom.

"Don't, Tom!" said Sophia.

"Why would I do that?" asked Cita. "Why would I not have all of you with me, fighting for the Earth? Imagine Artur Kasparov admitting how his technology hurts the planet! Picture you and JT arguing against future space missions!"

"I won't drink it," said Sophia.

"Nor me," said Tom, propping up JT.

"But how can you stop me?" ask Cita. "You can't run away from me – not from here."

Something clicked in Sophia's head. Running away from the Prometheus launch site...

"I know you," she said, turning to look at Vaughan. "You were here, then."

"What?" demanded Cita.

"Vaughan. He was here for the launch of the *Prometheus*: in the BCC record I saw him running away just before it exploded. They edited him out of the public version. But he was here, he was involved, he knew it was about to explode. Why would BCC want to keep that secret?"

"Nonsense. Captain Vaughan stayed with the boats," said Cita.

Vaughan nodded. "She's lying – I wasn't anywhere near the explosion – you know what happened, you remember."

"No, he was here. I saw him," insisted Sophia.

"Interesting," said Artur. "Another suspect; we didn't consider Vaughan."

"She wasn't here," said Vaughan. "She's making it up."

"It's not me but BCC. It was their recording. And it was different from the one they published global public."

Cita looked at Vaughan, considering.

"What do you remember?" asked Sophia.

"I remember Ben, I remember the explosion…"

"Who runs those cloud sticks?" asked Artur.

Cita looked puzzled, Vaughan annoyed.

"Captain Vaughan does," she answered. "He controls them via his bracelet; it's standard cloud tech."

"No, it isn't," said Artur. "It's AI-enhanced, linked to the BCC's in-house AI, the one they call Unverified."

"What?" asked Cita.

"Unverified is unstable," said Artur. "It was optimised to maximise news content for the BCC servers; it doesn't consider humans or their lives."

Sophia, trying to twist away from Nails, could see where her father was going.

"So if it considered the *Prometheus* explosion a good news story, it would work to that end, whatever the human cost," she said.

"Exactly. And Vaughan is an agent of BCC, working with Unverified, so he'd do what they'd say; he'd be its proximity vector to plant a device – explosives."

Cita looked from Artur and Sophia to Vaughan.

"AIs," she said. "All this comes from AIs – I told you they were evil."

The Defenders murmured their agreement. "Demons!" some cried.

Vaughan spat on the ground.

"You worked with them yourself," he pointed out. "You worked with Unverified to hack Sophia's cloud to get intel on Kasparov."

"What?" Even surrounded by nutters and with Nails leering by her head, Sophia found a teaspoon of joy. "I *told* you it wasn't me!" she exclaimed. "I *knew* it wasn't my fault Cita was in the *Prometheus* construct!"

"Ok, ok," said her father.

Cita was staring at Vaughan.

"But I never told you that," she said. "I never said anything about Unverified or how I got that intel."

Vaughan took a step back.

"If I didn't tell you, then it must have come from BCC. Then you *are* their agent, and maybe Kasparov's daughter is telling the truth."

Vaughan laughed.

"Truth? What is truth? What you tell the Defenders? When you give them Memory and Belief? What does it matter anyway? We stopped the *Prometheus* from launching, we have them as our prisoners: that is what we wanted; ignore what they say. Truth is what we publish, how we edit, like this stream."

Cita approached Vaughan.

"Truth? Memory? You ask what matters? What matters to me is Ben, and all I have of him is memories. And you killed him and rewrote the recording, the images which have become my memory of him. When I relied on those machines, the true memory was lost."

She grabbed a gun from one of the Defenders and pointed it at Vaughan.

"You are a traitor. You betrayed me and assisted an AI to sabotage the rocket, and in the explosion my son was killed."

"Lies," he said. "All lies."

"No," she said. "I don't believe you. You poisoned my memories of that day."

She indicated to Nails.

"Come here – we must disconnect him, quickly. Cut the command bracelet."

"No! Don't!" cried Vaughan.

Nails released Sophia and ran to Vaughan, his hand raised, nails glowing, buzzing, ready. He grabbed Vaughan's wrist with one hand and cut into the bracelet with his other.

"Stop!" Vaughan cried.

There was the shriek of polycarbonate on aluminium, sparks flying. Then all the cloud sticks stopped pulsing, flickered once, and went dark so they were lit only by the Defenders' torches.

"Engage," said Artur, and an explosion rocked the site.

51: Tom

Orange flames illuminated them all. In their light Tom could see the layer of sweat on JT's face and a grimace of pain. Instinctively he ducked down, taking JT with him.

"Easy, lad," JT cried.

The nearest lightning tower rocked, then began to fall – in their direction, tumbling down, sparks flying, lit by billowing fires. The Defenders on that side fled, their torches fading into the dusk. The tower crashed into the ground, so close that stones and wads of dirt and grass flew just over their heads. Tom could feel the heat on his cheeks, pebbles stinging his arms and head.

"I remember Earth as being more fun than this," muttered JT.

Further explosions followed, and out of the flames came waves of drones, battle-darkened, guns unsheathed: no holds barred now. The recoil from each shot flung the machines back, but they recovered and continued relentlessly towards the Defenders, pushing them away from the quartet of Artur, Sophia, Tom and JT.

But Cita remained, and with her stood Daniel and Nails. Vaughan had fled, lost into the night.

A pair of drones hovered on either side of Artur; a locker sprang open in one of them. He reached inside and took out a gun, which he pointed at Cita.

"Now we're going to leave, while you stay just where you are," he said.

Tom stood, taking JT with him, moving towards Artur, away from Cita.

"No, you don't," she said. She grabbed Daniel and pulled him close, protecting herself behind him. "Would you kill this boy too, child-killer?"

Daniel looked puzzled.

"But the water?" he asked. "When is he going to drink the water?"

Artur laughed.

"Hiding behind a boy? Is that what you've come to?" he said. He turned his head to look at Sophia as if this justified his actions.

That was when Cita fired: one shot into Artur's eye, flinging him back onto the ground, his head impacting with a crack.

The Defenders returned, waves of gunshot growing like a sudden tropical rainstorm, the drones flashing with impacts, some falling out of the sky, others exploding, flinging debris over Tom. He ducked again, and again JT winced.

A drone flew directly into a crowd of Defenders and exploded. Tom could see bodies fall, broken, bloodied. Another drone approached Cita and fired. She fell back, her face bruised and scared, Nails and Daniel with her, to be surrounded by armed Defenders, faint figures in the dark.

Tom crawled to Sophia, who was crouching over her father, finger on his neck. His face was a bloody mess, one eye missing, the other closed.

"Dad!" she cried. "Get up, Dad!" There were tears on her face.

"Sophia, we have to go!" said Tom. "We can't stay here."

"He's alive," she gabbled. "I can feel a pulse – he's still breathing!"

A salvo of shots from the drones, an answering hail of bullets from the Defenders.

"I don't know what to do," Sophia whispered. She looked at Tom, panic and fright full in her eyes and face.

"What about those bikes?" he asked.

"They're on their way," said one of the drones. A speaking drone? "But you should head towards them: it isn't safe here."

"No kidding," said Tom. "Sophia, grab his other side – sorry, JT."

Tom and Sophia hauled Artur up, one arm each around the body's shoulders, dragging him forward. JT followed, swearing with pain.

Another squall of shots, and Tom and Sophia dropped to the ground, dumping Artur like a sack. Over their heads drones engaged, a dance of fire, recoil, reposition, repeat.

Tom turned to check on JT, only to see him still standing, his mouth full of blood, bullet holes in his chest.

"JT!" he cried.

JT's eyes turned to him. Maybe he saw Tom, but then his knees collapsed and he fell to the ground.

"JT!" said Tom, crawling to him, keeping as low as he could.

JT twitched once, blood pouring from his mouth, then stopped, the eyes glassed and locked, fixed forever.

The moment had no meaning. How could this be happening? Tom froze. Nothing made sense; his eyes, the world, everything was crazy.

Except Sophia – she was real. She ran back, ducking, and touched JT's body, feeling for a pulse.

"I'm sorry, Tom, I can't feel anything."

The drone agreed. "There's nothing we can do; we should take the bikes."

"I'm not going," said Tom. He wouldn't leave JT, couldn't, not after all they'd been through.

"My father is about to die! We have to go *now!*"

Even with that scream, Sophia seemed a long way away. Everything did.

She shook him.

"Help us, help me, please!"

Tom looked at her and then snapped back to the now: dulled, grey and empty.

From the shadows around the launch site came a whine of motors, and then two electric bikes drove themselves towards the small group. One of the drones took a hit, starting to spin, grinding sounds from within, then sliding in the air away from them before exploding.

"We must go!" said the speaking drone. "I have sent a transport drone to collect Artur; you two must go on one bike."

"The other bike?" asked Sophia.

"That's a surprise. Get ready!" said the drone.

One of the bikes flicked its kick-stands out to come to a rest by them; the other hurtled by towards the Defenders, coming back at them, firing as it went. A large drone hovered over Artur, arms grabbing his body, lifting him up into the sky, two fighter drones flying either side. Then the bike exploded, deep in a cluster of Defenders.

"Go now!" said the drone.

Sophia pulled Tom up.

"Follow me," she said.

Tom seemed to have trouble thinking, moving or feeling. He seemed empty; even his fear of the bullets seemed to have gone. His sight seemed dark, apart from Sophia.

Sophia flung a leg over the bike seat and he sat on the back, behind her. She revved up the motor and they accelerated away.

Tom turned to look back at JT's body. He could see a crowd of Defenders around it and at its heart Cita, who was kneeling down, hand to the old man's neck.

Then they were gone.

Tom couldn't stop the tears filling his eyes – tears that led to shaky sobs, two hundred million kilometres of grief overcoming him.

He held Sophia tight and tried not to think, not to see JT in his mind's eye: his mouth full of blood, the body lying on the ground.

52: Sophia

Sophia was enveloped by fear. It grew, bigger than her, eating from within, then swallowing her whole. She rode as fast as she could, away from the craziness, towards what Humai promised was a way out of there.

But she could see her father's eye explode in blood again and again. She'd speed up to escape, then slow down in fear.

The bike twitched under her – Humai making a point, taking over control for a millisecond.

"We have no time, Sophia," it said. "We have to hurry."

She was sure the machine was right, and took a deep breath. She could smell smoke, burning and sea salt and feel Tom's warmth against her back, hear his gentle sobs. She was not the Sophia who had left Justinian; she had no choice, for now wasn't the time to think but to act.

In the battle view Humai projected into her goggles, she could see the track ahead and potential threats overlaid in red. Nearby was the track of the drone carrying her father, together with med-info. He was still alive!

"What's that cluster of red dots, the one just ahead?"

"Potential ambush," said Humai. "To avoid it we'd have to retrace your steps, which would be equally risky. I'll send a flight of drones in as a diversion, and then you should be able to speed through."

Should. Humai wasn't sure, then.

"Can you test road conditions?" she asked. No surprises, she hoped.

"It's pretty smooth, but will measure with lidar and plot the best route."

They were getting closer. In the battle view she could see drones matching her speed on either side, the threats resolving into individuals and a line marked out: her way ahead.

"Hold tight," she yelled out at Tom, and then to Humai, "Engage!"

The drones sped ahead, and she could hear explosions and gunshots. The red dots spread out on either side, and for a moment she thought they'd get through without trouble. Then bullets headed in their direction.

Sophia put her head down and gunned the accelerator, ignoring the real world, living in battle view, following a line, forgetting everything else. For a moment she thought they'd made it – then there was a jar to the bike, and Tom's arms tightened around her.

"Are you ok?"

They were through, she realised, but was Tom hit?

"It's my shoulder," he said. "I can't see, but it hurts like hell."

She could feel something damp on her back – warmth from his shoulder. More blood.

They were approaching the runway.

"Where's that plane?" she yelled at Humai.

"Incoming," it said. "Follow the track laid out; it will sync to you."

Crazy; there was nothing there. Sophia turned right, onto the runway, lines and tarmac stretching out ahead of her.

"Here?"

"Yes – speed up!" commanded Humai.

Tom said nothing, so she assumed he was ok and looked round for the plane. There was really nothing there, but the red dots were approaching: two groups, one behind and one ahead, to cut them off.

"Speed up!" it said again.

She accelerated down an empty runway. Crazy.

Then she felt the blast of jets, the roar of engines, and the SpecOps craft decloaked by her side, wheels touching the ground, matching her speed, rear door opening, ramp descending.

"Quick!" said Humai. "Drive in!"

It posted a route, a crazy path directly into the moving aircraft. Sophia gritted her teeth and focussed. This had to be right. *Align with the centre of the door, creep up, slowly matching speed, then when stable, gun for it, then – brake! Brake!*

She was in. They were in.

The drone carrying her father flew in as the door was closing, the engines already revving up, powering them away.

Sophia turned to Tom and inspected his left shoulder. It was bleeding, but was still a shoulder.

"Can you move your arm?" she asked.

"Ouch," he said, flexing his left arm, but he could move it; it couldn't be that bad. Was flesh-wound the right phrase?

Then her father: no, first look around.

There were rows of padded seats, racks of equipment, spaces for drones, and a medi-centre that looked like a coffin.

"It's an auto-medic," said Humai. "Get Artur in – he's lost a lot of blood."

"We have to get my father into that thing," she said to Tom, taking Artur's earplugs; the goggles were lost, somewhere back there.

Together they grabbed one side each and lifted him into the auto-medic. They had got him half in when the aircraft banked quickly, sending them and Artur tumbling to the floor.

"Keep it even!" screamed Sophia.

"Sorry, but we had incoming – had to evade," said Humai. "Try again."

The aircraft banked again, but this time it helped, lurching the body into the cylinder. Robot arms reached out, holding him in, one grabbing the wrist and injecting needles into it. The cylinder slammed shut.

"Warning," said Humai. "Incoming. Evasive manoeuvres imminent. Get into those seats!"

Sophia flung herself at the nearest chair. She had time to catch a deep breath before the aircraft lurched again.

53: Tom

The plane banked again, sending Tom sprawling into the seat next to Sophia. He reached for the restraints and pulled them tight. His shoulder seemed to be bleeding less, but his shirt was soaked red.

"Do something, Humai!" said Sophia. She wasn't talking to him but that machine.

"Deploying countermeasures," it said.

In front of them was a huge display. It showed them in 3D, flying away from a runway which was covered in red dots. On either side of them were two red triangles marked *Wolf Bats*, closing, matching speed, tracking.

Then the aircraft dived and banked, hard, pulling negative g, then positive, in rapid succession.

"Avoiding hypersonic railgun," said Humai.

"Have you got anything on their tracking method?"

"They may be detecting your airflow using metsat lidar. It's pretty sophisticated, but the satellite was designed by Bangalore Systems so there are ways and means."

Alarms sounded, and there was a series of bangs along the fuselage; Tom could *see* the holes the projectiles had left.

"Shit, shit, shit." They said the same thing together.

"Wear these," Sophia said, handing Tom her father's earplugs.

On the display at the front they could see two words. *Blip/out.*

"What does that mean?" Tom asked.

"Not good news. Humai?"

There was no answer.

More alarms sounded, and more impacts.

The display showed the two Wolf Bats following them, closing in. In the corner more words appeared: *Auto-navigation damaged. Manual flight mode on.* Control sticks appeared out of the seat's arms.

"What is it?" asked Sophia.

"Don't you know? They're used to fly a plane; I used one on Mars."

"Go ahead, then – time you did something."

Tom grabbed the stick and pushed it forward, and the plane dived. Then he flicked it left and it banked, hard. It was infinitely more responsive than the blimp, reacting instantly with a powerful, exhilarating feeling of freedom.

He kept his eyes on the Wolf Bats and flicked the plane upside down, diving towards the sea.

"What are you doing?" screamed Sophia.

With a twist, he rolled the aircraft through a right angle, the g-forces thrusting them down into their seats. Tom almost blacked out, blood draining from his brain, but the seat expanded, swallowing them up, cocooning them, squeezing his legs, forcing the blood upwards. It felt good, safe, as if back in a surface suit.

"Feel like I'm being swallowed by this damn seat," said Sophia. "Humai, can you hear me?"

The Wolf Bats had lost some ground but were closing in again now, machines able to pull turns that no human would survive.

"Humai, can you hear me?"

Tom ignored her but tried to fly randomly, unpredictably, pitching up to vertical and then corkscrewing back down again. It didn't seem enough; the separation shrank.

More gunfire headed their way, missing by what sensors identified as centimetres.

"Tom," cried Sophia, "I've had a blip from Humai. It's going to hack the metsat satellite's systems; be prepared to bank to the right and then dive as low as you dare, *now.*"

Tom followed her instructions, trusting her and the mysterious machine that seemed to be everywhere but nowhere. He pulled up just above the sea, able to see individual waves on the display. He could see the lethal lines of their followers' fire, intersecting at the point where they had been just moments before.

Then the Wolf Bats began to yaw, pointing from side to side like dogs hunting a scent.

Blipcoms on flashed up on the display.

"You're clear," said Humai.

"Get this stupid seat off me – I must check on my father," said Sophia. She headed towards the rear of the aircraft.

Tom took a moment to catch his breath, flying the craft easily, watching the displays until the words *Repair successful. Auto-navigation restored* appeared.

He felt slightly disappointed: back to being a passenger again. Tom turned to watch Sophia with her father, then looked away; it might be an idea to give them a moment alone.

Then the pain in his shoulder was forgotten as he remembered JT.

54: Sophia

Sophia woke with a start. She hadn't realised she had fallen asleep, wouldn't have wanted to, wouldn't have believed she could. Where were they? A quick look at the display showed they were close to Justinian; she must have slept for five hours.

She looked over to Tom. He had his eyes closed as if sleeping, a frown on his face, but his hands fidgeted restlessly. Maybe it would be best to let him be for a while.

That left her father.

"How's Dad?" she whispered for Humai to hear.

"Stabilised," was the response. "He will need a new eye when we arrive at Justinian, but otherwise the wounds are fixable."

Something eased within her, then tightened as she remembered the fight, bullets flying overhead. Her hands began to tremble. Why now, when they were safe?

"Your mother asked me to set up a blip-con when you woke up," said Humai.

She would be furious, but Sophia longed to talk to her. Furious with her dad, she hoped and feared, not with her.

Ahead, the display opened a window and her mother appeared. Behind her Sophia could see the Global Council: desks, displays, people moving, a background hubbub of talking.

"Sophia! Oh, dearest, are you ok?"

Sophia felt emotions well up and tears on her face.

"Mum, I'm ok, honest – we're coming home. Dad's wounded, but Humai says it should be fixable, and I'm fine."

"Your father... What was he thinking? Letting you into a war zone like that? Fighting, killing – him and that machine."

Sophia expected Humai to chip in, but for once it was silent.

"I will never forgive him, never forget – never," said Anna.

"Mum... are you sure?" Suddenly Sophia had another fear. "He's wounded, hurt bad – won't you help him?"

"He and Humai can make their plans without us. I won't have my children dragged into gun battles with the Earth Firsters, not now we've seen what they're prepared to do. No, no way."

She banged the table in front of her. Behind her Sophia could see faces turn round, watching, listening.

"What's going on?" she asked.

"We got an update from Humai while you were sleeping, and it's been absolute chaos ever since here at Justinian. Earth Firsters' use of illegal nano-drugs, BCC corrupting official records, Unverified hacking your construct, and all of them being behind the explosion of the *Prometheus*!"

Sophia could guess, and felt a bit better at hearing what they'd done. *Hah! Take that, Cita.*

"What's being done about it?"

"The Earth Firsters are falling over themselves to get some space between Cita and the rest of the movement. Mr Bevan has taken over as their leader and is currently helping frame a resolution condemning Stone and her use of memory-altering nano-drugs."

"And BCC?"

"Nothing; no denials, but no comment either. The official history of the *Prometheus* explosion has been updated, showing Captain Vaughan planting the device, but that's it. Unverified is, well, untraceable – off-cloud at present."

Alejandro; what about him? Sophia looked across at Tom and noticed that his hands had stopped fidgeting: he was listening in, and rather than annoying her, it felt like she wasn't alone.

"What about JT?" she asked. At that Tom's hands twitched, but he continued to be 'asleep'.

"The Earth Firsters have promised to return his body, so he can get a proper burial."

Tom would like that.

"Anna?" It was someone in Justinian, just out of view.

"I must go," said Anna. "I'm currently drafting text with Mr Bevan and Bina."

"Mum, don't be hard on Dad."

"We'll see," said Anna. Then she paused and gave her daughter a long look. Finally: "I'm proud of you, Sophia; even if it was wrong, you did good."

"Thanks, Mum."

"Love you."

"Love you."

And then she was gone, leaving Sophia to her thoughts.

It had been good to talk, to see her mum, but it hadn't been enough; the tension still burnt in every nerve. When she closed her eyes, she could see her father's eye explode, JT's mouth fill with red, feel the thud as the bullet hit Tom, the stickiness of his blood seeping into her shirt.

She needed a wash, fresh clothes, but what else? This wasn't something that she could wash away; her feelings and memories were too intense. She needed an escape, something wild and bad, something strong enough to make her forget, something her parents would object to.

Alejandro would know.

She wished she could scream, but she'd wake Tom from his pretend sleep.

And Tom? He could look after himself. He had a funeral to go to.

When she got in, after seeing Mum and Nina, she'd blip Alejandro. Maybe at some point they could even talk through what had happened. Afterwards, when the ache had eased, many drinks later, somewhere seriously off-cloud, off-limits. She'd have to dump Humai's tracking pendant.

Tom made a pretence of waking up. Should she go along with it?

"Where are we?" he asked.

"Nearly at Justinian, where we live," she said.

Suddenly she wondered what he would do next; maybe he did too.

"I've been told to say that Tom has an invitation to stay with the Kasparovs," said Humai.

It was back, or rather, no longer pretending not to be in the loop.

"Thanks," said Tom to Sophia.

"Hey, nothing to do with me, but you're welcome."

He was, too, but she wondered who had invited him: her mother or father?

He smiled but hesitated, as if wanting to bring something up. JT, she guessed.

"Did you hear all that?"

"Yes," he said, a bit sheepish.

"It's ok," she said. It was, too. Weird.

"We'd like to take Tom's pendant for examination," said Humai.

"It was given to me by my father," protested Tom. "It's all I have of Mars here on Earth."

"It could help us – help you – to get another mission. We don't need it all."

"Another mission… To rescue my mum?" he asked.

He started discussing orbits and spacecraft with Humai, and Sophia zoned out. Justinian; just get her to Justinian, then she'd let them talk resolutions and missions to their hearts' content. She'd be having fun off with Alejandro.

On the display ahead, she could see the familiar three linked islands. She was home.

55: Tom

They had to play the cards quickly, while their aces were still high, or so said Humai, though Tom would rather sleep. He was so tired and the shoulder ached, though less so.

After landing, as the aircraft taxied towards a stand, the auto-medic had opened, needles had unplugged themselves, and Artur was brought back to consciousness. His eye was covered in a beige bandage, and he reeked of disinfectant. Sophia helped him out of the auto-medic; he swayed as he stood, then raised a hand.

"Humai, give me an update." Artur closed his working eye as if lost in thought, then opened it, and he grinned at Sophia. "Nice work!"

"You should have a black eyepatch like a pirate," said Sophia. "After how you've acted. Mum was…"

She seemed lost for words.

"Furious?" said Artur, grimly.

Sophia nodded. "I've never seen her like that."

"That can wait, but we can't," he said. "We must get to the GC before they pass any of their resolutions."

The plane stopped with a jerk. The engine whine faded to nothing and the door at the back opened. Outside were three robocabs and a man – Dr Khujandi.

"Your pendant, please, Tom," said Artur.

Reluctantly, Tom handed the Origin Stone to Artur, who handed it to Dr Khujandi.

"Rush job, anything your lab can get on this; we'll stall as long as we can," said Artur.

Dr Khujandi nodded and took one of the robocabs.

"I'm off home," said Sophia. "You don't need me, and I have to get into something cleaner."

She turned to Tom.

"See you later," she said. "Check out the yew Athena statue: real auth!"

Then she was gone, and he was heading in the third vehicle with Artur, who was talking to the invisible Humai and delegates. Had he slept at all on the plane? It had seemed like a never-ending nightmare, but here he was, travelling between islands on Justinian, choices made by others now – not just him and JT, co-travellers for so long.

The buildings on A Island seemed like works of art. They told a story of power and history in a language that Tom couldn't understand, so unlike the familiar worn rocks and red dust of Mars. They approached the largest and the vehicle stopped at the entrance, a grand veranda.

They were met by armed guards, and Tom stiffened again.

"Relax, Tom," said Artur. "These are JustSec; they're here to keep us safe, they protect the GC."

It was difficult to get in, as Tom didn't have something called a quantum ID or qID, but Artur used some sort of emergency protocol to get him authorised with floor access to the Great Chamber, whatever that meant. It was all so new, so different from his old life on Mars.

In the entrance hall was a great crowd, a circle of delegates from all countries, who burst into applause as Tom and Artur entered.

"Technocrats and allies," whispered Artur.

Tom looked around and saw a huge wooden sculpture of a woman with a sword in one hand and display in the other. This must be the Athena that Sophia had talked of.

"Tom, at last," said a voice, and he recognised the woman from the blip-con.

"Bina," he said hesitantly, hoping he had the name right, and was rewarded by a smile.

"I'm so sorry about your colleague, Jim Trevelyn," she said.

"JT," Tom corrected automatically.

"You're just in time," she said. "We're about to pass a resolution condemning the violence."

"We have some suggested modifications," said Artur.

"Put them into the system; we shall see. I shall have to discuss them with... the others."

"My wife?"

"She is busy, or I'm sure she'd be here."

Tom wasn't so sure that was the reason Sophia's mum hadn't met them on arrival.

"First, a statement – an update," said Artur, pushing Tom forwards into the Great Chamber.

It was huge, space for thousands of people, rows of desks, huge displays, more art. Tom's head spun at the size. He'd been wrong, thinking they were going to *the* Earth. There wasn't one Earth; it was more like *Earths*, filled with different people, wild variations in dress styles, colours, genders, ages and languages. And that was just a tiny fraction of the diversity of the planet.

Then there were the politics. Once he had assumed it would be *the* Global Council, one group, but here there were factions, some friendly, some openly opposed to what he wanted – to rescue his mum.

What was he to say?

Artur led them to the desk with the animated flag of two rotating spheres, where on a display Humai had prepared text for Tom:

My mother, the Nobel Prize winner Mei-Li and two others remain on Mars. They are stuck in confined spaces I know only too well, every day at risk that some machine will fail. They cannot wait for months of debate: another mission must be sent, and quickly.

That matched how he felt, and Tom was relieved that he didn't have to conjure up words by himself for this audience.

At the front, Bina as the chair called for order and the murmuring quietened.

"The chair recognises Dr Kasparov," she said.

The hall darkened slightly, and a spotlight illuminated Tom and Artur.

Artur gave his statement, blaming Cita Stone for the violence, emphasising how they'd only acted in self-defence, calling for a rescue mission. Then:

"We have examined the Origin Stone brought by Tom Tesla to Earth. It shows signs of the first life on Mars, from a time before there was life on Earth. Maybe life started on that planet and made its way here? We must return to find out more. But there is another reason we must return. I have here Tom Tesla, born on Mars, who has made the long journey across millions of kilometres: let him explain why another rescue mission is so essential."

That was Tom's cue, and he read out the three simple sentences, then added one for himself.

"And we must return in memory of my friend, JT, who was killed on arrival…"

He had meant to say more, but he didn't trust his voice.

There was a murmur of support.

"The chair recognises the modification from Dr Kasparov to the proposed resolution," said Bina.

Giant displays flashed up the following words, or versions of them, in the many official languages:

Resolve 7: to authorise all necessary steps to investigate the potential for life on Mars, including return of the remaining colonists.

There was a vote, and it was agreed, to applause. Artur seemed to collapse in relief.

"We got here just in time. Now everything is possible," he said to Tom, "and finally I can go to hospital. Wait here: my wife will collect you."

As he left he looked tired and sick, as if feeling his wounds. Tom was alone, despite being surrounded by thousands of delegates. Even knowing who he was, they seemed reluctant to approach. What should he do?

A woman appeared out of the crowd.

"Hello, Tom," she said. He recognised the voice from the flight. "I'm Anna, Sophia's mother. Are you ok?"

He nodded. She was a reassuring presence, focussing on how he was, rather than Artur's drive for what he could do.

"You'd be very welcome to stay with us," she said.

"Thanks," said Tom, even though Sophia had said the same.

The session had ended, and delegates were beginning to leave the hall.

"Time to go home, Tom," she said.

Home?

They made their way to the Kasparov apartment, high up on one of the B Island towers. There he met Nina, who pestered him with questions about life on Mars, before getting frustrated at how backwards it was compared to the latest Earth tech.

"Where's Sophia?" he asked.

"She's out with that Alejandro," said Nina. "So dad can take me next time."

"No chance," snorted Anna. "Oh, and Tom, there's a message for you."

It was from Elena, with an update of life in the base after they'd left. With Tom on Earth and the world's eyes on a rescue mission, Victor had been on his best behaviour. It helped to know she was ok, but he would feel her absence and the guilt until she too was freed from Mars. He also had to go to Cornwall, for the funeral, to say goodbye to JT, however hard that would be.

Tom's room faced west, and through its windows he could see the setting sun. It was red: the colour of Mars.

The colour of his planet.

Thanks to Tristan Gooley for the feedback and the team at Rowanvale Books, in particular Emma O'Connell, Jaide Long, Ellie Owen, Day MacLeod, Gemma Butler, Billie Hastie and Cat M'Crystal-Fletcher.

Author Profile

John Pahl has designed a navigation and communication constellation for a Mars Polar Base and predicted mobile phone coverage within the Valles Marineris.

After he had the mental picture of a boy flying a blimp across the Martian plains, he began to wonder the hows and whys behind the image. This developed into *Martian Blood* and the *Noctilucents* trilogy. He first saw noctilucent clouds while sailing a yacht down the east coast of Greenland, but since then he has seen them from his home in London. This is his first novel.

rowanvale
books

Publisher Information

Rowanvale Books provides publishing services to independent authors, writers and poets all over the globe. We deliver a personal, honest and efficient service that allows authors to see their work published, while remaining in control of the process and retaining their creativity. By making publishing services available to authors in a cost-effective and ethical way, we at Rowanvale Books hope to ensure that the local, national and international community benefits from a steady stream of good quality literature.

For more information about us, our authors or our publications, please get in touch.

www.rowanvalebooks.com
info@rowanvalebooks.com

www.ingramcontent.com/pod-product-compliance
Lightning Source LLC
Chambersburg PA
CBHW020944260626
47169CB00006B/1810